ANDRÉ BRINK

# Praying Mantis

## VINTAGE BOOKS
London

Published by Vintage 2006

2 4 6 8 10 9 7 5 3 1

Copyright © André Brink 2005

André Brink  has asserted his right under the Copyright, Designs
and Patents Act, 1988 to be identified as the author of this work

First published in Great Britain in 2005 by
Secker & Warburg

Vintage
Random House, 20 Vauxhall Bridge Road,
London SW1V 2SA

Random House Australia (Pty) Limited
20 Alfred Street, Milsons Point, Sydney,
New South Wales 2061, Australia

Random House New Zealand Limited
18 Poland Road, Glenfield, Auckland 10, New Zealand

Random House (Pty) Limited
Isle of Houghton, Corner of Boundary Road & Carse O'Gowrie,
Houghton, 2198, South Africa

Random House Publishers India Private Limited
301 World Trade Tower, Hotel Intercontinental Grand Complex,
Barakhamba Lane, New Delhi 110 001, India

The Random House Group Limited Reg. No. 954009
www.randomhouse.co.uk/vintage

A CIP catalogue record for this book
is available from the British Library

ISBN 9780099488941 (from Jan 2007)
ISBN 0099488949

Papers used by Random House are natural,
recyclable products made from wood grown in
sustainable forests. The manufacturing processes
conform to the environmental regulations of the
country of origin

Printed and bound in Great Britain by
Bookmarque Ltd, Croydon, Surrey

The name of Hottentot will be forgotten or remembered only as that of a deceased person of little note.

John Barrow, *Travels into the Interior of Southern Africa* (1806)

The non-believers need the believers. They are desperate to have someone believe [ . . . ] It is our task in the world to believe things no one else takes seriously. To abandon such beliefs completely, the human race would die. This is why we are here. A tiny minority. To embody old beliefs. The devil, the angels, heaven, hell. If we did not pretend to believe these things, the world would collapse.

Don DeLillo, *White Noise* (1984)

Erasmus prompts the question: Can a man choose to be mad? But there is another, equally important, question: Can a man choose not to be mad?

Philip Edge, *A Fool in his Wisdom* (1992)

*Praying Mantis*

is dedicated to my readers

without whom I could not have been a writer

# ONE

*c.*1760–1801

## Koup to Kamdeboo

# I

# A Kind of Birth

CUPIDO COCKROACH WAS not born from his mother's body in the usual way but hatched from the stories she told. These stories took many forms. One of them had it that his mother was a virgin, as skinny as a thong, and that nobody even suspected she was pregnant until the puny baby arrived. In another version she was in fact visibly and hugely pregnant for an outlandishly long time, something like three or four years, before the mountain brought forth a mouse. Depending on her mood and the phase of the moon, she might aver that he wasn't her child at all but had simply been deposited in her hut, newborn and with the umbilical cord still attached to the afterbirth, by a stranger who'd happened to pass by in the night and whose face she had never seen. (The only thing she could confidently say was that, unlike herself, an indentured labourer, he was 'a free man' who could come and go as he pleased, like the wind.) From this account it was but a short step to the assertion that the stranger had been no human being at all but a night-walker, one of the *sobo khoin* or 'people of the shadows' who stalk the living, or a phantom from a dream. Many of her listeners favoured the version that Cupido had been one of twins and, being very obviously the weaker of the two, had been laid out in the veld according to the immemorial custom of the Khoikhoin (or, as they were commonly known late in the eighteenth century when it happened, the Hottentots). At some stage, the story goes, an eagle came diving down from the heavens, a magnificent bateleur from the distant mountains, scooped up the barely wriggling infant in its talons and then, in the way these birds would kill a tortoise, lost – or dropped – it very far from there, in the godforsaken upper reaches of the Great Karoo known as the Koup, where distance loses all meaning and pure space takes over. The baby landed in the lap of the woman who was sleeping in the veld, and when she woke up, the child was there, and hers.

As for his name, 'Cupido' was a common enough name given to slaves and indigenous men by their white masters. 'Kakkerlak', that is, 'Cockroach', is more problematic. We know that to this day there is a Kakkerlaksvlei (or Cockroach Valley) in the Eastern Cape, not far from the present town of Port Elizabeth, where Cupido spent the middle part of his life, but that may be neither here nor there. It is more likely that the place was named after him than the other way round.

There is a more plausible explanation for his birth (or his miraculous appearance, depending on one's point of view), which may, without much certainty, be said to have occurred around the year 1760. In this version, his mother had simply taken the day off from her work on the lands, without asking permission. She was an ordinary woman of the Hottentot tribe, indolent and dirty like all of them (as the farmer would have attested), but without deceit or malice. Her baas had found her years before in the region of Namaqualand, where he had gone with a number of his neighbours in search of game and labourers. The journey had been a great success. On their way the commando had shot the following:

eleven lions
forty-two elephants
seven hippopotamuses
ninety-eight springbok
twenty-three hartebeest
two rhinos
seventeen zebra
thirty-one wildebeest
a single camelopardalis (a rare beast, almost as
     improbable as a unicorn)
and eight Bushmen

Several Bushmen children were captured and strung on a long *riem* by their necks, tied to the commanding farmer's horse, and brought back to be tamed as field labourers and wagon leaders. On the way back, inland from Saldanha Bay, a small band of marauding Hottentots was also rounded up and persuaded, one way or another, to accompany the farmers back to the Koup where they were to be indentured. It turned out that this particular woman was something of a trouble-maker, as she had an unfortunate tendency to abscond, which meant that valuable time had to be spent pursuing her, bringing her back and duly punishing her according to the Word of God. The farmer took great pains (and also, it must be said, inflicted great pain) in his efforts to inculcate in her an appreciation of her condition as an indentured labourer. And in the end, it would seem, his perseverance bore fruit as she appeared in due course to peel off her early resentment and resistance like an old skin and become more compliant. At last she seemed to accept that for the rest of her life she would be confined to that farm. And surely there was space enough, even for a person belonging to a tribe that was used to wandering across the wide land through the changing seasons, following game, new rains, the stars and the wind.

The farm was huge, extending from the small stone house in the middle to the horizon on all sides: at the dawn of time the farmer had personally staked it out on horseback from sunrise to sunset one near-endless midsummer day. So there really was no reason for anybody to feel constrained. And as time went by the woman must have learned to adapt. Perhaps she simply had no will left to resist. Which was all the more reason for the farmer to feel perturbed when she did not show up in the bean fields that day.

He arrived at her hovel with his brand new hippo-hide horsewhip to enquire after her absence and encourage her, in his tried and tested manner, to return to work. Faced with the wretched and wizened little creature on the lap of the woman who sat surrounded by potions and food offerings from all the neighbours, he swallowed his anger; and deprived of the occasion to break in the splendid whip all he could do – for he was a fair-minded man – was to mutter, 'These goddamned creatures multiply like bloody cockroaches, they must be drawn by the smell of food.'

Whereupon the farmer turned on his heel and left, peevishly slapping the virgin whip against the bottoms of his moleskin trousers. Behind him, and unbeknown to him, the baby whimpered, shuddered, went into a quiet convulsion, and died.

# 2

# Instead of a Funeral

THE BURIAL COULD only take place after dark, as the workers on the farm — two slaves, seven male Hottentots and five females, and a couple of tamed Bushmen (not all the children from the long-ago raid had survived) — were obliged to wait until, in the deep dusk, the day's work was done before a grave could be dug; the earth was as hard as rock. By that time the moon was out, a mere sliver of light in the sky, the Milky Way strewn with star dust that marked the route followed by the evil god Gaunab as he fled from the spot of the last in his long line of battles with the good god Tsui-Goab, to die out of sight in peace. The dead baby was rolled in a tattered old coat stripped from a scarecrow in the bean field and placed on the edge of the shallow grave so that the men could partake of some refreshment before proceeding with the ceremony.

The refreshment was believed to have included some *karie* beer brewed from honey and potent enough to dissolve an ostrich shell, a fair amount of dagga or wild hemp, and a sheep removed from the kraal of the Baas (an act for which, in the days to come, ample use would surely be found for the farmer's new whip of hippo hide — but in their delirium of grief and celebration they could not care much about the morrow). Whether this had anything to do with what followed at the end of the festivities, as the sky already began to show the first bloody streaks of dawn, is difficult to tell. But by the time the workers, now considerably more vociferous than before, repaired to the grave where the tiny bundle still meekly awaited their arrival, something extraordinary brought an unexpected twist to the event. As the small crowd, dancing and singing with complete abandon, arrived at the crudely scooped-out hole and the mother bent over to lay to rest her dead child, she staggered back in awe. On top of the shapeless little bundle, still tightly wrapped in its scarecrow shroud, a bright green mantis sat in fervent prayer.

In the world of the Khoikhoin, as everybody knows, the mantis is revered as the harbinger of good fortune; its Afrikaans name, *hotnotsgot*, even means 'Hottentot god'. The people recoiled, suddenly struck sober. Then they shuffled out of the way and eventually sat down to wait. The sun was just showing itself on the ridge of low koppies that marked the eastern horizon, when somebody uttered a high-pitched shriek and pointed. Everybody looked. Everybody saw. The mantis had disappeared. Perhaps it had never been there. Except that everybody had seen it. It had been *there*.

What was more, as the mother approached the bundle for the second time, it stirred. As if to make quite sure that they would not be mistaken, it even uttered a feeble little sound of whining. And when the black tatters of the scarecrow's tailcoat were unfolded, the baby was alive and staring up at them in mild amusement. The mother drew a breast from her clothes and pressed the puny child to it. Unhesitating, it started tugging greedily at the nipple that lay against its little mouth like the scaly head of a tortoise. By this time the sun was already two handbreadths above the hills, long after the time the day's work was supposed to have begun.

As if in a spell, the people started trundling towards the dingy little raw-stone house of their lord and master. When they reached the backyard, he emerged from the stable door, rubbing his eyes as if he had just woken up. Never before had he overslept; and he seemed oblivious of the fact that they were all late for work. Just as he never noticed that there was a sheep missing from the kraal. Truly, there were miraculous things let loose in the world.

'And all because of the mantis,' said the mother in a manner not so much resigned as luminously knowing, inspired perhaps by the dregs of the *karie* beer. Looking down at the squirming little creature at her breast, she added, 'This little one is going to go on a long walk through this world. Right past the ends of this farm, past the hills and ridges, past everything. If you ask me, he has been chosen to become a man like no other. He will not be like me, or like any of us, he will be a free man.'

# 3

## Voices in the Dark

AFTER THE BIRTH, if birth it had been, when all the people were back on the lands in the early dawn, the woman tied the child in a carry-doek on her back and took him far away into the veld, to a narrow passage between the hills, where there was a pile of stones erected by her people, a *heitsi-eibib*, one going back to the beginning of time, when the world was still new and wet with birth. Because those were the days when the hunter-god Heitsi-Eibib was still going about freely among the people, dying many times and in many ways, and getting reborn all over the place. And whoever passed such a mound was required to add a stone to it, so that one could form part of the people who had lived before, and those still living, and those yet to come, united in the death and life of Heitsi-Eibib. This ensured that one's days would be blessed. So the woman added a stone for herself, and another, a mere pebble, for the child.

That night, after everybody had gone to bed, she remained sitting in the darkness of her hut. She had the gift of seeing, and she saw the whole length of the road her people had come, past all the cairns built for Heitsi-Eibib throughout the length and breadth of the land, to arrive where she was now, propping up in her lap the little thing she had not wanted or expected but which somehow was now hers. In her eyes were many things. Not only what had happened, but what was still to happen in the years to come. For example: how one night, six years from now, or perhaps eight, the boy goes on playing outside by himself under the moon, long after all the other children have come in. And how finally he comes slinking inside carrying something shiny in his hand.

'What is that shining thing?' she asks him.

At first he tries to hide it, but then he says, 'It's a star, Ma. I picked it.'

'How did you manage to reach it?'

'This time of the year, in summer, they hang *mos* so low that they get in one's way.'

'Then go and put it back.'

'You cannot put a star back once you've picked it.'

'You're not supposed to pick it at all. Not while it's green. You should wait for it to get ripe and fall off by itself.'

'But what do I do with it now? I've got it right here.'

'Then go and put it outside so that it can find its own way back. There are two things one never brings indoors: a star and a mantis. They bring good luck, both of them, but if you bring them inside, they cause trouble. Outside, they belong to Tsui-Goab. But inside Gaunab takes them away to the black sky of night where he lives.'

'Yes, Ma.'

But it is dark and the woman cannot see how he disposes of the star.

Another vision that passed before her eyes must have come from very far into the future, because in it she could see her child as a wizened old man trudging across an empty, arid landscape. He is moving his arms up and down, up and down. And as she watches, she can see his long spindly arms sprouting feathers, long quills, brown ones and others striped with white, like those of a bateleur eagle, and turning into wings, and before her eyes he takes off from the ground as he begins to fly, higher than the wind. And in some inexplicable way she found herself alongside him, seeing whatever he saw, foreign rivers and mountain ranges moving past far below, distant lands and places inhabited by weird people and animals. She could see flying elephants, and bustards with the horns of rhinos, and people with heads protruding from their chests, and tall women with enormous shiny diamonds on their big toes. She saw what she would never have thought possible: a lion and a lamb lying together, a goose suckling a hartebeest kid, a leopard tending a brood of chickens, an eland and a praying mantis mating.

At first she was upset by the sights. But soon she decided simply to abandon herself to them without trying to ask any questions. All she knew for certain was that this baby of hers was an extraordinary child. What lay ahead of him not one of her ancestors could have had an inkling of.

On the night it all came to her, she could only sigh. She tried not to think any more. Whatever was to happen would happen anyway. She thrust her nipple back into the baby's mouth. While he sucked, she went on talking. People passing outside might well have stopped to listen to the voices. For with this woman one could never be sure if she was having visitors or talking to herself in different voices; and if you should bother to ask, you couldn't count on the answer. 'It was Heitsi-Eibib,' she might say. 'He came to see his son.' It was a night when one could clearly make out the deep bass of a male voice. But it might just as well have been a stranger, like the wanderer who had stopped by nine months before to plant the seed of the child in her womb. Or even the bateleur eagle that had delivered him. When it came to events like that, many people believed that the world was still as it had been in the times before time, when everything could speak: man and baboon and mouse and mantis and eagle and snake and stone, as Heitsi-Eibib had made them, following the decree of Tsui-Goab.

'And what did Heitsi-Eibib have to say?' someone might ask.

'He said this is a child to be brought up with great care, because he is going to be a great man.'

'It is hard to believe, looking at him like this. He is barely the size of a cockroach.'

'That's true.' Another sigh. 'But don't forget, in the beginning Heitsi-Eibib was just like that. It's not for us to question or make fun of it.' Then she would quietly and resolutely cover up the wretched little gnome again, announcing, 'It is time for you to go. I'm expecting visitors.'

Casting meaningful looks at one another, the people would prepare to leave. A few of them might still linger outside for a while. And sure enough, the voices would start up again inside.

# 4

# Feathers for an Eagle

THESE ARE THE voices Cupido Cockroach will grow up with. For his mother always keeps him close to her, scared that something might happen to him. One never knows, with a little thing as frail as that, when someone might just give him a shove in passing – and what would happen to him then?

On most days she takes him with her to the farmer's home where she is now the housemaid, after working on the lands with the others for years. Here, from a very early age, he can give her a hand with the sweeping and dusting and washing, emptying the piss pots, sprinkling dishwater on the floors to cause the dust to settle, chasing flies with a leafy branch, shooing away chickens and Muscovy ducks, or fetching wood for the large hearth in the kitchen.

Sometimes when there is too much work to finish before sunset, he and his mother sleep over in the kitchen, in the far corner by the hearth, where the heat still lingers like a large indolent dog. On those evenings they have to attend the prayers that follow the frugal supper of bread and milk, a scoop of pumpkin or sweet potato, occasionally a hint of meat, of which they are granted the leftovers. Cupido cannot make head or tail out of this ceremony. All he gathers from it is that it must have some connection with the gods. Then his mother has to explain, even though she too is largely in the dark. What he does make out is that this Jesus the Baas talks about must be related to Heitsi-Eibib, since he also died and was resurrected. To Cupido this sounds blasphemous. Surely, if Heitsi-Eibib were to meet this interloper in the veld, he would kill the man with one blow of a flintstone.

What he does like is the singing that accompanies the talking of the Baas. For Cupido singing is like rain on a hot day. In spite of all his mother's efforts to rein him in, the moment the Baas, his wife and their seven children begin to sing, Cupido joins in at the top of his voice, following his own melody, and his own words too, which he learned from his mother:

> O Heitsi-Eibib
> You our grandfather
> Bring me good luck
> Bring me game
> Let me find roots and honey
> That I can call on you again
> You who are our great-grandfather
> O Heitsi-Eibib!

High above all the others his voice rings out, clear as a reed flute, a voice much too big for that spindly little body. And in due course the Baas must tell him to shut up, he is disrupting their communion with God. Then he falls silent, keeping his singing for later, when he is alone with his mother again, or wandering in the veld, beyond all the familiar rocks and ridges and plains, where the world is still empty, awaiting a word to cover it with its shadow or its weight.

There is something else he likes about these prayer meetings. It is the fact that the man who stood in for the father of Baas Jesus was a carpenter. Because this is an activity which has taken hold of him like the glare of hot coals you stare at, unable to turn your eyes away. Whenever there is some carpentry being done in the farmyard, he is sure to be there. The smell of wood shavings turns his head, like the *karie* beer of which he sometimes surreptitiously drains the dregs when the labourers dance in the farmyard on new-moon or full-moon nights. The mere feel of a piece of wood under his fingertips, its smoothness or graininess, sets him dreaming about what it may become – this slightly curved piece is surely meant to be the leg of a chair, those two wide boards cannot but be used for a table, that hardwood stump discarded in the backyard is destined for the hub of a wagon wheel which will outlast the most bumpy stretch of veld. It is very seldom that the Baas allows him to give a hand with the carpentry, but that does not prevent him from watching enthralled, imprinting everything in the deepest recesses of his mind.

'One day,' he tells his mother, 'one day I shall make us a wagon and we'll go off, just the two of us, and nobody will ever find us again.'

She glances round furtively to make sure no one has heard. 'Shut your mouth, Cupido,' she tells him. 'If the Baas hears you he will kill you dead.'

'I can't understand how you can just sit here,' he says. 'Heitsi-Eibib didn't just give us backsides to sit on. He also gave us feet to walk. We've got to walk.'

When his nagging becomes too much, she tells him about her many attempts to run away in bygone years, how she went farther and farther every time, and how the Baas came after her to bring her back, beating her nearly to death, until she no longer had the strength to try.

'You shouldn't have given up, Ma,' he says.

'You haven't felt that man's horsewhip on your body,' she says. 'You just keep your feet off that road. That is the way to certain death.'

'What was the furthest you went?'

'Far.'

'Further than this farm?'

'Much further.'

'Further than those hills?'

'A hell of a lot further.'

'And what does it look like there, Ma?'

'Same as here. Only different.'

'How different?'

'It is a bare place.'

'How bare?'

'Just bare. No word has come to lie on it yet to say how bare it is. So it is just bare.'

'I want to go and look for myself, Ma.'

'You stay away from there. It will be the death of you.'

'I'm looking for life, Ma.'

'What do you know about life?'

'All I know is what we have in this place. And this cannot be life.'

'You don't know anything yet.'

'What I know I have learned from you. Life must be like Heitsi-Eibib. Here today, tomorrow somewhere else, always in a different place, always a different body. A man, a lion, a duiker, then a mantis or a butterfly or a tortoise or a bleeding rock; one day he is a moon, the next a star. He never remains the same, and he never stays in one place. You've got to let me go, Ma.'

She hasn't meant to say it, but suddenly it bursts from her lips: something she has been cherishing inside her since the day of his birth: 'You'd better wait for the eagle to come and take you away.'

'What eagle?' he asks.

She would prefer to remain silent, but she knows he will

allow her no peace unless she tells him. 'Look, Cupido, you remember that bird I told you about, the eagle?'

'There were so many stories you told.'

'Yes, but the one about the *arend*. The eagle that carried you in its talons high up in the sky, and then dropped you in my lap.'

'Was that what happened?'

'Cupido, I cannot tell you for sure if that was what happened. All I'm saying is that if that was what happened, then you have to wait until another *arend* comes to fetch you again one day. Then you needn't bother about a wagon any more. Once you can fly, you'll go much further than you'll ever get on a wagon.'

And then she tells him another of her stories: about the farmer who trundled far and wide on his farm in search of a stray calf after a storm and who found a newly hatched fledgling eagle that had fallen from its nest in the mountains. The farmer took the little thing home, where it grew up in the backyard with the chickens. It scratched for seeds and worms with all the other poultry, and at night it roosted on a beam. Until one day a man came who gave one look at the strange bird and exclaimed, 'But this is not a chicken, it is an *arend*!' The people tried to stop him, but he shook them off and took the eagle with him to the mountains. At first the bird refused to make the slightest attempt at flying. But at last, at sunrise one glorious summer's morning, the man took the bird up to the highest summit and there he told him: Look, that is where you belong. Up there in the sky with the sun, not down here on the earth. And with that he flung the bird up into the sky, just as the huge red sun drifted free from the horizon. And the *arend* spread its mighty wings and began to soar, as free as a cloud and as high as the wind, far beyond the sun. Because by now it knew at last what it meant to be an eagle.

Cupido sits listening without batting an eyelid, almost without breathing. The story sets off a train of thinking in his mind that will go on for years and years. He starts exploring the veld from horizon to horizon, gathering all the feathers he can find, and hiding them in the thatch of his mother's hut. Until at last he decides that he has enough. Then he rubs the gum of thorn trees and sticky roots on his shoulder blades and his arms, and – just to make sure – takes honey from a tall red anthill to add to the glue. Covered with feathers like a very rare bird indeed, he cautiously climbs the rocky outcrop behind the farmer's homestead, takes up position on the highest ridge, shuts his eyes and jumps.

When he starts limping about again three weeks or so later, he immediately goes off into the veld to start gathering feathers once more.

After the third fall he sadly resigns himself to take his mother at her word and wait for the *arend* to come for him.

# 5

## Pomegranates and Quinces

ONE DAY, WHEN Cupido has more or less recovered, he is
sent with a basket of pomegranates to the neighbouring farm
where the Nooi's sister lives. It means walking from before
sunrise until the sun sits right overhead. The Baas cannot take
a grown-up out of his work, and the Nooi cannot go herself,
as she is in bed with newborn twins. So Cupido has to go.

A basket filled with twelve shiny red pomegranates is what
she sends, and with it a folded letter to give to the woman
on the neighbouring farm.

He walks and walks and walks. When he gets tired of
walking, he rests in the shade of a big rock on an outcrop
on a hill. After carefully thinking it over, he eats two of the
pomegranates. No one will ever know.

That is what he thought. But when he reaches the neighbour's farm and hands over the basket and the Nooi's sister
unfolds and reads the letter, she comes back to the kitchen
door to ask, 'Where are the other two pomegranates?'

'What are you talking about?' he asks, ashen with fright.
'These are the only ones she gave me.'

'This letter says your Madam sent twelve pomegranates
in the basket. Now there are only ten. So I want to know
what happened to the other two?'

Cupido is struck dumb by the power of the letter. So
dazed, in fact, that he is barely aware of the twelve blows of

the neighbour's sjambok that cuts into his buttocks and his back like slashings from a knife. All the way home – and it is only then that the pain comes alive in his body – his mind keeps teasing and unravelling the mystery of the folded letter. But he never says a word to his mother and keeps it hidden inside himself. When she asks him about the cuts and welts on his back, he refuses to answer; and familiar with the inscrutable ways of white people, she does not press the issue.

And then, it must be about a year later, he is once again sent to the sister on the neighbouring farm on an errand. This time it is because of death in the family (one of the children has been bitten by a *geelslang*) and there are twenty quinces in the basket. And another folded letter.

Along the way he is overcome by weariness and hunger. The taste of a quince is nothing compared to the sweetness of a pomegranate. But he cannot resist the temptation. He knows he cannot rest unless he has tasted a quince. But this time he won't be caught out as before. So he first takes the letter the Nooi has sent along and hides it under a flat stone behind a large boulder. Only after he has finished the quince and carefully obliterated all signs of his feasting does he remove the folded letter from under the flat stone and set out on the rest of his journey.

And then, true as Heitsi-Eibib, they catch him out again and enquire after the missing quince.

There are tears in his eyes as he explains to the woman all the precautions he has taken to hide the letter. It must have been Gaunab, he says, who impregnated the letter with evil to damn him. To his amazement the white woman bursts out laughing, until her own face is also streaked with tears.

'Now listen, Cupido,' she says, and from her voice he can hear that there will not be another flogging. 'It was not the letter that spied on you. It was your Madam who wrote that she was sending you with twelve pomegranates the last time, and twenty quinces today.'

'But that letter is mute,' he protests. 'It hasn't got a mouth, it cannot talk.'

'No, it doesn't have a mouth. But let me show you its way of talking. Look.' And she spells out, word for word, what the letter says.

Cupido can still not quite understand. All he knows is that this is something bigger than himself. And that in some mysterious way the letter is holding hands with the big brown book the Baas uses to speak from at prayers in the evening, holding forth about God and Baas Jesus and a host of other people nobody has ever heard of.

This time he does discuss it with his mother.

'I also want to put down words on paper, Ma,' he says. 'This is strong magic. There is life in this thing they call writing, and it can run further and faster than you ever did.'

'This will be the death of you, Cupido,' she warns him, as always.

But at the very first opportunity that presents itself, he fearlessly faces the wife of his baas. She finds it so funny that, like her sister on the neighbouring farm, she begins to laugh. But he stands waiting patiently until she has finished, and then he says, 'So will the Madam now teach me how to write?'

'No,' she says.

He can feel life dribbling from him like spittle in the sand. 'Madam!'

She doesn't have time for such nonsense, she says. But she will ask her older daughters, Cornelia and Jacoba. Perhaps they can give it a try.

# 6

## Encounter with a Lion

BUT IT DOESN'T LAST LONG. The two girls – Cornelia is fifteen, Jacoba thirteen – thoroughly enjoy teaching him. For them he must be something like the little monkey they brought up after the dogs had killed its mother in the veld: they could spend days teaching it tricks and games, until he just became too cheeky and unruly and had to be beaten to death by the boys. Cupido is surprisingly quick in picking up whatever they will teach him, and actually becomes something of a nuisance because of his eagerness. He starts neglecting his duties on the farm. So the Baas very soon puts an end to it all.

'What does a Hottentot want with reading and writing?' he demands. 'That's just asking for trouble. One of these days he'll start thinking he's white, then he won't know his place any more. He's got work to do. And if he's got time to waste on reading and writing, I have other ways of keeping him busy. This has got to stop right now. If you girls don't listen, you're going to get a thrashing just like him. Is that understood?'

That is the end of the lessons, but not of the unbearable desire burning in his chest like a live coal that is lodged there and cannot get out. He still tries to persist on his own, but it isn't easy and there is no one to help if he gets stuck. He has neither slate nor pencil, let alone pen and paper, and it is heavy going to scratch the words on a patch of sand smoothed in the backyard. Yet, he persists. But the burning just gets worse.

It lands him in trouble too, especially when he is supposed to tend the sheep and goats far away in the veld. That is a good time for writing. But if there is a sheep missing when it is time to go home in the late afternoon, there is hell to pay.

But even that does not deter him. Following the trail of his mother's stories he continues to wander across the barren tracts of the farm, tending his goats and sheep. That is when something happens to break the monotony of his days. One afternoon, when he kneels as usual over a sandy patch trying to shape his letters, somebody comes to sit beside him. It must be the ferocious heat that causes his eyes to blur with drops of perspiration, but he cannot quite make out who or what it is. At first it seems to be a tree. Then it changes into something shadow-like. After a while, when he glances at it obliquely, it changes shape again. A huge mantis. No. It is a human being after all. A very big, muscular man.

'Who are you, creeping up on me like this?' Cupido ventures to ask.

'I am Heitsi-Eibib,' says the man.

Cupido gets such a fright that he nearly falls over backwards. But he is too numb to move. Like a mouse paralysed by a snake, he just sits there.

'Don't be scared,' says Heitsi-Eibib. 'I brought you something.'

Between thumb and forefinger he holds the something out to Cupido: it is a lion's tooth.

'Wear it round your neck,' he says in a deep, low, rumbling voice. 'It will protect you against all evil.'

The following day, and the days after that, he gradually

becomes used to the big man. They start talking. Heitsi-Eibib can tell stories like nobody else in the whole world. Slowly, all Cupido's fear filters away like water in dry sand. And from then on, whenever a sheep or a goat happens to stray, Heitsi-Eibib brings out his medicine horn filled with fat, and dips a thread torn from an aloe into it so that only a thumb-length protrudes. This he sets alight and holds against the wind, and following the direction of the smoke, Cupido is sure to find the strayed animal. Never again does he get a beating from the Baas for losing the sheep and goats in his care.

From time to time, when he has to spend the night in the veld, Heitsi-Eibib teaches him about the stars. Just after sunset, he is told, he should watch very closely. The moment the small cluster of the Seven Sisters appears, he must start singing at the top of his voice. That is guaranteed to bring him luck. And he should take care to be very respectful to the moon, as it is not only Heitsi-Eibib himself but also, in some mysterious and convoluted way, the good god Tsui-Goab who in the beginning of time made all the rocks and stones from which people were later hatched. And the snakes. Every little spring in the veld, Heitsi-Eibib shows him, is guarded by a snake. This snake must never be killed, as that will cause the spring to dry up, bringing death to everybody who draws life from it. Once a fountain has dried up, one may as well move away. Only stone remains.

But it is when it comes to hunting that Heitsi-Eibib really takes him in charge. It begins with small buck – oribi, grysbok, suni, steenbok (never a hare, as this repulsive creature with its split lip is the messenger of death). These he catches in ingenious traps. Then follow larger antelopes: springbok, blesbok, hartebeest. Heitsi-Eibib helps him carry those home, so that there will be food for him and his people. They are amazed by the boy, but he refuses to tell them anything. He knows that if anybody were to find out that Heitsi-Eibib has been hunting with him, the Great Hunter will never come back.

One day, he must have been about fifteen or sixteen, he comes upon a lion in the veld beyond the tract of red earth mottled with anthills where there is a patch of dry bush. Nothing ever seems to grow there, yet new shrubs and undergrowth constantly appear overnight when one breaks out firewood. This is a place where even on the most blazing day one is conscious of a thin stream of cold air coming from the bushes. That afternoon, as he follows a stray goat, a meerkat suddenly appears before him. Nothing strange about that. Except that the meerkat begins to speak.

'What are you doing here?' asks the meerkat, in a voice curiously deep for such a tiny creature.

'None of your business,' says Cupido.

'That is what *you* think.'

All of a sudden it is no longer a meerkat standing there but a great eland.

'*Now* are you scared of me?' asks the eland.

The antelope stands about twice his own height in front of him, but Cupido can be quite impertinent for his size.

'Why should I be scared of you?' he sneers.

And unexpectedly, in a flash, there is no longer an eland but a lion. A magnificent male. Its sleek body pale brown, the black mane wild and tousled, its deep golden eyes smouldering like live coals. And huge. Larger than any lion Cupido has ever heard tell of.

Cupido can feel fear clutching his tight little balls, squeezing until there are tears in his eyes. Turning back is impossible, as the lion will then charge from behind. Approaching is also out of the question. All he can do is stand his ground and hope that it will be over quickly.

But then Heitsi-Eibib is beside him. He cannot see him, only hear him. The sound of a great tree with wind and birds in its branches.

'Look at the lion,' says Heitsi-Eibib, so softly that it may have been the wind.

'This is no time for looking, it's time to shoot,' says Cupido.

'Look him straight in the eyes and say, "Whaa!"'

Cupido looks. But in his throat where the sound is supposed to lodge, there is a lump as big as a tsamma melon.

In front of him the lion slowly lowers his great head. His tail is swishing in the tall yellow grass.

Cupido can feel fear dribbling down his legs like piss.

'Look at him,' says Heitsi-Eibib. 'Talk to him.'

At that moment the lion begins to charge. Cupido stares straight into his yellow eyes. From somewhere, he has no idea where, he finds a shard of sound in his throat and shouts, 'Whaaaaaaaa!'

Without meaning to, he closes his eyes.

When he looks again, the lion is lying on the ground, about ten paces in front of him, dead. Heitsi-Eibib has vanished. The only movement left in the wide veld is that of the wind, like a man whispering.

He has his knife with him. Not much of a knife, a rather useless thing that can barely skin a frog. His mother told him that his father gave it to her. Whoever his father may have been. But at least it is a knife with a blade.

With the piss going cold against his crooked legs, Cupido goes closer. He squats beside the lion's head. He can see lice moving in the mane. That reassures him. The louse was the first creature to take the moon's message about death and resurrection to mankind, before the hare messed it all up. He starts palpating the lion's body. Rolls him over on his back. Then starts hacking away with the knife. He has to work right through the night to skin the beast. Fortunately the moon is big and bright overhead, and he knows it is Tsui-Goab looking down on him beaming benevolence. He isn't even aware of fatigue.

At the break of day, as the sky turns red, Cupido is finished. He rolls up the skin, the smooth wetness inside, and slings it over his shoulder. Looking up, he sees his flock of sheep and goats, including the stray, approaching.

He begins to walk back. They follow.

By mid-afternoon he arrives at the farmyard.

The Baas emerges from the kitchen door, shielding his eyes from the sun with his hand.

'Cupido!' he calls. 'Where the hell have you been? What in God's name have you been doing?'

He shrugs the skin from his shoulder. In the background, his flock looks on impassively.

'I brought you a lion,' he says placidly. 'He tried to catch one of the goats.'

'How did you kill him?'

'I shouted Whaa.'

'What?!'

'I shouted Whaa and then he dropped dead.' He gathers confidence. 'He can't *mos* catch our goats like that, Baas.'

'You're lying to me, Cupido.'

'It is the truth. This skin cannot lie.'

The Baas takes the skin and spreads it open on the ground, carefully examining it from mane to tail. There is no sign of violence.

'I can't see any holes or tears,' he says, flabbergasted.

'I told you.'

'How did this madness get into you?'

'It was a tree told me, Baas.' For Heitsi-Eibib's name is not to be spoken in front of strangers.

'Cupido, don't play the fool with me. I'll break your neck.'

'You can break as much as you like, Baas. The truth is the truth. And now you can take the skin.' He scrapes together his courage. 'You can count the sheep and goats. There's nothing missing.'

# 7

## Death of the Hunter

THAT WAS THE BEGINNING of Cupido Cockroach, hunter. The Baas wasn't sure what to make of the lion skin without mark or blemish, but he didn't want to take any chances. Secretly he believed that the lion must have died of hunger or illness, although it seemed unlikely, given the prime condition of the skin. But that made him even more firmly resolved to discover the truth. The only way to do so was to take Cupido with him on his hunting trips and not allow him out of his sight. It is hard to tell whether it worked or not. Because from that day, whenever Cupido was present on a hunt, their success would be spectacular: antelopes, from small buck to the very large and stately ones, kudu, eland, oryx (these, too, were plentiful in the Koup in those days, if the Bushman engravings on the rocks or the paintings in every cave, on every overhanging cliff are to be believed). But they brought back more than antelopes: rare giraffes, as well as lynxes, leopards, jaguars, hyenas, the occasional lion (though never as majestic a specimen as that first one). Hippos quite often, less frequently rhino, and on three occasions elephants.

And yet no one would vouch that he'd personally seen Cupido bring down an elephant, a lion, a kudu, or even a springbok, whether with bow and arrow or the Baas's elephant gun. It could be that they'd just missed it every time, happening to look away the moment he shot something. But

there was something curious about it. Magic, some of them
– labourers, or neighbours – mumbled behind cupped hands.
But how could one tell for sure? Yet the evidence was there:
the rhino that was stopped in mid-charge, dropping in its
tracks. The hippo opening its jaws as wide as a wagon door,
then suddenly slamming them shut again, sinking in a spray
of water, as dead as only death can be. The leopard jumping
down on Cupido from its high perch in the skeleton of a
tree, then collapsing in a fearsome tumble and landing, dead,
a few yards from its obvious target.

Had he or hadn't he? Not even the Baas could tell with
any certainty. And yet they all knew that he was keeping his
eyes peeled on Cupido, as ardently as any jealous husband
spying on another man approaching his wife. Could all of
them have been mistaken? Every single one? And every single
time?

It simply happened too often to be mere chance. And all
that mattered in the end was that they were bagging a plethora
of animals whenever Cupido was present. And only then.

It would happen that a man who had been out hunting for
weeks or months on end without any luck at all would finally
come to the Baas to beg, hat in hand, for the loan of Cupido
so that he could bag something, to save his starving wife and
children. Then a price would be agreed on – so many sheep,
so many bags of wheat, so much firewood, so much soap, so
many skins – and Cupido would go off with the would-be
hunter, returning after a couple of days or a week or two,
possibly three, their wagon groaning under the load of meat
and skins and horns and feathers.

In due course strangers would turn up on the farm from
very far away, once – honest to God – all the way from Cape
Town, which was almost as far as heaven or hell, lured by
the name of Cupido Cockroach. Stories were spread far and

wide, covering the land like the first stain of green on the veld after the rains (the very green that had originally inspired Cupido's mother's people to name that tract of land the Koup).

And time and time again Cupido struck them dumb on the hunt. No one who had ever gone into the veld with him returned with innocence intact. Only one man was not impressed. And that was Cupido Cockroach himself.

It was good to have bagged the lynxes and the lions and the three elephants. But not good enough. Deep inside him the ember still lay smouldering. If only there were someone who could have explained to him where it came from. But there was no one. Not even his mother. There was only one being who could have told him, and that was Heitsi-Eibib. But he would not talk of his own accord, and he had a habit of not readily replying to questions. All Cupido could coax from him was:

'Just wait. It will come in its own time. You will know it when you see it.'

Perhaps it was this feeling of impatience, of disgruntlement, that brought the turning point. There was another hunt, perhaps the biggest of them all, well past the reaches of the Wilgerbos River or the Sandleegte or even the Nuweveld Mountains, beyond Koppiesfontein and Skilpadfontein en Palmietfontein, past the Sak River and the Nontees Mountains, over the Kaiing Hills and the Lat River and the Hartbeest River, all the way to Donkerhoek Stream and the orange-brown flood of the great Gariep, where in those days only a few white men had yet set foot. All the way there they hunted, until the wagons were threatening to collapse. And it was there, up against the Gariep, the furthest extremity of the known world, that they found the elephants, a great herd of at least forty or fifty.

'My God,' exclaimed the Baas. 'This can be trouble. What do you say, Cupido?'

'We can turn back, Baas, or we can take them on. Look at those tusks. That bull in front: they're scraping on the ground.'

'That bull is mine. Can you get him for me?'

'I can try, Baas.'

'Then bring him in.'

Cupido inched forward, followed by the others. In a broad crescent, trying to keep a patch of *withaak* between them and the elephants. But what they didn't notice was that they were now wedging in between the group in front – the big bull, and a few younger ones, and some cows – and another group that included a number of calves.

Slowly, slowly, one didn't take chances with these beasts.

Crouching, Cupido edged still closer. The big bull started flapping its ears, raising its long trunk.

'Take my gun,' said the Baas, thrusting the unwieldy thing into Cupido's hands. 'This is no time to make mistakes, Cupido. I'm counting on you.'

'It's not I, Baas. It's Heitsi-Eibib.'

The moment he said it, he knew it was a mistake. He had spoken the name of the Great Hunter. But it was too late to undo it.

At that very moment the bull charged. Normally one would expect the bull to stop after a few yards, perhaps raise his trunk, trumpet, throw up sand, a final warning. But not that time. Perhaps because the name of the deity had been taken in vain, that was the only explanation. The bull just went on charging, coming straight at them.

Cupido could feel his reed legs trembling, but he stood his ground, as on that first time he had faced the lion. Believing – knowing – that at the last moment Heitsi-Eibib would take over. But this time the bull went on charging, followed by the rest of the main herd. It was like thunder rolling across the veld, churning red dust up to the clouds. The earth rumbled. They could feel it shuddering under their feet.

Up to the very last moment Cupido did not flinch. Desperately believing that Heitsi-Eibib would come to his aid. Like every other time. He just *had* to intervene.

But he didn't. That was when Cupido knew it was all over. This was what death looked like.

# 8

## Home Again

ONLY AT THE VERY LAST MOMENT Cupido manages to jump out of the way, hurling his body sideways into a clump of thorn bushes. A number of the guns are discharged. People are shouting. The elephants trumpet.

The Baas also jumps. But not quickly enough, and not far enough. Grabbing him in his huge trunk, the elephant bull flings him into the air like an old skin. It makes one's guts turn to hear him hit the ground, like a heavy branch falling. And immediately afterwards the elephant swings round, incredibly fast for such a huge animal. Then he starts stomping and trampling on the broken body with his feet as large as the boles of trees.

Only then does Cupido remember the gun. He grabs it in both hands, swings it to his shoulder, aims upward – the elephant looming above him like a mountain   and fires. At a spot behind the left ear. The kick sends Cupido flying back several yards before he lands flat on his spine. But he does not take his eyes off the bull. For a while it seems as if nothing is going to happen, as if the beast is going to shrug off the bullet like a horsefly. But then, just as he picks up the limp and bleeding, dusty body to hurl it into the air again, higher than the surrounding trees, the great legs start crumbling under him. Everything begins to happen more slowly, Staggering, staggering, and then the whole huge body caves in and subsides in a heap. Right on top of the hunter. Who quite fortunately is no longer alive. Every bone in his body is shattered.

It is the first time they have actually witnessed Cupido firing a shot. A perfect hit too. Which confirms what they have always believed about him. Except that this time it has really come too late.

They chop out the tusks to take home with them. Sixty-five pounds apiece, the scales will register. The men lay the Baas down inside his own wagon, on the pile of skins of all the game they have shot so far. Then they turn back, away from the Gariep, on the long way home.

After three days they have to bury the man as the smell has become unbearable. The grave is quite shallow, in a spot where the earth is not as rock hard as elsewhere. Then they stack branches and rocks on top of the grave to keep away the jackals and hyenas. A pile which from a distance rather resembles the cairns that have come to commemorate, over the centuries, the lives and deaths of Heitsi-Eibib.

It is the apotheosis of Cupido's life as a hunter. But in his beginning, he knows, is also his end. He will never be able to trust Heitsi-Eibib again.

And the first sign of the god's withdrawal (though one can of course never be entirely sure) comes when they arrive home again on the farm in the Koup from the long trek, to discover that his mother has disappeared from their derelict hut. No one has the faintest idea of what might have happened to her. But after the many years in which she has ceaselessly spoken about going away, it does not really come as a surprise.

There is such consternation on the farm following the death of the Baas that no one even thinks of going in search of her. That is to say, *if* she has run away like years before.

How can one ever tell? Perhaps she has simply been taken away by a whirlwind. All they can say for sure is that she has gone. And Cupido's loneliness is beyond all reach of words.

# 9

# The Man with the Many-Times Face

WE ONLY HEAR ABOUT Cupido Cockroach again when two wagons turn up on the farm one day. Both of them creaky and decrepit, one with a front wheel buckling precariously, the other sagging in the hips. They are escorted by a couple of Hottentot men and two small Bushmen boys leading the two teams of a dozen oxen apiece. From their looks one would think that they have trekked all the way from the Cape without a rest. On the seat of the front wagon sits a man with a sad long face, wearing an inordinately tall top hat. His clothes look shabby, yet he has the bearing of a man born to command. His name, he informs the people in the front yard, is Servaas Ziervogel. He is a teller of tales. He is also a musician, and an itinerant trader, and his wagons are loaded with everything people in the deep interior may need, or not need. Down in the Cape, he tells them, commodities are getting scarce, as a result of fewer and fewer ships arriving in the Bay, what with the new war against the English. Which makes his load exceptionally valuable. It comprises:

sugar and coffee
many rolls of tobacco and tins of snuff
several half-aums of arrack, stoneware bottles of
    brandy and Dutch gin
needles and cotton

steel nails
gunpowder and lead
tinderboxes and flintstones
hats and stockings and buttons of every description
bolts of chintz and linen and corduroy
kerchiefs and bowler hats
salt and spices
ladies' clogs and shoes from Amsterdam and
    Amersfoort
a chest of leather-bound books in languages no one
    has ever heard of
jewel boxes and tool boxes
enemas and tubes for every orifice of the body
fiddles and wooden flutes
hatchets and handsaws and cross-cut saws and two-
    man saws and drills and pliers
delicate necklaces and heavy wagon chains
anvils
a smelly sandal that once belonged to St Paul
cutlery and pocket knives and sabres
quills, stoneware jars of ink powder, reams of paper
binoculars and magnifying glasses
etchings of figures from the Bible
heavily carved chairs in dark wood
spiked neck-irons for recalcitrant slaves
copper wire
bags and barrels with all imaginable kinds of seeds
lanterns and hanging lamps in copper and brass
a stuffed Bengal tiger
vats and iron pots for boiling soap and kettles and
    casseroles
medicine chests
various bits and pieces – behind glass – of the Cross

an obstetrician's forceps
a cluster of pocket watches and two ship's clocks
rolls of Brussels lace
hinges and doorknobs
bellows
a fishing net
pails and buckets of metal or teak, with copper
    fittings
a small skull of St Peter as a child
numerous chamber pots decorated with leaves,
    flowers and cherubs
two white-plumed wings of an angel from Macedonia
and mirrors: hanging mirrors, cheval mirrors, hand
    mirrors, all draped in black

But above all, the man in the top hat informs them, he is a
servant of the Lord of Hosts, sent to spread the Gospel in
the interior of this heathen land. He pauses for a moment to
wipe, with a red kerchief, perspiration from his face which
is reminiscent of the brow of Moses coming down from
Mount Sinai. (For a land as dark as this, the sun is merciless
to the eye of the beholder.)

He offers to lead the people on the farm in a prayer
meeting – perhaps after some refreshment has been served
– which he concludes with a long and ringing invocation
to God. As he rises to his feet, he indicates his willingness
to proceed forthwith to the baptism of any unbaptised
members of the farmer's family, in view of the terrors of
hell awaiting the unredeemed; and even without being
asked produces from his wagon chest a collection of parch-
ments to prove that he has been properly ordained to
conduct all rituals and sacraments of the Church. The
mother and her children (who now number nine, no longer

seven) throng around him, reverently fingering the imposing documents of which they do not understand a word. Even the few who have learned to read are unable to make head or tail out of the Latin (if Latin it be); but it all seems impressive enough.

The children, not one of whom has been baptised before, are summoned to form a procession, followed by servants and slaves. To the eye of a fountain below the rocky ridge against which the farmyard was laid out many years before. Before anyone can utter a warning, the man of God wanders straight into the water, still wearing top hat, tailcoat and shoes, unaware of the steep decline of the bank into the fountain. As his foothold suddenly caves in under him, he disappears unceremoniously in front of their eyes. Only the top hat remains floating on the water. Struck with awe and the fear of God, everybody remains transfixed on the bank, possibly in expectation of a miracle. Only a number of bubbles rise to the surface. It is some time before the stricken widow appears to realise that drastic action is called for. She shouts at the labourers, Cupido among them, to come to the rescue. Not one of them being able to swim, and with an ingrained apprehension of water, they show some reluctance. But when it becomes clear that a catastrophe is looming, Cupido ventures a few steps ahead of the rest, not without trepidation. Like all his people, he knows only too well that in every fountain lurks a serpent, whose favour first has to be won with the sacrifice of a bundle of entrails from a newly killed sheep. If not, he is sure to come and get you. Moreover, in this fountain below the tall ridge, his mother has warned him ever since he was a baby, there is also a water-maid. Upper body of a human being, with long hair like strands of green slime, and breasts as round as calabashes. Lower half scaled like a snake or a fish. If you got involved with her, she is bound to come to visit you in the night and then you won't ever be seen again.

But this is a matter of life or death. The serpent will just have to understand. And the water-maid too. Without waiting any longer, Cupido leans far forward and begins to churn the water with his outstretched hands. Much to everybody's surprise, he catches hold of the waterlogged holy man, and with the help of many other fluttering hands he is dragged to the side and laid on his back like a strange pale water creature.

Nobody knows quite what to do next, and some of the men are already muttering about having to dig a grave in the rock-hard soil; but then it is once again Cupido who resolves the matter by jumping impulsively and quite irreverently with both feet on the nearly drowned man's stomach. With spectacular results, as an incredible quantity of muddy water comes spouting from the man's mouth. The next moment he sits upright, splutters, turns his eyes up, and begins to look about him. The widow hurriedly sends some of the children to the farmhouse for various concoctions and remedies while Cupido wades back into the water to retrieve the still floating hat; and after a period of intense activity the saved soul is helped to his feet to say another prayer. They are not quite sure whether he will be prepared to go through the whole ceremony again, but it seems that the mishap has merely strengthened his resolve, so that the rites can resume their interrupted course.

Servaas Ziervogel immerses himself into liturgy and sacrament, though not quite as deeply into the fountain as before. As he goes on, he acquires momentum and conviction, building to such grandiloquence that the two last children brought to baptism are very nearly drowned in the enthusiastic immersion. Cupido watches everything from the semicircle of servants and labourers, enthralled. After another ample dose of reading and prayer the visitor is invited to outspan his wagons in the farmyard, Cupido is instructed to slaughter a sheep, the women in the kitchen are ordered to prepare a gargantuan meal for the evening, and just after sunset Servaas Ziervogel betakes himself indoors with the family to partake of more food than is usually consumed in a week on that farm, accompanied by further devotions.

While the white people are occupied inside, Cupido keeps close to the wagons, too intimidated to touch anything, but too inquisitive to withdraw. From a distance he gawks at everything piled up there, a greater quantity and variety of wares than he has ever set eyes on before; most of it may just as well have descended straight from Tsui-Goab's red sky, if not from Gaunab's black abode.

Soon after the evening's prayers, back in the farmyard, the stranger in the tall hat becomes aware of this exorbitant interest; and since the young man has, after all, saved his life, the older one cannot but feel some affinity for him. But Cupido keeps his distance. He is wary of strangers, particularly white ones, having never quite got used to their presence.

But his diffidence makes no impression on the visitor. Servaas Zicrvogel knows how to handle people. The very next morning he calls Cupido to give him a hand with unloading the wagons – and an order from a baas cannot be ignored. Moreover, as he makes his cautious approach the stranger already holds out his hand in greeting.

'I have something for you.'

'Baas?'

The stranger opens his hand, palm upwards. A hunting knife with an ivory handle and a long curved blade.

'Baas?' His voice is strangled in his throat.

'This is for you. But for you I would have been dead today.'

'For me?'

'As a token of my gratitude.'

For a long while Cupido just stares at the object in his hand. He cannot fathom it.

'Au, Baas.'

Faced with this tall, thin man who stands in front of him like a herder's staff, he feels like an insect – harvester cricket or mantis or grasshopper.

That is the beginning. There are three magic tricks, he will soon discover, which the stranger employs to make Cupido quite malleable in his hands. The mirrors are the first of these. Music is another. And the third is stories.

First the mirrors. Even while they were unloading the wagons Cupido was intrigued by those objects so carefully wrapped in crape. He wasn't sure whether he dared to ask, and Servaas Ziervogel did not volunteer anything, pretending to be unaware of it all.

That night Cupido cannot sleep. He knows he should be on the lookout for the revenge of the serpent and the water-maid. But uppermost in his mind are those shapes covered in black. For all he knows they may be ghosts, motionless ancestors, grey-feet, emissaries from Gaunab.

Before daybreak he steals from the hut he once shared with his mother and where he now lies alone at night. A thin wind is approaching across the yard, right through his clothes, through flesh and sinews, into his very bones.

There stand the things in black, like corpses wrapped in skins for burial. He cannot go any closer, yet he cannot stay away either. Round and round the wagons he creeps, like a dog lured by a good smell, but too scared to risk a dash for it. Round and round, until the sun appears behind the distant hills, causing the objects to cast long shadows.

That is how the man in the tall hat finds him, when he comes stooping from under his wagon hood.

'What is going on here?'

'Just looking, Baas. These things. They don't move but they look alive.'

'Do you want me to show you?'

'I want to see, Baas. But I'm scared.'

'There's nothing to be scared of. Come and take a look.'

The man bends over and pulls away the cloth from the first object. Nothing happens.

'Come closer.'

Cupido obeys. Stripped of its shroud the thing no longer looks quite so intimidating. Until Cupido bends over to look more closely.

He utters a scream that wakes up the whole farmyard as he nearly topples over backwards.

'No, Baas! This thing is alive.'

'Take a good look.'

This time he approaches on all fours, from the side, cautiously glancing round the frame. The same face looks back at him. A live face with sharp eyes like a meerkat's, black tufts of hair on its head. Cupido raises both hands to hide behind them. The face before him does the same.

Cupido takes a few steps back. The man in front of him becomes smaller and makes no attempt to follow him.

Now Cupido creeps up behind the flat object. But there is nothing at the back. He ventures round to the front again. Now the face is back. They stare at one another. The thing in the frame imitates whatever he does: if Cupido pulls a face, the stranger does the same; if he raises a hand, so does the other.

'Come here,' says the man in the tall hat, approaching to remove the black shroud from the second object. Then the third, the fourth, until all twelve of them stand uncovered in the early sun. From each of the frames the same face looks back at him. He starts scurrying from one to the next, trying to surprise the stranger, but every time the face is there, imitating him, moving away when Cupido does, returning on cue. Whenever he steals round to the back, there is nothing. In the front, the face keeps on returning.

After a long time Cupido dares to ask, 'Who is this thing with the many-times face?'

'Don't you know him then?'

'Never seen him, Baas. He cannot be from these parts. He came with you on the wagon, didn't he?' He shakes his head. From where he is standing, he can see six or seven of the strange faces also shaking their heads: the rest are too far away, or stand sideways. 'They must belong to the grey-feet,' he says. 'The *hai-noen*. Perhaps they are shadow people from the other side. *Sobo khoin*. But they don't look too dangerous. Only, one can never be sure.'

The tall man keeps a straight face. 'That's true. If you mind your step, he won't harm you. But don't make him angry. When I am away he looks after the wagon for me. Then you must take special care.'

'I think the Baas must rather cover him up again, before he starts wandering about on his own.'

He helps the man to cover up the mirrors again, one by one. Now he can breathe again. But he most assuredly will not risk it near the wagons on his own, especially not in the dark.

Only when the other labourers turn up for their morning coffee does Cupido regain his self-assurance. He tells them what he has seen, uttering dire threats about what will happen should anyone dare to venture too close to the mirrors. To make quite sure that they will respect his instructions, he asks the tall man to escort all the others to the apparition, one by one. They are very subdued when they come back. No one will set foot near those wagons again.

The second kind of magic used by the stranger to control Cupido and his people is music.

After evening prayers he usually comes out into the farmyard and selects one of the instruments he has brought along on his wagon – fiddle, accordion, flute – and starts playing with such verve that all the people are drawn to listen. Sometimes it grows so wild that they break into dancing until moon and stars are covered with a blanket of dust. On other occasions the music becomes slow and sad, causing thrills to run down one's spine with the quivering ticklefeet of insects and creepy-crawlies: spider or gnat, chameleon or mantis. It feels as if death has come to lie heavily on the farm. And the labourers are not the only ones to come and listen: all the white people are there too, the Nooi and her whole brood, big and small. As long as this music is playing, they seem to be held in a tight noose that draws them all together.

The third kind of magic lives in the stories the stranger tells.

Mostly about his travels. All the places he has visited with his wagons over many years. Up and down through Africa, to the most distant places in the world. To the Kingdom of Monomotapa. And even further, to the land of Prester John and the empire of the Queen of Sheba, or to Ur of the Chaldeans, and the city of Samaria, and Ephesus, and the land of Nod which lies to the east of Eden, and the land of Kush. All the way, he assures them, to the New Jerusalem, a city paved with gold and silver and jewels, diamonds and sapphires, jasper and ebenezer: all these things he has beholden with his own eyes. (And if anybody present doubts that, they can go and ask the Man with the Many-times Face, he has been there too, he can confirm it all under oath, so help me God.) He tells them about regions where lions and tigers grow on trees, and of cannibals with eyes between their toes and their teeth and in their armpits, people with three heads or no head at all, dragons that spit fire, and a monster bearing on his back a woman clothed in scarlet, with forty breasts on her body, of people with the heads of men or women and the bodies of lions or eagles. He shows them the wondrous things he has brought on his wagons and tells them where they all came from, mostly from far beyond the Red Sea and the Sea of Galilee.

No wonder that after the first night or two the Nooi of the farm invites the stranger to come down from his wagon and make his bed in the house. In the beginning they prepare a bed for him at the kitchen side of the long narrow house. There she sometimes visits him in the night to tell him about all her woes and pains, since he has a cure for everything. Pain in the legs, cramps in the stomach, backache, a congestion in the chest, migraine, female complaints. Worst of all, nightmares. In earlier times she never suffered from those, but ever since the death of her husband on that ill-fated hunt, she has had no rest or peace of mind. He keeps on haunting her in her empty bed.

This news seems to entice the visitor to deep reflection. He has been casting glances in her direction ever since he first set down his long feet on her farm. Such a young woman still, in the full bloom of her years, probably just turned thirty; and only nine children: she has a long way to go. And an attractive woman too. Get thee gone, Satan. But he keeps on looking and glancing and leering, trying to sound out God's feelings about it all. And late one afternoon he approaches her where she is roasting crackling in the hearth, and he clears his throat and says: He has been considering her situation and yes, he is prepared to bring her husband back to her. Not permanently. But at least overnight. Would she be amenable to that? She blushes and nods. Yes, she would be amenable. There is a new tone in her voice. How soon can he make the miracle happen?

Servaas Ziervogel notices her eyes as he has never done before, and he swallows so hard that his Adam's apple moves up and down his long thin throat like the cud of a herbivore. There are a few strict conditions, however, he points out. There should be no light in the house, as it may scare off her late husband. No lamp or candle of any description, and the shutters of the two windows must be closed tight. The children have to be sworn to silence beforehand since the slightest sound or whisper may have unspeakable consequences, as will an attempt by any of them to approach her bed in the night. And should the husband indeed come to her in the dark, she is to receive him without addressing a word to him. Is that clear? Not a word, otherwise he will promptly return to where he came from. If he comes, it will be to comfort her in the way a husband comforts his wife, not to indulge in conversation. If she has any messages for her husband, she can convey these to Servaas Ziervogel in the daytime. But under no circumstances is she to address him directly. Is that understood?

It is understood.

The following morning the widow appears unusually shy, but her previously pallid cheeks bear an unmistakable flush.

To Servaas Ziervogel's enquiry after her nocturnal visit, she is evasive at first, keeping her back to him as she energetically kneads the dough for the day's batch of bread. But after a while she admits: Yes, her husband has been to see her. But it was rather different from what she had expected. Different from what she had been used to.

How different?

Just different.

But in what way? Did anything go wrong?

No, not wrong at all. Actually, it went rather well. Only . . .

Only what?

At last she admits: She could not recognise her husband's smell. It was – well, different.

It is the smell of Beyond, he says promptly. Remember, he comes from the realm of the dead. She will just have to get used to it. Otherwise he can arrange for the husband not to come again.

No, no, she assures him. He is most welcome to return. She blushes again. It is so much better than lying awake in the wide bed all by oneself.

Is that all that bothered her?

Yes. Except – if he would forgive her for talking about such private matters – her husband had – well, gone about things rather differently.

Gone about things?

Now her back is turned squarely to him, while she belabours the dough as if she wants to hammer it right into the table. Her husband – may the good Lord have mercy on her – but her husband always tended to be rather hurried, rather rough. But last night it was almost as if he didn't quite know his way any more.

She has to bear in mind, he says, that it was a rather new experience for her husband too. After such a long absence among the many dead. She should give him some time. He should soon recover his confidence.

All right, she promises, returning to the dough with more compassion. She is prepared to accept anything. She wishes to thank him from the bottom of her heart.

It has been only a pleasure, Servaas Ziervogel assures her.

# 10

# On the Road

FOR A MONTH, TWO MONTHS, the nightly visits continued. Even three or four, for all we know. In those days time was not important. Only when it became clear that the Nooi was putting on weight — a miracle if ever there was one, with her husband so long dead and buried on the plains — did it become time for Servaas Ziervogel to load his wagons again and set off on the road to God knows where.

From the moment Cupido got wind that the Story Man was preparing to leave, he had to wage a battle against himself. He was raring to go, but at the same time he wanted to stay. Suppose he left and in his absence his mother came back as quietly as she had gone: what would become of her? On the other hand, from the day of his birth she had been telling him that he was going to roam the world one day: how could he become untrue to his own nature?

If only there were a way of knowing what Heitsi-Eibib had in store for him. It would have helped so much. But ever since the cursed day he'd taken the hunter's name in vain, he lived in ignorance. Also, it worried him that the tall thin newcomer to the farm was beginning to turn his head with his stories. He could no longer be quite sure about Heitsi-Eibib any more. Not even about Tsui-Goab or Gaunab. It was beginning to look as if there might be more to the world than he had known before. The very thought made his chest contract. At the same time he was aware of a kind of hunger inside him, the kind of hunger a man feels when he needs a woman, a hunger for a tender kind of heaven-flesh he had not tasted before. But what about his mother, what about his mother?

Then, one morning, just after he has seen the Story Man coming from the narrow door of the homestead – stepping rather high, as if trying to avoid some invisible obstacle – Cupido turns away so that the man won't notice what he is staring at. There are the two wagons loaded sky-high, and on the front part of the nearest wagon the small assembly of shapes wrapped in black, all the repetitions of the man with the many-times face, and among them, on the seat, perched exactly in its centre, standing high on its hind legs, its front legs folded in devotion, in a green so intense it makes the eyes dazzle, a praying mantis.

This is the sign he has been hoping for.

He turns back towards the house, the wagon now behind him, and waits for the skeletal man to approach.

'I'm going with you, Baas,' he announces. With no trace of impudence, a simple statement of fact.

'What are you talking about, Cupido?'

'If the Baas is leaving, I am going with.'

'What makes you think I'm leaving?'

'I been watching you.'

'Even if it was so, and I'm not saying it is, I already have my helpers, my team leaders. What must I do with another mouth to feed?'

'I have two good hands, Baas.'

'So?'

'I need you to take me with you. But I think the Baas also needs me.'

'What for?'

'I know this land like I know my footsole, Baas. There are dangers everywhere and if you don't know where to put your foot without stepping on a shadow, it may cost your life.'

Mijnheer Ziervogel is inclined to believe him. And he has no wish to tarry much longer. Over the past few weeks the girth of the farmer's wife has increased alarmingly.

Before the day is over he informs her of the guidance he has received from Above to proceed into the hinterland again. There are other people who require his services: saved souls who need confirmation of their chosen way, the unsaved yearning for redemption. Her late husband, too, he informs her, has been in touch with him, urging him to resume elsewhere his ministrations in the service of the Lord.

Does that mean, she asks quietly, that he will never ever . . . ? He cannot tell for sure if there is dread or relief in her voice.

Not her husband, no, he affirms. But who knows, somebody else . . . ? By the time her child is due, she should consider going on a journey on her own wagon, he suggests, perhaps to the Cape. He has a feeling that God may be waiting there to provide for her needs. A handsome woman such as her will never be left to herself.

In that case, she announces, let God's will be done. She has by now had ample time to consider her situation. Perhaps it is not such a bad idea after all to have her bed to herself again.

It almost makes him change his mind. But there is, in a manner of speaking, a time for coming, and a time for going.

Before the end of the week (in the remoteness of the Koup no one is quite sure about the days of the week anyway), he wants to leave, and take Cupido with him. His other servants are not overly pleased at the prospect, but they do not dare complain openly.

But first the wagons have to be prepared for the journey. New rims where necessary, one new hub, several spokes to be replaced, repairs to both draught-poles, new yokes and thongs, a new lid for one of the chests. Cupido is sent into the hills to cut wood in the dense kloofs; afterwards he sets to work with saw and hammer and chisel (even the new hunting knife proves its worth), until every joint is a perfect fit, every tongue matches its groove, a pleasure to behold. As good as new. At last everything is ready.

After Servaas Ziervogel has made a selection of the gifts he wishes to bestow on the widow (a barrel of arrack, chintz and linen, a string of beads from the New Jerusalem, toys and sweets for the children, sugar and coffee, and one of the hand-mirrors still lovingly wrapped in black), Cupido is instructed to subject all the remaining mirrors to a final polish. Once again he gapes in awe at the Man with the Many-Times Face, both relieved and alarmed by the realisation that they will accompany the trek. And long before dawn one morning the entire farm gathers to see them off: the bulky Nooi and her gawking children, the labourers and their offspring, even the goats and sheep and the five cows and their bull, the chickens and Muscovy ducks, the three turkeys, the pigs and a small hand-reared springbok.

And so they ride off, a prelude – although Cupido will not realise it for a long time yet – to other turning points in his life. It will not be his last wagon journey into the vast interior.

The journey takes him very far indeed from the farm on which he first came into the world: all the way from the Koup to the region just beyond Graaff-Reinet.

On a map, with some guessing and wishful thinking, one may today attempt to trace their route from one outspan to the next, but at some stage the journey might well leave all

familiar landmarks behind and end up in a wilderness on the
other side of names. There is no straight line on this journey.
When, one evening, Cupido ventures to ask where they may
be heading for in the morning, the mournful traveller replies,
'How can I tell you in advance? All I know for certain is this:
when we come to a fork in the road, we'll take it.' And this
is why the route they follow may well look like this:

across the Jakkals and Dwyka and Gamka Rivers
past Vyevlei, or Fig Valley, along the course of the
    Sand River
over Droëberg, the Dry Mountain, and Witberg, the
    White Mountain,
up the Droëkloofberge, that is, the Dry Kloof Range,
to Bakoondlaagte, Oven Plain, and Groenpoort,
    Green Gateway,
past Kwaggapoel, the Quagga Pool, and Rietkuil, the
    Reed Hollow,
past Eensaam, which is Loneliness,
to the Boesmanpoortberg, the Bushman Gateway
    Mountain,
below Trompettersberg, Trumpeter's Mountain, to
    Graslaagte, Grassy Plain,
and on to Platbosch and Bloupoort and the Klein
    Winterhoekberge
through the barren stretches of Vaaldraai and Snake
    Fountain
up the high road to Plum Hill and Olive Fountain
and not forgetting Horse Fountain and Garlic Fountain
or otherwise along the low road to Hoogenest and
    Oukraalleegte
followed by Speelmanskraal and Vaaldraai and
    Gwarina

drawn by names like Kootjieskolk and Wagendrift and
    Windheuwel
that is, Kootjie's Flood and Wagon Ford and Windy
    Hill,
past Sandkraal and Voorspoed and Kwaggasfontein
as far as Goedverwachting, which means Great
    Expectations,
and then Gans Fontein, or Goose Fountain,
to Bossieskraal, Scrub Kraal, and the Dakklipheuwels,
    the Roof-Slate Hills
or possibly Fisanterivier and Vinkfontein and Bulwater
    and Rooiheuwel
or through the Murderer's Karoo at Middle Lake and
    Mud Dam
past Scoppelmaaikraal and Skoorsteen and Die Puts
and Wolf Fountain and Jackal Fountain and Jurie's
    Fountain and Herb Fountain
and Kleinkraalvoëlkuil and Grootkraanvoëlkuil and
    Hannekuil
to Bakoond and Gannahoek and Poffertjiesleegte
and then Two Fountains and Bulrush Fountain,
Rhinoceros Fountain and Wild Duck Fountain: all
    those many fountains
(each with its serpent, most of them with a water-
    maid)
then onwards to Riem and Luiperdskloof
further down to the Onder-Sneeuberge and the
    Moordhoeksberge
and then perhaps to Geveltjie and Wilgerbosch and
    Gemora
followed by Gannalaagte or Noordhoekskloof
and, who knows, says Servaas Ziervogel, Samaria and
    Damascus

and the Khyber Pass and Uzbekistan
past Vladivostok and Nizhni-Novgorod and Samarkand
and the Dead Sea and the Caspian Sea and the Black
 Sea
past Uranus and Saturn and Pluto
and the Sun and the Moon, and Tsui-Goab's Milky
 Way
responding to the lure of the Blomfonteinsberge, the
 Flower-Fountain Mountains
and Nardousberg, down to Aasvoëlberg, Vulture
 Mountain,
or Slechtgenoeg, Badenough, and Goedgegund,
 Wellbestowed
where once again the fountains give birth to lethal
 maidens and lovely serpents:
Paardefontein, Blinkfontein, Vlakfontein,
 Boesmanfontein
— and that is where they make a halt.

All along the almost-endless road the two of them are
thrown on each other's company, the team leaders and assistants always keeping their own counsel. Servaas Ziervogel can
go on spinning his tales for days on end: mostly from the
Bible, but freely embroidered from memory and imagination;
and in exchange Cupido plies him with stories his mother
told him in his childhood. Sometimes they sing, mostly hymns
the pious man has taught him, otherwise monotonous, intri-
cate tunes Cupido tries to teach him, usually in vain. Whenever
they pass a ridge or a mountain, Cupido hurls his voice against
cliffs or boulders to hear it echoing back to him. A voice that
never ceases to astound Servaas Ziervogel, because it is unbe-
lievable that such booming organ-tones can be produced by
such a little sliver of a human body.

'You should become a preacher,' he says many times. 'A voice like that was made to be *heard*, you cannot hide it here in the veld among stones and aloes.'

Then Cupido, embarrassed, merely grins. Sometimes he says, 'I am a Hottentot, Baas.'

What the tall thin man regularly resorts to for inspiration is Holy Writ, from which he reads at the fireside at night, his great brown State Bible open on his bony knees. There isn't much of it Cupido can understand, but he is enthralled by the mere sound of the words. More and more he wonders whether he shouldn't shake off the world of Heitsi-Eibib and enter into that of the Book. But then they happen to trek through a narrow kloof again where there would be a cairn erected for the god; and without fail he feels obliged to scamper from the wagon to add his own stone to the heap; and the other Hottentot servants immediately follow his example. Even though Heitsi-Eibib has been hiding himself from Cupido ever since that day on the hunt, one can never be sure. Somewhere he may yet be lurking, nothing can escape him, and one day, who knows, he may return to demand an account of Cupido's life.

There is another duty he very assiduously observes: on the long trek he stops at every *spruit* or stream or fountain or river, to offer his sacrifice of innards or wild fruit and bulbs in order to win the favour of the serpent that lurks there.

He also continues to hunt. Sometimes with the wagon drivers, but more often than not on his own. Carrying only the long hunting knife Servaas Ziervogel gave him, he sets off on a spoor in the veld – no one can track an animal down as relentlessly as Cupido – returning many hours later, sometimes a full day, with his quarry of blesbok or rietbok or quagga.

Once there is an old lion, a toothless, limping old male undoubtedly vanquished and driven out by a younger contender in the pride, that stays on their heels for days. At night they stack two tall fires and sleep between them, but one never knows when the predator may be driven to such an extreme as to jump right over the flames. No one dares to shut his eyes. That is when, one early morning, Cupido announces, 'You go on with the wagons. I must have a word with that lion first.'

Servaas Ziervogel does not say anything, but he turns white around the gills; the Hottentot servants snigger, but Cupido ignores them. He resolutely takes hold of his knife and strides in among the *ganna* shrubs which in that region grow quite tall.

'Take one of my guns,' Servaas Ziervogel calls after him.

'No, the knife will do.'

The wagons proceed without Cupido. At a very leisurely pace they continue until evening, looking round from time to time or casting their eyes upward, then walk on. Until just after sunset, as the dark comes down, when Cupido approaches from the bushes behind them, seemingly without a care in the world.

'Well?' asks Servaas Ziervogel. 'Where is the lion?'

'He won't bother us again.'

That is all he says. But there is no further sign of the lion.

Whenever they stop at farms on the way it invariably lengthens into a long stay. Servaas Ziervogel is never in a hurry, particularly not when upon their arrival it turns out that the farmer is not home. Perhaps he is on a journey to Cape Town to sell and barter his produce or to buy slaves or provisions, or he may be off hunting in the deep interior, or on a raid against Bushmen – in which case the man of God finds a way to insinuate himself into the position of the absent husband. Widows he finds especially irresistible. They also provide useful opportunities for trading his own wares.

On such occasions Cupido begins to follow his employer's example with the slave and servant women on the farm, developing quite a taste for the business, and increasing proficiency in the exercise of it.

He soon discovers that on these sojourns on different farms Servaas Ziervogel proves himself commendably generous with the half-aums of arrack in his load. During the journey Cupido, too, begins to acquire a taste for liquor, and with drink and women freely at his disposal, life is turning into a rolling feast. It does not always work out well: possibly as a result of his inexperience, his involvement with women sometimes leads to bad quarrels. Twice his hunting knife causes quite serious trouble. The first time his opponent only sustains a flesh wound. But the second time the man is nearly killed, a blade between two ribs. Servaas Ziervogel has no choice but to pay compensation to the complainants, which leads to a lamentable cut in Cupido's liquor rations. But by that time he has learned how to unplug the barrel, help himself and refill the vat with water, so the sanction does not make much difference in practice. And just as his fame as hunter and tracker and singer begins to precede him on the journey, his renown as a womaniser and a fighter and a drinker also spreads. The great future his mother once predicted for him is slowly turning into reality.

But best of all for him is Servaas Ziervogel's readiness to teach him to read. Not that there is much time for lessons, as there always seems to be something more urgent; but slowly, very slowly, he starts mastering the principles of writing. And by the time they finally arrive in the region

Servaas Ziervogel has been heading for all along, he has made sufficient progress carefully and almost reverentially to nudge the words on a sheet of paper with an outstretched forefinger the way a dung beetle moves along its precious little ball.

Their provisional destination in the Eastern Cape is a farm in the foothills of the Renosterberg. Followed by another in the Agter-Sneeuberg. Then another in the Bouwershoekberge. And at long last they end up in the environs of the Tandjiesberg or Small-Tooth Mountain, somewhat closer to the little village of Graaff-Reinet. There, at some stage, Cupido remains behind while Servaas Ziervogel moves on. It is a sad parting, as by that time he has grown fond of the man with his stories, his music, and the many curiosities on his wagons. But he has found employment with a farmer who can use him for tracking and hunting and cutting wood in the dense vegetation of the mountain kloofs blessed with such magical names. (Perhaps it is no coincidence that this farm is also where Servaas Ziervogel finally runs out of liquor.)

One event softens the blow of parting, and that is Servaas Ziervogel's decision, as he takes his final leave, to present Cupido with one of his miraculous mirrors. With this artefact in his possession, Cupido is prepared to face whatever the future may hold for him. Through many years he will keep the mirror carefully wrapped in its shroud of black crape, removing it only on very special occasions to confer with that ubiquitous stranger who also, inexplicably, turns out to be another self.

The story master, musician and blessed of God goes his own unpredictable way to moon and stars and foreign lands. Cupido Cockroach settles on the farm.

As far as it is possible to assign a date to that momentous

parting, it must have been about the year of Our Lord 1790, give or take a year or two, when Cupido was some thirty years of age.

It was about the time when he found himself a wife. And this is how Anna Vigilant enters the story.

# I I

# The Woman of the Sparks

SINCE WE ARE CONCERNED with the truth, the whole truth, and nothing but the truth, something else demands to be narrated here. Cupido was not only the greatest hunter in his part of the world, but the greatest singer, the greatest storyteller and, in due course, also the greatest womaniser.

It went back a long way. The first time it happened was not recorded, and just as well. It must have been in the years before Servaas Ziervogel when, tending the goats in the veld, the youngster would make a finger-deep hole in a patch of sand, moisten it with spit, and thrust his little member into it. Nothing special about that. But when he came past the spot a week later, once again following his flock of goats, there would be a plant growing from the hole. And not just any common little *ganna* bush either, but something that looked as if it might turn into a tree. And before the end of the year it was indeed a tree. With a tall straight trunk and dense foliage and birds in the high branches, a tree of a kind not seen in those parts before. And soon it was no longer a single tree, but a whole copse of them, a sure indication that Cupido had been making the most of his talents.

There is no need to enter into more embarrassing detail, except to mention that in the course of the following years Cupido also availed himself of every willing girl-child on the farm. As well as of a selection of ewes from the goat and sheep flocks, the three turkeys, and whatever else it pleased the heavens to place within his reach.

At some stage his interest must have extended to females beyond the domain of the natural. Water-maidens, for example. On the logistics of an entanglement with a creature that was a woman down to her navel, and a scaly water-snake from there on, it is preferable not to put too fine a point. But that might have been one explanation for the fact that he escaped unscathed on the day he saved Servaas Ziervogel from certain drowning without stopping to ask permission from the resident water-maiden: some prior acquaintance may well have saved the day.

By the time Cupido Cockroach left on his journey with Servaas Ziervogel, he must have been well equipped for what lay ahead. And while his lord and master confined himself to the sporadic solace of a widow or a single woman, one might safely conclude that for Cupido there was no lack of opportunity to vent his desires. It may not be too far-fetched to conclude, with one reputable historian who calculated that on that journey – which stretched, as we now know, from Jakkals River to Dwyka River to Gamtoos River, to Platbosch and Noupoort, to Riem and Luiperdskloof, to Shiny Fountain and Shallow Fountain and Bushman Fountain – he fathered some 134 offspring. Quite apart from the considerable number of trees he planted along the way.

And after he had settled on the farm in the Agter-Sneeuberg, he conscientiously continued to enhance his reputation. At a given moment people stopped counting. As a matter of fact, to all but himself it became rather boring. Until one day rumours start filtering through to the Tandjiesberg about a woman on the far side of the mountain, in the direction of Platberg, the Flat Mountain, who is reputed to be a match for any man.

ely grins and shrugs when he first hears these
ey continue, becoming ever more persistent,
ng his mind. In his own neighbourhood people
o whisper: You think you've got something to
There is one woman you can never match.
, grate. Gategrategrate. Like a twig in the
h.

make enquiries – first cautiously, indirectly,
lly.

at woman think she is?

Anna Vigilant, he is told. Lame in one leg,
ther here nor there. Brought back from the
long ago, when the Baas went to catch chil-
n his farm. Now she is a soap boiler of promi-
. But above all, above all: a woman guaranteed
man so utterly that he is fit to be buried in
No man who thinks himself a man can last
le night with her.

dy who is in the know.

Cupido begins to lose his composure. Perhaps
it it to the test.

be that he has had too much to drink. Ever
Ziervogel left, Cupido has been abandoning
imaginable kind of liquid refreshment. From
e farmer on whose farm he lives at the time.
ing. Concoctions of *kougoed* and *gli* roots and
d devil's tobacco. As strong as lye prepared
of soap. Enough to burn out your intestines
lowing and causing you to see stars at the
nd it is in that kind of mood, stumbling some-
sun and moon and stars, that one reckless
o takes the momentous decision to meet the

woman. They have to get past their own stories and meet each other as they really are, naked, man and woman, person and person.

It is no quick or easy task. They have to wait for a time when all the inhabitants of the Tandjiesberg can gather without raising suspicion among the farmers. There is only one time to match this need: the few days surrounding New Year's Day when all the farmers take a rest and the farm work comes to a temporary standstill. For months on end messages have been exchanged, followed by an unbearable, churning silence of waiting.

Not that it is much help to the others, for there is one thing Cupido impresses upon them from the beginning: this meeting concerns him and her alone. The others may have their own celebration, but that must be separate, on the farm of the Baas, in front of their own huts and hovels, while he and the woman meet on the mountain, where he can be only he, she only she.

But how will they know the outcome? the people want to know.

They will find out.

And Cupido sends a message to the woman. How does he send it? With a young boy, some people say: a boy as old as he was when he was sent to the neighbours with quinces and pomegranates.

But others say: No, it was no boy.

Then what was it?

It was a hare, of course.

Oh no, others argue. Not a hare. What about a chameleon?

No, not a chameleon.

What then?

It was the wind. When there is a great message to be delivered only the wind can be trusted to do it safely.

So we decide: All right then, Cupido sends his message with the wind. And the woman asks the wind to take back her answer. She says: Yes. We shall meet on the mountain, at the very top where there is a small even patch, as if a great hand has flattened it. On the night when the old year merges with the new.

This allows Cupido Cockroach a few days to consider how to set about it. For it is not simply a matter of storming in. A whole life is at stake. Two lives, for all he knows.

During this time of waiting Cupido Cockroach first consults his mirror. This happens one evening after dark, in the tenuous light of a candle in the obscurity of his little hut, his back turned to the entrance. That is how it happens that as he sits peering into the shadow eyes of the stranger he sees a shooting star behind his head, exploding in a spray of foam. This must be what brings him to the idea. Impossible to say how and where he finds the fireflies, and so many of them, and where and how he manages to hide them, but this how it is.

On New Year's Eve the people begin to gather where the labourers' huts stand huddled together, irresolute and self-conscious, like guests summoned to a baptism or a wedding or a funeral but reluctant to appear too eager. That is where they all converge, from near and far, over hills and plains and ridges and ranges, men and women and children in a crowd such as those parts have not yet witnessed, not even for Nagmaal. And as it happens, the moon is full, a sign that Heitsi-Eibib and Tsui-Goab have chosen to attend in person, which even under ordinary circumstances would have been an occasion to dance and celebrate.

That night, when the moon sits in the middle of the sky, all the people are gathered in row upon row around the clearing in front of the huts. That is when Cupido emerges from his own hut and shakes hands with each one of them, as if he is taking his leave, before he goes off on his own, across the bare veld, then up along the slope of the mountain, towards the moon. At the very top, where the slope levels down, he has already built, during the preceding days, a small shelter of dry branches: not very spacious, but big enough for two, with two cowhides covering the entrance.

That is where he arrives, draped in his kaross of jackal skins. And from the far side of the mountain the woman comes, covered from head to foot in her kaross of dassie skins. She is dragging one foot behind her.

Far away, down at the farmyard, the people are waiting, buzzing like a beehive. Music begins to sound, a number of *ghoeras* and reed flutes and oxhide drums. Everything happens very slowly and deliberately. No one is in a hurry. No one really listens. All ears are tuned inward, where the silence is taut as a thrumming string. All talk dies down, all movement freezes.

Up on the mountain top, where it grazes the lower stars, the two contestants duck into the shelter. Neither of them says a word. From now on their only witnesses will be the full moon, and the stars of course. And the wind, most likely. For if it was the wind who first carried their messages to and fro, he will also be the one to spread the story in the world afterwards.

Just inside the entrance they shake off their karosses. Both bodies must have been greased with lard and buchu, for in the brief moment before the cowhides are dropped over the dark entrance there is a glimmering of bare limbs in the moonlight.

Sssssssss, say the stars, as if water has been poured on their embers. Sssssssssssss.

There is something like two whirlwinds of moonlight and darkness churning about inside the shelter.

Ssssssssssssssss.

The woman begins to make music deep in her throat. Cupido growls like a leopard.

In the most distant distance, where the people are waiting in a throng, the drums cast a rumble of thunder up at the sky, the flutes sing, the *ghoeras* whine and drone.

Inside the hut there is no moment of rest or respite. The whirlwinds keep on whirling.

Overhead the moon begins its slow descent, the Milky Way spirals past, the Great Hunter strides on. Inside the shelter the shadows spin and whirl. No end to it.

It must be halfway to the morning when something extraordinary happens. As they come careening once again past the kaross Cupido has thrown off, in some obscure way, he grabs a clutch of fireflies, lowers his hand to where their bodies are joined, and releases a fly. It gives off a small, bright foaming streak of light.

There's a spark!

Sssssssssss.

A panting, thrusting, tumbling interval. Then: Another spark!

Ssssssssssssssssss.

From the depths of her throat the woman warbles like a night-bird winging up into the sky.

More sparks!

Neither of them can have much life left in them by now, but still they go on. Now. Now. Now!

Ssssssssssssssssssssssssssssssssssssssssssssssssssssssssssssssssssssssss ssssssssssssss.

He bellows. The woman screams. And in her scream she shapes herself into a name, Anna Vigilant.

He releases a whole handful of fireflies between their thighs. They chatter like shooting stars, like a rain of comets in the night sky which is already turning red at the edges.

Heeeyyyyyy! shout and roar and yell and thunder the stars. Anna is on fire! The shelter is going up in flames!

If for a moment they are petrified with fright, it does not last long. For as they look around them, there are no flames to put out. The dry branches of the day before are covered in young green shoots and foliage, livid with flowers.

And Cupido Cockroach and Anna Vigilant emerge from the entrance, modestly covered once again with their karosses, walking hand in hand. Together they start going down the incline, back to the people where the music is still keening and rejoicing, back to the everyday world.

# 12

# For the Whitest Wash

ONCE CUPIDO COCKROACH and Anna Vigilant have come together as man and wife, they begin their connubial life on the farm against the Tandjiesberg. There have to be negotiations between the farmer who hired Cupido and the man with whom Anna has been indentured since he first caught her in the Bushmanland as a child. In view of her earnings as a soap boiler he is reluctant to let her go. But Cupido's Baas desperately needs his sawyer, and after making some shrewd calculations about Anna's worth, and several months of bargaining during which a number of foul threats are traded, a deal is struck and a fair amount of rix-dollars, draught oxen and wheat change hands. Anna is allowed to join her new husband, who has built them a hut, and they start a family. He hunts, and drinks, and saws wood, and together they sing and spend long nights talking about his people and their people and the white people. And she boils the soap for which she has become famous.

There is nothing about making soap she does not know.

First, she will tell you, comes the lye. For this one needs *ganna* bushes, nothing else. In these parts they grow quite luxuriantly, and easily as tall as a big man. These shrubs are burned to provide ash. What is added, is lime. It can be dug out from the ridges in the mountains, but to her taste nothing is as good as burned shell-grit — which means making an arrangement with somebody on his way to the sea, either at Algoa Bay or all the way to the Cape.

To prepare your lye you boil your *ganna* and your shell-grit in your soap pot in the yard. And don't use just any kind of woods to kindle a fire. What you need is long, thin branches, as these can be easily pulled out from under the pot should it get too hot and threaten to boil over. You keep on adding water, stirring and stirring until it is ready. Once it has come to the boil you keep stirring from time to time, allowing the lye a chance to cool off and become clear. This lye is then transferred to another pot. The old one is filled up with new ash and lime and water, and these are brought to the boil again, and the new batch is transferred to a third pot. This one is kept apart from the other, as its lye is not as strong as the first.

Then comes the lard. The best lard Anna has ever used for soap came from a hippopotamus. Nothing else can match it for richness and whiteness and smoothness. But it goes without saying that there isn't always a hippopotamus at hand on the farm. So she has learned to make do in other ways. When there is no hippo lard, she spends up to a year collecting sheep fat. Beef is also acceptable, provided the animal is still young. Sheep fat yields a soap as white as snow, while beef tends to be yellowish, like cream. Sometimes, if beef or sheep is hard to come by, one can fry the fat from the carcasses of game found in the veld, preferably wildebeest or antelope, but even then it is wise to add beef or sheep. Pig too, of course, but this should never be mixed with anything else, it should be pure pork. To the fat you may add a measure of eggshell, ostrich eggs ground between two stones, which gives a very fine, smooth texture to the soap. Prickly pears brought from the environs of Algoa Bay are a prized ingredient to add lustre to the finished bars. It is worth one's while to pay attention when Anna is talking, it is evident that she knows what she is saying.

Now what you do with the fat, once you have enough, is to boil it in your big iron cauldron in the yard over a slow fire, with enough of the first lye added; and once it has boiled dry you start adding the second batch of lye, until the cracklings turn a pale, even colour, not too dark. Then you get two men to put a long pole or an iron stave through the handles of the pot, and have it carried away from the fire to settle for a while. To this concoction you add milk, a small dose at a time. This allows the cracklings to burst out of their dry shells and turn pure white. But if you try to hurry in any way, the stuff will soon boil over, which will burn you all the way to hell and back.

At last the cauldron can be returned to the fire for the final cooking. Still slowly, even more slowly than before, until the soap is as thick as honey and just as golden. All of this takes time, takes patience; if you try to speed things up, you should keep away from soap, you will never get it right. The word to remember is *slow*. And all the time you keep on stirring with the long ladle that has a rounded end for a good, slow motion; don't even think of stopping for a rest, or the colour will turn mottled.

By this time, supposing you started well before sunrise, it will be late afternoon. When the soap begins to separate like curdled milk and the water starts boiling over the top of the pot, you know the soap is ready. Now you can scoop out the remaining embers from under the cauldron. But don't stop stirring for a while yet, until it has properly cooled off. That is when you cover the pot with sacks to keep the warmth inside, because you must take your time with the cooling too. Until the following morning. That is when you can come with your big knife to cut the soap loose from the edges of the pot. You cut out a number of big blocks, remove them from the pot and pack them away. Six weeks or two months later they are dry enough to divide into smaller blocks.

But all this is just the outline of the process. For someone like Anna Vigilant it is only the beginning. Because now it depends on the kind of soap you want. You can add pumpkin, or potatoes, for a smoother and more delicate texture. She occasionally adds blood too, if the boiling can be timed to coincide with a slaughtering day. Ox or sheep, or even a whole, live chicken. Once a hare. To be added while the fat is still boiling and bubbling like an angry beast. The results are astounding. This part she never discusses with others, her recipe remains her secret. Which is why Anna Vigilant's soap is sought after all over the colony, even from the Cape.

Laundry washed with her soap is guaranteed to come out white. Not your everyday white, but white as the inside fibres of a sheep's best wool. White as the snow that covers these mountains in winter. And white is what Anna Vigilant is after. She loves what is white and absolutely clean. She is infatuated with cleanness. In her hut and on her yard no speck of dust is allowed to settle. Everything has to be white, the way the world came from its mother. All that is not white has to be burned clean away. Which is what she feels about white people too, even if one can hardly call them white, they tend more to pink, like suckling pigs or a cow's udder. But this is still better, she argues, than being brown. Because ever since she was caught, as a very small girl, in the Bushmanland, she has known that brown isn't something one wants to be. There is nothing one can do about it. But no one in his right mind would choose it of his own free will.

As a child she used to think that she could change her colour to white in the soap pot. Luckily she first tried with one foot only, and it almost killed her. Since then she has been lame in one leg, and she is still not white. But this does not diminish the yearning.

# 13

# The People from Beyond

BOILING SOAP IS NOT the only thing Cupido has learned from Anna. She can tell him about everything under the sun from the lore and the customs of her people. About making arrows from thin reeds that one bends straight and smoothes and allows to dry before attaching a feather to the top with *tkwai* juice and a fine thong, and covering it with the venom of a puff adder. About curing and dressing small skins in the manner of the San. About how one takes a girl at the first flow of her blood to isolate her in a hut, waiting for the arrival of the rain-bull. About how to make an overture to a young woman who has softened your heart, working for her parents until you have proved your virility. About the moon. All those stories without end. Stories about encounters between skunk and eland, lion and snake, meerkat and mantis, all of a size, all equally strong, sometimes equally weak. Stories about which she finds it impossible to say who first told them: stories simply blown from afar by the wind. Resembling the ones Cupido's own mother used to tell, but different. About how the mantis got angry because the meerkat had killed the eland which he, the mantis, had created, and how he had stuck an arrow into the gall bladder of the dead eland to make the world grow dark, and how he had then gone blind himself and lost his way in the dark. And how in his blindness he threw his shoe into the sky to become the moon, a moon that shows red in the gloom, from the dust that settled on the shoe in the time when the mantis wore it to walk in his slow, deliberate passage on the red earth.

Still no end to Anna Vigilant's stories. About the god of her people, the one they called Tkaggen, and whom the white people call Devil. Like Heitsi-Eibib, suggests Cupido. Yes, she says, except that he is *not* Heitsi-Eibib, he is Tkaggen. But what about Tsui-Guab and Gaunab? he asks. No, she doesn't know about them, she says, and so she cannot believe in them either. Long arguments that spin through many nights. He becomes more and more confused: the stories his mother told him about the Khoi people, the stories told by Servaas Ziervogel on his wagon, about a god who is Father, Son and Holy Ghost all at the same time and lives beyond the clouds, and now Anna's stories about Tkaggen and his kind. What should a man believe in, what is the truth?

We are going about on these flat plains, she tells him, but above us and below us are other, invisible, plains. Behind the rocks and cliffs of the mountain those plains open up into foreign worlds densely populated by the spirits of the dead. And provided you know how to walk, you can step over from one world into another at any place, any time. All you have to do is to dream the right dreams. It all starts with dreaming. Suppose you're going on a hunt tomorrow, then you should dream tonight of the eland you plan to shoot, or the wilde-beest, or the warthog, or the elephant, or the hartebeest. (But don't ever think of offering *her* some of the hartebeest while she is still rearing children: haven't you noticed that the head of the hartebeest looks exactly like that of the mantis? That would be looking for trouble and darkness.) And once you have succeeded in dreaming it, the animal you have dreamed about will walk straight into your arrow in the morning. Everything you see around you, she says, every person and stone and animal and moon and stars, began as a dream. Which means that it is in your power also to change anything in this world, just by dreaming it.

'What about you and me?' Cupido once asks her. 'That night on the threshing floor? Surely that just happened the way it happened. There was no dreaming.'

Anna gave a small, wise smile. 'What makes you think I didn't dream it before it happened?'

'It was I who brought the fireflies.'

'But it was I who dreamed the fireflies so you could catch them.'

In the beginning he refuses to believe her stories. But then, on a few occasions, a strange thing happens to Anna which makes him wonder. She would squat down and start thinking without uttering a word, her eyes gazing straight ahead. Then they would turn up, showing the whites. She would no longer hear anything he says. She would start thrashing about on the ground, covering herself with dust and dried grass and twigs, uttering strange sounds, foaming at the mouth.

Once, twice, three times he becomes so scared that he runs to other people for help. But unperturbed they shake their heads and tell him to leave her alone: she has always been like that, they assure him, it is something that came to her from the medicine men of her people.

Does that mean she is bewitched?

No, not bewitched. All that happens is that she sees what we cannot see and hears what we cannot hear. She will tell you when she comes back.

And that is exactly what happens. Anna is eager to tell him everything: it is as if she starts spinning, she explains, and then everything around her also begins to spin — trees, people, stars; and humans would change into lions, spirits would wander about freely, there would be snakes everywhere. It feels as if she is entering into deep water, struggling to breathe. At the same time she is becoming lighter and lighter, until she starts floating, flying. In these dreams she usually goes back to the Bushmanland where the white people caught her as a young girl who had just begun to bleed. She tells him in great detail about all the people she spoke to on her journey, the living and the dead. Or when she does not return to the world of her childhood, she travels to where the rain comes from. And in times of drought she would bring rain back with her, leading a rain-bull on a thong across the farmyard to the high hills, where she would unleash a storm that causes a flood to come raging down the slopes. On other occasions she would bring a rain-cow, just as big as the bull, and just as dun-coloured, but with longer, thinner legs that reach down from the clouds to the earth, bringing gentle, soft rain without thunder, lasting for nights on end.

If somebody falls ill, usually caused by the poisoned arrows the dead would shoot at them for this reason or that, it is Anna who fetches medicine. She burns shrubs or the shells of ostrich eggs, or grinds dry leaves and roots to a fine dust, which she then mixes with blood or gall or piss, and feeds to the sick person, who is healed in almost no time. So it is much more than boiling soap that Anna Vigilant has brought to this place with her. She keeps the farm in good health, she wards off the bad spirits, she makes Cupido Cockroach a happy man.

It is she, too, who tells him one day: It isn't good or right for them to stay on this farm and work for the white people. Here they will grow old and useless. At the moment they are still strong and vigorous, they can earn enough to lead a reasonable life on their own. She can boil soap, and heal the sick, and he can saw wood and make wagons and furniture. They can be perfectly self-sufficient.

Cupido is tempted by the idea. But before deciding anything he first withdraws into their hut to have a consultation with his mirror. The black crape is ceremoniously removed and neatly folded up. Then Cupido seats himself cross-legged in front of it to gaze thoughtfully into the man's now familiar yet ever-strange bright eyes. He sits in involuted silence. Now you must tell me, he says in his mind. This thing that Anna has brought to me, is it a sound idea? Or is it bad?

No, the mirror replies in his head. It sounds like a good idea. If your hands are able to work for yourself, it does not seem reasonable for you to spend your life in the employ of someone else. All your life you have been wanting to go further. Not just further, but *further*. You have been waiting for that *arend*, that eagle your mother used to talk about. But you cannot just sit here, waiting for him. You should go out, go somewhere, so that he will find you when he comes.

With a small sigh Cupido rises to his feet, covers his mirror with the black cloth again, and once more hides it behind the pile of grass and rushes that forms their bed.

So one day in the autumn they prepare to leave the farm on the slope of the Tandjiesberg. At first the Baas tries to resist. Cupido arrived here on his own, and if it really is his wish to leave, then so be it. But Anna is indentured, he paid much money and cattle and grain for her, don't ever forget that.

But Cupido and I belong together, she tells him. The Baas can see that with his own eyes.

Where will I find another woman to boil me soap?

All these years I have been boiling soap for farmers and washed the world white for them. Now it is time I did it for myself.

You will stay right here.

Don't talk like that, Baas. Suppose a big wind comes to blow away everything in this yard?

Don't you try to threaten me, Anna.

Then the wind comes and blows away the yard, house and shed and stables and all. Will the Baas now allow them to go in peace?

You think I'm a bloody fool?

Baas must watch out for locusts, she says.

And the next day they come like a black blanket spread out between them and the sun, from horizon to horizon, sweeping down on the fields and consuming every sign of green.

How about giving them a Yes now?

Anna, I'll flog you until you lie there trembling like the skin of the water in a bad wind.

Watch out for your oldest son, Baas, she says quietly. There are many spirits of dead people gathering around him.

The next day, without a moment's illness, with no crack of thunder, no sign of beast or bird of prey around, the eldest son collapses in his tracks in the backyard, stone dead.

What about letting us go now, Baas?

Go to hell and never come back, he shouts.

And that is how, near the turning point of that year, Anna Vigilant and Cupido Cockroach and their children leave the farm and move to the little village of Graaff-Reinet, with its sprinkling of whitewashed homes and its ostentatious drostdy and its long, narrow irrigation plots, to start a new life.

# 14

## An Unruly Knife

THOSE WERE TURBULENT TIMES along the eastern frontier
of the Cape colony. In unforeseeable ways events in Europe,
half a globe away, were influencing what was happening at
this rim of the world. Who could have thought that an
upheaval in France would inspire inhabitants of the villages
Graaff-Reinet and Swellendam in the frontier districts of the
Cape to address each other as *citoyen* and *citoyenne* in their
dusty streets? Or that the arguments of philosophers like
Voltaire and Rousseau would inspire citizens of the Cape to
rise up against their own authorities? Or that revolution and
war in Europe would encourage the Khoikhoi of the frontier areas to take up arms against their white masters?

Throughout the eighteenth century the Dutch East India
Company continued desperately to cling to life like a cancer
patient turning increasingly cantankerous and mean-spirited
as he feels his force and energy relentlessly draining away.
And when yet another war between England and the
Netherlands in their rivalry over the fabulous power and
riches vested in the spice and cotton trades was unexpectedly complicated by the military ambitions of Napoleon,
England succeeded in 1795 in wrenching the Cape from the
convulsions of the Company. From Table Bay to the Great Fish
River in the east, doughty burghers, who for a century and a
half had suffered the exploitation of greedy and merciless

masters, at last saw an opportunity to cast off their yoke. In the Cape England soon enough succeeded, through military rigour and the cajoling of Lady Anne Barnard, to restore the good order; but in the remote districts of Graaff-Reinet and Swellendam 'republics' were suddenly declared, the liberal landdrost Maynier, who had been suspected all along of supporting the cause of the rebellious Xhosa and the Khoikhoi against the frontier colonists, was forcibly expelled and replaced by a man of the farmers' choice, one Gerotz, and for a while it seemed as if everything would be permanently turned upside down. It was not a matter only of politics. The congregation of Graaff-Reinet were grumbling because the sermons of their minister, Dominee von Manger, were too abstruse for their liking and revealed too little understanding of their problems, as a result of which he, too, was summarily dismissed. But that was just the beginning.

As the Xhosa incursions from across the Great Fish River became more and more unstoppable, the general feelings of apprehension and open distress were aggravated by stories of San raids in the north and even a slave rebellion at Stellenbosch. British troops were dispatched to Algoa Bay overland and by ship, colonist leaders were arrested and taken to the Dark Hole in the Cape castle, Khoi chiefs in the Suurveld – Stuurman, Trompetter, Boezak – joined ranks with the Xhosa and went on the rampage, setting fire to farms all the way to the Winterhoek and Bruintjieshoogte, less than a day's journey from Graaff-Reinet. Entire farmer families were massacred, all their names duly recorded in official registers. Numerous Khoi and Xhosa were shot, unrecorded.

By the time Cupido Cockroach and Anna Vigilant and their children moved into the *kaia* of Ma Martha, an old Khoi woman, the village – according to the traveller John Barrow – was still in its infancy, consisting of barely a dozen little

clay houses occupied mainly by tradesmen, the church and
its vicarage, in addition to the barracks of a modest garrison.
Soon after their arrival the church was destroyed by fire. It
was hurriedly rebuilt, but before it could be consecrated it
was requisitioned as headquarters for a detachment of
*pandoers*, Hottentot troops.

This was also the time when the first emissaries of the
London Missionary Society arrived from abroad. In the midst
of war and rumours of war they tried to establish a small
measure of peace and stability with their tireless preaching
to white and brown alike; but in other respects their very
presence brought dissension and made the situation worse
than it had been. More and more colonists dislodged by the
upheavals from their farms between the Sunday's River and
the frontier, the Great Fish River, came to find refuge in the
town. Moreover, many hundreds of Khoi people, caught
between the colonists and the blacks, flocked there too in
search of a safe haven in the turmoil. And between white and
brown tensions were coming to the boil.

Anna resigned herself to whatever was going on around
her. War or peace, she reckoned, people would always need
clean clothes, so there would always be a demand for her
soap. And the wood Cupido brought from kloofs and distant
hills was more and more urgently required. As he became
more skilful in carpentry, it added significantly to his income.
In a modest way they even began to flourish.

But in his heart Cupido could find no rest. That live ember
which for years had been keeping him awake at night and
driving him on by day was still smouldering. For the first few
months after their move to the town he was somewhat more
at peace with himself. But the restlessness was only biding
its time, looking for a way to break out.

He was driven more and more to seek satisfaction with

other women. And this town, flooded by hordes of people from the remoteness of the frontier, was like a verdant little paradise after the dry scrub he had been used to. Every time Anna so much as dared to look at him in disapproval, he would decamp in search of someone else. If she tried to speak to him, he would hang his head in abject contrition and assure her that he didn't know where this urge came from; it was something that just took possession of him, he was power-less to resist.

I am your wife, she would persist. You've got children. You're not a chicken any more. Come to your senses before you bring shame on us.

He would say: I know, I know.

And perhaps he might leave off for a while, but then the fire would flare up in him again. Or if he tried to stay out of temptation, he would turn to drink. Once he even stole a half-aum barrel of brandy from a trader's wagon that had stopped to offload behind the drostdy. Had they caught him there, Anna assured him, they would have taken him straight to the Cape. Cat-o'-nine-tails and Dark Hole, if not the gallows, once and for all. And he'd better not come to cry on her shoulder.

Then Cupido would become terribly sorry for himself. Sometimes he would stay in bed for days, bursting into tears if anyone tried to remonstrate. But sooner or later he would get up again and go off to the nearest drinking place. Or the nearest female flesh. Worst of all was when he could not find what he was looking for. Then nothing would be too disgraceful to contemplate. He might even go to the drostdy's livestock kraals and pick a nanny goat, as in the old days when he took whatever crossed his way.

You can't go on like this, Cupido, Anna would berate him. It's a shame to me and our children.

I can't help it, Anna. I was made like this.

Then it's time for a makeover. Nanny goat! For goodness' sake, man. Where's your decency? If your mother knew about this . . .

Leave my mother out of this.

If your mother knew. You can't keep your hands off any live thing that comes your way. Only a hare, perhaps, but that's just because it is too fast.

Leave me alone, let me be. You don't know what is going on in my head.

I know what is going on in that thing of yours, and that is bad enough.

Anna, stop this now.

No, I won't. Because it is my business. I am your wife. Don't you care about me?

Then he would plunge back into misery. Because of her. Because of himself. But not for long. Soon he was back at it.

It did not always end peacefully either. Twice, three times, it landed him in big trouble. Once when he got involved with another man's wife he was trapped right on top of her and the man pulled out a knife and swore he was going to castrate the miscreant on the spot.

But naked as a snake Cupido rolled off the woman and crouched to await his attacker. It was like when the urge to drink got hold of him, or the woman-urge: it made him blind, he couldn't see a thing. All he did was to lower his head and go for the man. The knife gashed Cupido's shoulder, but this only made it worse. The woman started screaming. Other people arrived on the scene. When they grabbed hold of Cupido, he was sitting astride the wronged husband, both his hands clutching the man's throat. He was a hair's breadth from strangulation when they managed to drag Cupido away. He arrived home in a sorry state. And without his clothes.

Tried to hide away from Anna. But she pulled him from under his kaross and started ranting at him. Not even the Sunday's River in flood could wash him clean again. Until the remorseful Cupido broke down in tears once more. She had no answer to that.

The second time Cupido had his own knife with him, that beautiful gift from Servaas Ziervogel. The woman he had found in the veld while she was actually gathering *ganna* bushes for Anna. Her husband set on Cupido from behind. But Cupido disentangled himself and started stabbing blindly with his knife. The furious husband hit back. Just missed Cupido's jugular. But there was blood everywhere. The attacker himself had to help Cupido home, where he could weep and lament and rant and rave in agony and misery, before he went off to drink himself into a stupor and then spend three days in bed in Ma Martha's *kaia* like a dying man.

The third time it was murder. On this occasion no one intervened while he and the woman were at it. But afterwards, overcome by regret, she confessed it all to her husband. He first thrashed her to within an inch of her life, then stormed out, still clutching his *kierie*, and went to find Cupido in Ma Martha's *kaia*. Without bothering to ask for an explanation or do any talking himself, he started belabouring Cupido on the head and shoulders. Three, four times around the *kaia*, all the women in the neighbourhood cackling and ululating and trying to keep the screaming children out of the way. Then Cupido dashed back into the *kaia*, and when the wronged man ducked to follow him, Cupido was waiting for him with the beautiful hunting knife. A single thrust, forward and up, and the man was dead.

Loud lamentations in the *kaia*. How were they going to save Cupido from the gallows this time? It was one thing to pick a quarrel with a stranger in the road and leave him behind for dead (Cupido had told Anna about his travels); but to commit murder in a white man's town was something else. There was no soap in the world that could get you white again.

'Anna, you got to help me,' Cupido pleaded, trembling all over, his knees, his arms, his whole body, huddled beside the dead man that lay in a pool of blood which grew bigger and stickier, darker. Flies were beginning to buzz around the edges. He could already feel the noose around his neck. Was this what his mother had brought him into the world for? This what he had hoped and suffered for? This what he had travelled for, all the way from the Koup, over mountains and plains, past stars and remotenesses? With this hunger still unsatisfied in him, this fire that lay embered within him? He still did not even know for sure whose child he was. Who *he* was. He knew nothing. Except that he could not possibly die now, it would be just too unthinkable.

'Anna, you must help me,' he moaned again. 'You are my wife.'

'You should have thought about it before you ploughed another man's wife. You deserve no better.'

'Anna, help me,' he sobbed. 'Help me, Anna.'

And her heart softened. She couldn't do otherwise, this was the man she had chosen, the man who had baptised her with fireflies, she had to take care of him.

'Go outside,' said Anna Vigilant. 'Take the children with you. You too, Ma Martha.'

'You have no right to send me out of my own house.'

He shook his head, too confused to argue. The children held on to his legs, whimpering and crying. In all his life he had not felt as terrible as this.

Yet he knew in the deepest depth of his heart: if a beautiful woman were to come past at this moment, he would follow her. Even if they killed him ten times for it, the noose around his neck.

At last he managed to calm the children by telling them stories, sitting flat on the ground in front of the hut. His mother's stories, Anna's stories.

Ma Martha sat listening to him without saying anything, legs outstretched in front of her. She refused to look at him.

It must have been an hour or more before Anna opened the rickety door sagging from its thong hinges.

'You can come in now,' she said.

'Where is the man?' he asked in a smothered voice.

'There was no man here,' said Anna in a flat voice. 'Get this into your head.'

'Anna, Anna.' It was as if a whirlwind passed through him, a dust devil, *sarês*, the messenger of the dark god Gaunab.

'Just tell me,' he asked her again, that night when they were alone – after she had boiled him a large pot of water and watched while he washed himself from head to toe, in front of her, with a brick of her very best hippopotamus soap.

'There is nothing to tell.'

'I killed a man. You took him away.'

'I took the unruly knife away too.'

'How did you do it?'

She did not look at him. 'I dreamed,' she said after a long time.

He shook his head. He knew it was no use talking.

'How can I thank you?' he asked softly.

'You can thank me by never doing something like that again.'

'I wish I could promise you that. By how can I? You know how I am.'

'I shall help you, Cupido.'

He pressed his head against her breast. He so wanted to.

There was nothing he could wish for more strongly than that. But already he knew. Tomorrow, when the new sun rose over the world, if he saw another calabash of wine, or a beautiful woman coming past with swaying hips, or felt a knife fitting into the palm of his hand, the urge would be back. He was not ready yet to dream her kind of dreams.

But at least he would make the effort. He had his pride after all. Look where he was today. He was living in a town among other people, white and brown. He had work for his hands. In a way he was respected. It might not be what his mother used to wish for him. But it was something. Wasn't it?

And things were indeed beginning to look better for him, with Anna Vigilant at his side.

In the tumult of those days competent tradesmen were in high demand. And no less than the new landdrost, Frans Bresler, who had moved into the drostdy to replace Mijnheer Maynier, and his temporary successor, Gerotz, drew up a contract with Cupido Cockroach, sawyer, in terms of which he would be remunerated with the sum of sixteen rix-dollars (no less than four English shillings) per year, plus food and clothing, to provide the drostdy with timber – the highest wages any official was allowed to pay a tradesman in those days. It sounds somewhat less impressive if one considers that white Capetonians at that time paid six rix-dollars per month to send their daughters to school. But that is beside the point. Cupido Cockroach was not white and his children did not go to school.

# 15

# Uproar in the Church

THE TURNING POINT COMES on a Sunday in June when Cupido is on his way from the upper end of the village to Ma Martha's *kaia* after delivering a batch of soap on Anna's behalf. On his way there he has already become aware of a buzz as if the whole place has become a beehive. Over the previous months there have often been protests and scuffles as people gathered in the streets for one reason or another, but today it is worse, more threatening, angrier. White men, he notices, huddling in small knots and herds in front of this house or that, are all armed with muskets. Even among the groups of Khoi in the vicinity of the church guns are conspicuous, something that has seldom been seen before.

At the gathering in front of the church he stops to enquire what is going on.

'It's this church business,' says an old man, spitting a squirt of yellow tobacco juice right past his face.

'What church business?' he asks. In recent weeks Anna has insisted that he keep off the streets: it is not their place, she argued, for them to get mixed up in other people's fights; that is just asking for trouble. Particularly when the white man's church is involved, seeing that no fight is ever quite as bad as a fight about gods. Whites know nothing about Tsui-Goab or Tkaggen and it is no use trying to talk about it; much better just to let every man believe what he wants.

'It's about the tall man.'

'What tall man?'

'How can you live here and not know about him?'

'I want to know now.'

'The tall man, the one called van der Kemp, the missionary. He's preaching for us Khoi people here in the church every week. And he's invited everybody who is baptised to come and share in wine and bread.'

'How does wine get into it?' Cupido asks with new interest.

'All the baptised people are given wine. He says it's the blood of his Tsui-Goab, the one they call Jesus.'

'He can keep the blood,' Cupido decides. 'But if there is wine I'll come and listen.'

'You can't just drink. You must get baptised first to be a child of the Lord.'

'Then he gives you wine?'

'Then he gives you wine.'

'Nobody has ever told me whose child I am,' says Cupido. 'My mother gave me a different answer every time. It could have been Heitsi-Eibib. Or a stranger who came past in the night. Or one of the grey-feet, the *hai-noen*, or one of the spirits, the *sobo khoin*. For all I know it could even have been our Baas, it was the kind of thing he often did. Everything about my father is dark. So if it comes to wine, it might just as well have been this Jesus person. How could she tell? It happened in the dark.'

'You'd better come and hear for yourself,' the old man suggests, aiming another jet of spittle past Cupido's left ear. 'It is almost time for the service to start.'

Cupido still hesitates. Wine is one thing, but he has heard enough tall tales, from Servaas Ziervogel and others, to feel diffident about the whole thing.

'Are you coming inside or not?' asks the man. 'If you come, you can decide for yourself.'

Whereupon Cupido ventures into the small whitewashed church with the others. What makes him feel uneasy is that all the Khoi people are thronged together in this end of the church, and all the white men in a solid mass at the far end. The guns are still all over the place. Perhaps it would have been better to stay outside, wine or no wine. Beginning to feel stifled, he darts his eyes in all directions to see whether he could still make a quick getaway.

But before he can dash to the door a long thin man in a black tailcoat and a gibbous bald head enters from the front, and the crowd opens to let him through, like a narrow kloof in the mountains. He proceeds to a trestle table at the front. On the table Cupido notices a few silver platters stacked with bread. And several shiny jugs.

'Wine,' the little old man beside him whispers.

Not very much for such a crowd, thinks Cupido, but by now he feels so thirsty that a single swallow will seem like a fountain.

The tall bald man flings his long arms wide. It seems as if he were preparing to fly, and for a moment Cupido is convinced of it. But at the last moment it does not quite happen, although Cupido keeps on expecting something of the kind. The man utters a few sentences which in the general noise Cupido cannot understand: he is ready for anything. But then, without preparation or warning, the Khoi congregation bursts into song, and Cupido joins in with gusto, his big voice resounding like a bell – his own tune entirely, as he used to do at prayers on the farm of his first Baas, a rain-song for Heitsi-Eibib. Only much later will someone inform him that it was Psalm 134 that was intoned that morning:

*Behold, bless ye the Lord, all* ye *servants of the Lord, which by* night stand in the house of the Lord . . .

Even before their ringing voices have quite died down, the white people at the far end of the church rise to their feet to reply from Psalm 74:

*Thine enemies roar in the midst of thy congregations; they set up their ensigns* for *signs . . . They have cast fire into thy sanctuary, they have defiled by casting down the dwelling place of thy name to the ground . . .*

For a few minutes it seems as if the opposing groups are going to do battle right there in the church. But wholly unperturbed the tall man in front raises his two long arms and calls in a loud voice, 'Let us pray.'

And in that way a confrontation is avoided which for a moment Cupido has thought a foregone conclusion. What a pity, though, that in all this upheaval no wine has been poured.

But the event continues to haunt him. He goes to tell Anna about it, not immediately, but after it has been turned and turned in his mind like a pebble in a whirlpool after a sudden downpour.

'You must not meddle with such things,' she answers laconically. 'That's the white man's business. It's got nothing to do with us.'

'There were many of our people there too.'

'Your people, perhaps, not mine. Not San people. We know better.'

'You pretending to be better than me now?' He puts a hand on his *kierie*. He has never raised his hand against her; but she should not try his patience. And she knows it.

'Not better. Sometimes worse. But we, the Khoi and the San, we got our own road before us. If we land under the feet of the whites they will trample us.'

'We are under their feet from the day we are born. We don't want it to be that way, but that is how it is.'

'We can't change anything about how we came into the world. But what we doing *now* we can choose. And I don't like it, Cupido.'

'There was something about that man,' he says, still troubled, his eyes half closed. 'I don't know what it was. All I know is that it could have turned into a bad thing. There was thunder in the sky, but that man wasn't scared at all. His face seemed to shine.'

'Makes no difference.'

'The man can fly,' he announces in sudden inspiration.

'What?'

'He can fly.'

'How do you know that?'

'I saw him, Anna. With these two eyes.'

'That's a lie.'

'Hear what I am telling you, Anna.'

'I shall hear, but I won't listen. Not when you're chewing stale dry tobacco.'

'We shall see,' he says.

'Yes, we shall see.'

And there, for the time being, the matter rests.

# 16

## The Day of Almost-War

CUPIDO MUST BE WITH another woman again, Anna Vigilant concludes, disgruntled, as he regularly disappears from home over the following weeks, even when he is supposed to cut wood or fit a wagon wheel or plane a table for the landdrost. Or otherwise he must be drinking again. If only he isn't getting into scrapes. But in fact it is to the church he goes, or to the little hall nearby where the Reverend van der Kemp or one of his assistants – the sickly Reverend van der Lingen afflicted by a hunchback and a weak chest, or the ruddy-faced young Reverend Read – is employed in the ministrations of the Church. Read, who only recently arrived from England and is still struggling with Dutch, is mainly occupied with teaching children arithmetic and writing. The two older missionaries are involved with catechism of the thirty-two Khoi people eager to learn more about the Bible so that in due course they can be baptised.

Cupido does not mix with the others. But he is always around. Mostly to be at hand when somebody is needed to carry a chair or a table, or fetch a pile of spelling books from the vicarage, or run errands. He is usually greeted very heartily by the reverends, although the long thin man in the black corduroy coat and trousers is often too deeply wrapped in thought to notice anybody, as he moves in long, stiff-legged strides like a heron.

His absent-mindedness, Cupido is told by one of the cathe-
cumens when he has gained enough confidence to start asking
questions, comes from his being such a learned man. He can
speak every language known to man or beast, including
Xhosa, which he learned while working with Chief Ngqika
across the Great Fish River; and now he is even beginning
to pick up the Khoi language.

But what is a man like that doing in this place among them?
It is a long story, which is only pieced together for him
over time. But from what he can make out, the man is a very
learned person from far across the waters, a town much
bigger than Cape Town. But a difficult man too. They say it
was something terrible, the way he used to drink and smoke
and gamble and brawl. And women! Still unmarried, he had
a child with a girl he had picked up from the streets (strings
of children, some of the other people assured him), but then
he hauled another girl from the streets and married her while
still persisting in his wicked ways. Until the Lord decided to
call him to order. And here he is today, in Graaff-Reinet, near
the turbulent eastern frontier of the Cape Colony.

No one can guarantee the truth of these stories. But something in the account strikes a *ghoera* string inside Cupido.
Particularly the bit about women, and drink, and cavorting
in the big city. A man like that, he tends to think, may be
worth listening to. Surely he must know what he is talking
about.

For some time he is still reluctant to take the step. But
then a few things happen which set Cupido thinking again.

The first comes hard on the heels of that Sunday on which
Cupido first ventured into the little white church. It starts
with rumours that a whole horde of the farmers, driven
from their homes on the frontier by marauding armed Xhosa,
have drawn their wagons into a laager near Swaershoek, just

beyond Bruintjieshoogte. Almost three hundred wagons, he is assured. They have sent a message that they've had enough of Hottentots desecrating their church in Graaff-Reinet, and unless it is stopped immediately they are going to burn the whole place down. They demand that all the pews be washed, that the paving around the church be dug up and a fence be erected around the church to keep out that bunch of heathens, and that the pulpit be covered with a black cloth as a sign of mourning because they have no minister of their own.

Van der Kemp goes to discuss the demands with Mijnheer Maynier, who has recently returned to the town, now as commissioner in charge of its security. Things do not look too good. Should violence break out, there are only twenty-one lightly armed dragoons, nineteen *pandoers*, or Hottentot soldiers, about eighty armed Khoi, a handful of white inhabitants and four small field cannon to defend the town. For his part the missionary agrees to withdraw his Hottentot congregation from the church to restore peace: in future they will gather in his vicarage. Any whites who wish to attend the services will be welcomed. But as far as he is concerned he will never again set foot in a church from which a congregation of native people has been expelled.

In addition to these demands the farmers want all Hottentots suspected of having been implicated in attacks on farms handed over to them. But here Maynier refuses: if there are Hottentots in town accused of such crimes, he will have them arrested and tried according to the country's laws – but there is no way in which he will surrender them to a lot of farmers who insist on taking the law into their own hands.

At that stage the rebellious farmers are gathered a few hundred yards from the town, sheltered behind a round hill.

The available troops form a crescent at the lower end of the town, ready to attack,

Cupido is also there. Here is a big thing coming, he thinks. The air is heavy with murder and fire and brimstone.

At the moment when it seems the shooting is going to break out – the field cannon are already drawn up in a row, the soldiers positioned to load and fire – the long-legged stork van der Kemp comes ambling towards the troops. At the vicarage he turns into the yard, goes round to the back of the house and returns on horseback. Some of his people try to intervene, but he motions them to stand back and proceeds at an easy pace down the wide dusty street.

Halfway down, exactly opposite the spot where Cupido stands staring, the missionary suddenly draws in his horse, remains seated in the saddle for a while peering down at the ground before him, then slowly dismounts, goes down on his bony haunches and picks up something. For a moment he gazes about him with a vague, myopic look, then notices Cupido and comes towards him on his long reedy legs.

'Here,' he says, as if mumbling to himself.

Cupido mechanically puts out a cupped hand. The missionary carefully places on it what he has just salvaged from the road. A bright green mantis rocking on its delicate rear legs.

'Put this little thing in a safe place. If war breaks out today I shouldn't want it to be trampled to death.'

Without waiting, he turns back to his horse, mounts with a somewhat ungainly swing of his awkwardly hinged leg, and resumes his course down the street in the direction of the round hill just beyond the town, shimmering in the sweltering sun. Behind it, everybody knows only too well, lie the colonist forces, ready to attack. Surely that missionary, all alone against the hundreds of colonists, is riding towards his death. There is no hope of seeing him alive again.

Cupido feels his heart throb like a finch trying to escape from a trap. Folding his left hand cautiously over the one that cradles the insect, he goes to the edge of the road, into the nearest garden, where he delicately shakes off the mantis into a large tuft of dry grass.

Something of ineffable importance, he realises, has just happened. His body grows quite still, gathering itself around the secret inside himself.

He returns to his place among all the other people, brown and white, thronged at the side of the road.

For a long time the town remains as quiet as a graveyard. Here and there a dog barks, a single dove is cooing heart-rendingly in the distance, down by the river the weaver birds are twittering. Any moment now, they know, hell itself is going to be unleashed on them.

And then the missionary comes back, as leisurely and unperturbed as before, this time accompanied by two of the colonists in moleskin clothes, with beards and broad-rimmed hats. Together, they enter the drostdy, with Maynier and his councillors, the *heemraden*, in tow.

Only after Maynier and Landdrost Bresler have emerged again, with the Reverend van der Kemp between them, to announce that peace has been agreed on and that the farmers are prepared to withdraw, does the crowd disperse and the townsfolk withdraw in small groups to their homes. Most of the Hottentot congregation repair to the vicarage for a thanksgiving service. And this time Cupido cannot be restrained. He goes inside with all the others. And, as is his wont, he sings more loudly than anybody else.

After the service the missionary leaves to join his colleagues in the little school. Cupido follows on his heels, still in the spell of all that has happened.

'Baas,' he says as he catches up with the man in black.

Van der Kemp stops. He turns round slowly. Below his heavy black brows that form two upside-down carpenter's squares on his domed forehead his eyes peer at Cupido.

'What did you call me?' he asks.

'Baas,' mumbles Cupido, suddenly choking in trepidation.

'You must never call me that again,' the missionary reprimands him in a very low voice. 'No man is another's baas in this world. We are all slaves in sin.'

'Baas?'

'No, I do not want to hear that word from your lips again.'

'Then what must I call the Baas?'

'You may address me as "Reverend". If you must.'

'Reverend,' Cupido repeats slowly, as if tasting the word. 'That must be a very high word.'

'It is not a high word. It is just a name.'

'It sounds like a name much too high for someone like me. It is too big and too white.'

'Not at all. If you really wanted to, you could become a reverend yourself.'

'I can't believe that,' says Cupido with an embarrassed chuckle.

'In the eyes of God there are no distinctions between men.' A pause. 'I told you we are all slaves of sin. But in the blood of Our Lord Jesus Christ we can all be washed clean from sin, freed by His infinite mercy.'

'How does one do a thing like that?' asks Cupido, his voice catching in his throat.

'Come to my catechism class tomorrow. Then we can start working on your soul.'

Cupido stares at him open-mouthed.

When he comes home, Anna is waiting for him beside her huge black cauldron in Ma Martha's yard.

'Where have you been?' she asks, sighing. 'With another woman this time of the day?'

'You see that soap?' he asks quietly.

'What about the soap?'

'You know how white the clothes come out of a wash with that soap?'

'Of course I know. You trying to teach me about soap now?'

'Tomorrow I am taking you to that reverend man's church. When we come out of that place we'll be white.'

'I tried once before to make myself white in a pot like this,' she reminds him. 'I'm still limping from trying to be white.'

'It is not your body or mine I am talking about, Anna.'

'Then what are you talking about?'

'There's something they call the soul.'

'Just let me be,' she says, turning her back to him as she starts stirring with the long ladle again.

'That man talks a lot about washing,' he says. 'Like you, he also believes in mixing blood with the soap. He says it makes the washing whiter than anything else.'

Anna cannot help glancing askance at him, to make sure he is serious. But she is still obstreperous. 'What does he know about soap?'

'Why don't you come with me, then you can see for yourself?'

She gives an angry click of the tongue. 'You don't know what you're talking about, Cupido Cockroach.'

'Just wait,' he says. 'One day people will call me Reverend.'

She laughs, a long laugh stretched out like a gut.

'Reverend my arsehole.'

Undeterred, Cupido persists: 'I am going to be a child of the Lord,' he says.

# 17

# In the Name of Father, Son and Ghost

THE NEXT MORNING they all repair to the *heemraad*'s home
close by the church where the catechism takes place: Cupido
and Anna and the four children, Vigilant, Geertruid, Rachel
and Jan. Cupido and Anna do not speak. Once, as they are
leaving Ma Martha's house, he glances at her putting on her
red doek, she gives him a look that carries a dire warning:
Just say a word and I'll fix you with the soap ladle.

And she is. There is nothing subservient in her attitude.
On the contrary. One has the impression that she has been
lying awake all night, thinking: I first want to take a good
look at this thing. I am a San, and I'm not going to get caught
so easily. But if this so-called reverend can truly fly, and if
he can keep you away from other women and from drink
and fighting, he may not be so bad after all.

In the front room of the *heemraad*'s house she takes a seat
on a straight bench right at the back, with a few of the other
women; and the children squat down in front, on the floor
of peach stones, inlaid in pretty patterns in a layer of dung
and honey. Cupido is seated right in front, as straight-backed
as a meerkat. He is not going to miss anything.

First the young Brother Read addresses them. He is
clearly still struggling hard with the intricacies of the Dutch
language, his tongue still tied by English, which turns his
young ruddy face even redder. Still a bit unripe for a

reverend, thinks Cupido, like a green peach. Poor thing, the sun of the Kamdeboo seems much too hot for him. What Cupido does approve of is the way in which the man's pale blue eyes survey the women in the group, especially the young ones. That is something he can relate to. He decides to give the brother a chance with his soul. One never knows.

But it is the tall reverend he is waiting for. And when van der Kemp at last makes his appearance, picking his way through the many seated bodies like a cat walking in mud, Cupido casts a quick glance over his shoulder to make sure Anna is watching.

And she is. This missionary has a way of speaking which immediately grabs hold of one. Without any beating about the bush he starts talking about hell. About the pool of fire and brimstone, which reminds Cupido very strongly of a soap pot frothing and bubbling and boiling over in the yard. About the screams of the damned and the gnashing of teeth. He flails with his arms like a bustard trying to work up speed on the plains. Any moment now, Cupido feels, just like the last time, he is going to take off, over the heads of the assembled people, through the open door, away.

What does take flight and float is his voice. Higher and higher as he mounts the rungs of sin – drinking, blaspheming, gambling, fighting, whoring – until the very highest, where the whole house is reverberating with the sound. Followed by a total, deathly silence as when a windstorm in the Koup goes to ground among the hills. And then his voice begins again, like a small breeze stirring among leaves. Softly, as he tells them of mercy and caring and peace, of faith, and hope, and charity. Soon the tears are streaming down his pale, furrowed cheeks. Many of the men and women in the group are also weeping.

He talks to them about the years of his youth in the city of Leiden. About excesses and sin and heathen self-indulgence. And then about the day in the small rowing boat on the River Meuse, and the storm coming up. The howling wind, the screams of his wife and child. Once again his voice attempts the ascent into heaven, higher and higher. And this time Cupido is so transported that the miracle happens. He sees the reverend starting to swing his long arms once more, rowing and rowing, like two great wheels beginning to turn, two enormous wings, and then he sees the reverend floating up, very slowly at first, then accelerating, with larger flailings of his arms. And not only the reverend, but Cupido too: he can feel his body coming into motion, his arms sprouting feathers as they are transformed into wings, the huge wings of an eagle, a trembling that begins in his feet and moves up through his thin legs, and higher still, up along his spine, the vertebrae of his neck, still higher – and now the movement is spreading from him to the rest of the people, all of them, men and women and children, up to the high ceiling and out through the windows, like a flock of birds wheeling and spreading out over the whole town and heading for the mountains, high above all hills and koppies and ridges and heights, along the sluggish meanderings of the Sunday's River, and still on, to the blood-red sea, following the coastline past the mouths of many rivers, the Bushman's River and the Riet River and the Great Fish River, beyond the border, beyond all imaginable borders, impossibly far away, and still higher and higher, past the moon and the stars, all the way to the sun, and then right through the sun, one blinding light to all sides, a flood of purest light that shines through them, cleansing them like the brightest soap Anna has ever boiled, and then back, more and more slowly, reluctantly, languidly, until at last he can make out the town below them again, the broad streets bordered by water furrows, the oblong gardens, the sparse trees, the sprinkling of houses, the drostdy, the church. And at last they are back in their seats, and the reverend comes down among them from the heavens above, flapping his wings a few last times, one last time, shuddering to the tips of his long feathers, and coming to rest in a final quiver. His face is aglow, he is wet with perspiration, his huge domed head like the egg of some outlandish bird from another space is shining wet. Many of the people are sobbing with uncontrollable emotion. Cupido sits gasping, open-mouthed, it feels as if he has been with a woman who has drained him of every last drop of moisture in his body, every last thought in his mind.

*Praise ye the Lord*, he hears the holy man's voice still coming from afar. *Praise the Lord, O my soul. While I live I will praise the Lord: I will sing praises unto my God while I have any being.*

And that is only the first morning.

That evening, long after they have put the children to bed like a row of small, newly baked loaves of bread on the floor, he and Anna are still talking.

'I'm glad you went with me,' he says in the dark, when their intimate business is done.

'I had to go. You are my husband.'

'But you did it for yourself too.'

'Yes, for myself too. But that missionary is a dark man. His words are a danger to us.'

'He is a good man.'

'He may be good. But is he good for *us*?'

'What do you think about the flying?' he ventures.

For a long time Anna lies quietly beside him. Then she says, 'I'm not sure about the flying, Cupido. But he has a strong way of talking. That much I can say. And if he can help you give up the women and the drinking and fighting, he may be doing good. But I'm not sure if it is right for him to turn us away from our own believing.'

'Like what?'

'What will become of us if he turns me away from Tkaggen, or you from Tsui-Goab? What will happen if I can no longer dream the way I am used to?'

'Who says that will happen?'

'He speaks about his own Lord-God. He doesn't belong among us.'

'Don't you think there is enough space around for Tsui-Goab and Heitsi-Eibib and Tkaggen together with his Lord-God?'

'No, Cupido. Soon you will see there is no longer enough space for them all. The day will come, just you wait, when he will tell us: Now you must choose. It's either the one or the other.'

'We can think about it when that day comes. All I can think about now is to fly.'

She does not answer.

'What about you?' he insists.

'I been flying from the beginning, in my own way. Inside my head. And you know it.'

'But I want you to be with me. All the way.'

She sighs, grasping his hand in the dark. 'I shall be with you, Cupido. I shall walk with you. But when it comes to flying, you must not push me.'

The next morning she goes back with him. So do the children. For them it is a big adventure.

From then on they do it every day. Cupido continues with his sawing and cutting, Anna boils her soap. But in the mornings they attend catechism.

Some days there are only stories. That usually happens when Brother van der Lingen or Brother Read is in charge. Stories as they have never heard before. About Adam and Eve and the serpent. About Noah and his ark. About Daniel in the lions' den or Jonah in the whale or David and Goliath. Or about Our Lord Jesus Christ. Who could change water into wine and heal the sick and call a four-day-long dead Lazarus from the grave, and who was nailed to a wooden post with a cross-beam and then was resurrected just like Heitsi-Eibib, and who invited people to stick their fingers into the holes in his hands.

Then they sing again, services that go on for many hours. A singing which encourages Cupido to hurl his thundering voice against the walls, a singing that causes grown-up people to sob and children to piss on the floor and men and women to crawl on all fours with foam frothing from their mouths.

*Bless the Lord, O my soul: and all that is within me, bless his holy name. Bless the Lord, O my soul, and forget not all his benefits: who forgiveth all thine iniquities; who healeth all thy diseases; who redeemeth thy life from destruction; who crowneth thee with loving kindness and tender mercies; who satisfieth thy mouth with good things; so that thy youth is renewed like the eagle's . . .*

The children stare in awe at the grown-ups. They do not understand much of what is happening, but it is like potent liquor being poured into them, they are carried along by the flood, they cannot resist. They grasp at threads and snatches of stories. The singing transports them.

Throughout the winter months and the dusty spring when the trees begin to blossom, into the raging heat of summer. Until just before the New Year, when there is to be a large church service on the banks of the Sunday's River to baptise the recent converts, praise the Lord, hallelujah.

Over the previous days there has been torrential rain. In the river the current is flowing strongly, forming muddy swirls and eddies. As the Reverend van der Kemp wades into the edge of the stream, the angry tide reaches higher all around him. There are anxious voices calling from the bank. Should they not wait a few days for the flood to subside? There may be disaster lurking in the churning brown water.

But from the raging torrent van der Kemp calls out in a booming voice: Oh ye of little faith! The Lord of Hosts is calling you!

Anna Vigilant has been standing to one side all along. She is not ready for this thing yet. So far, she told Cupido, but no farther. At least not now. She needs time to consult with Tkaggen. How can she just turn her back on him? She still needs him. For all she knows, he may need *her*.

The children are passed on from hand to hand. Two of them start howling, trying to cling to Cupido's legs in fear, but he tears their hands away and pushes them down the steep bank into the waiting arms of the reverend. He cannot be detained by them at a moment like this. This is his day. His thoughts race on ahead of him. Perhaps he will take wing again, flying up to the bosom of God.

One, two, three, four, the missionary baptises the children. Vigilant, Geertruid, Rachel, Jan.

They scramble up the steep bank again, shivering and their faces streaming and shiny with tears and snot. Safe at last.

Now it is Brother Cupido's turn.

Over the raging water the voice of the man of God comes thundering: '*Behold, I was shapen in iniquity; and in sin did my mother conceive me . . . Purge me with hyssop, and I shall be clean: wash me, and I shall be whiter than snow . . .*'

Like Anna's soap, he thinks. One last time he looks back. Anna is staring transfixed from the top of the high bank, surrounded by sobbing children. She is waiting for a miracle.

But what happens is no miracle.

On the incline below the bank Cupido stands bedecked in his Sunday best, tall collar and all, an outfit Anna bought with her soap money. The missionary is engrossed in his peroration, waving his arms.

'Before this joyous day,' the pious man booms, 'before his conversion, our brother Cupido Cockroach was as notorious a sinner as was ever known: famous for his swearing, lying, fighting, lewdness, but especially for drunkenness, which often brought him up in a sick bed, being naturally weak. At such times he always resolved to leave that practice and lead a sober life. He was, however, surprised to find that no sooner did his health return than his sin again prevailed. Now, on this momentous occasion, he abjures it all, in front of the witnesses of the congregation of God.'

He throws his great head back: 'In the name of God, the Father, and the Son, and the Holy Ghost,' he calls in his stentorian voice, 'Brother Cupido, come down to the water.'

This is Cupido's moment. Everybody has been waiting for it.

Now, he thinks, now is his turn to fly.

He hurls his body from the slope of the bank into the river. The long missionary grabs at him, but misses. The furious torrent catches the frail body of the man who has flung himself so fearlessly into it. It thunders in his ears. This, he thinks, must be what Anna has so often spoken about, the moment of entering one of her dreams, when it felt as if she was going under water. Dream, Cupido, he thinks, for God's sake, dream! Now! Hurry! Dream! But in the churning waters all thought is washed from him. He can no longer breathe. There is water everywhere, outside, inside. Brown, tumbling, rushing, booming water on its way to the sea. On its way, for all he knows, to hell.

Cupido feels it clutching him, overwhelming him, turning

him upside down, dragging him into a flood of darkness. This is worse than flying. And incomparably more wonderful.

Hallelujah, he thinks. So this is the end. Here he is dying for the third time in his life, this time for good.

Here I come, Lord Jesus!

# TWO

## 1802—1815

# The Reverend James Read

THE FIRST TIME I may be said to have properly made the acquaintance of Cupido Cockroach (although I had been afforded glimpses of him before) must have been at his baptism in the Sunday's River at Graaff-Reinet on that stormy day at the end of 1801. How ironical that having restored him to life from the raging flood I should have been the one ultimately to abandon him in the wilderness; and that having assisted in inducting him into the life of the spirit, in the end I was to be driven from the church for succumbing to the temptations of the flesh myself.

I always thought him a little bit mad. But if madness it was, it was of a challenging and engaging kind, which constantly pressed me to examine the foundations of my own manner of judgement and thinking. Was not my own decision mad when I chose to forsake the security and predictability of life as a humble carpenter in the small village of Abridge in Essex, preferring a missionary career in foreign and dangerous parts at the extremities of the earth? Was it not madness to cling to Luther in boarding the good ship *Duff* to depart for the southernmost shores of Africa? — *Not the deed which thou choosest, but that which befalls thee against thy will, and thy mind, and thy desire; that is the path thou must tread, thither do I call thee, there be thou his disciple, that is thy time, that is the path thy Master trod.* Consider the outcome: a voyage of fully two years, taking us first to the coast of Brazil where we were captured by the French pirate ship *Le Grand Bonaparte*, and then to Montevideo and Rio de Janeiro on another ship which in its turn was intercepted by a Portuguese fleet that deposited us in Lisbon; then back to London, downcast and destitute, from where a mere seven of us were still determined to proceed to the Cape. Today, in truth, I must confess that I know not whether this was in pursuance of Luther, yielding my own wish to whatever God might have in store for me; or a blasphemous clinging to my own will, when so many of my companions had perceived in our adversity a clear sign of God's desire to prevent us from reaching the Cape of Good Hope, as it is called (whether providentially or ironically, remains to be seen). Are signs ever clear? Does the soul ever know its own blind reasoning? Where does the inscrutable will of God end and the stubborn self begin? I was still so young, barely twenty-three, when we stepped ashore in this wild land. How could I ever, then, have foreseen what tribulations still lay ahead?

I raise all this because it is pertinent to my acquaintance with Cupido Cockroach, who may be said now – too late, perhaps – to have been the bane and burden and the blessing of my life.

As I now remember it, my first encounter with him must have occurred some months before the ambiguous day of his baptism when it appeared to be God's will for me to save his life. It was in the small whitewashed church of Graaff-Reinet, where there was a spectacular confrontation of Hottentots and colonists in the congregation. Our Father van der Kemp preached the sermon, but he refrained from interfering when the clash, expressed in the raucous and defiant singing of opposing psalms, broke out. He was not always so passive and peaceful! But on that day he seemed intent on allowing the raging emotions to subside of their own accord, as the two parties appeared to become ashamed of themselves in his serene and almost saintly presence (if it is not a sin to speak of a man in such terms). On that occasion I noticed Brother Cupido among the others only because of the way in which he joined the singing, and because of his huge voice that resounded like an organ, even if wholly off-key and out of tune, in that small and austere building.

A mere few weeks later, as I now recall, the tensions threatened to erupt in war. That was when I noticed Brother Cupido once again, in a cluster of people thronging the main street that led from the church out of town, to where the colonist forces had been mustered behind a hill. Fearless, and ignoring my own entreaties and those of other Christians, our Father rode out on horseback to negotiate with the enemy (after all that has happened in the intervening years it is with much sorrow that I must indeed acknowledge the colonists as our enemy). That was when, noticing a small green mantis on the road before his horse, our Father pulled in the reins, alighted from his steed like the noble warrior he had been in Holland before ever coming to these distant climes, picked up the insect and almost lovingly deposited it in the hands of Cupido Cockroach before proceeding on his way. I am quite sure that our Father did not even notice the individual he handed the small green creature to; nor do I believe Brother Cupido was much aware of it. He might well have disposed of it immediately afterwards without being in any way aware of the significance of the moment. But I had witnessed it, and to this day I cherish the memory, which is so perfectly consonant with everything I observed in our Father from the day of my arrival on these shores until his deeply lamented death a dozen years after the occasion of Brother Cupido's baptism. (How often, when he could be persuaded to take a bath in the small basin placed on his floor for that purpose – something that happened only rarely, as his mind was always set on much loftier things – I would enter his dingy rooms to find him still gaunt and naked beside the basin, the water in the pitcher long gone cold, as he tried to coax some ants out of the bath, one by one, accompanied by many a muttered prayer, to avoid the risk of drowning them.)

This was so unlike Brother Cupido's own approach to life, and to faith. Head over heels, tempestuous, passionate, extreme. All of this was epitomised, I believe, on the very day of his baptism, when as the moment for his immersion in the river approached, he precipitated himself down the steep bank and took a flying leap, head first, into the raging waters. (Several of us, Brother van der Lingen and I included, had tried to caution our Father van der Kemp and recommended that the ceremony be postponed to a more propitious occasion when the waters would have subsided, but he refused – obstinately, if I may use the word – insisting that once the hope of salvation, coupled with the profound experience of baptism, had been kindled in a Christian's breast, no man should thwart that prospect and escape the wrath of God.) He hurled his insignificant body into the churning brown waters and promptly disappeared. A cry of anguish went up from among the assembled crowd. Some women began to weep, others collapsed in prayer; the four newly baptised children of the new convert were screaming.

As it happened, I found myself some little distance downstream where items of clothing lost or discarded by the children in the course of their immersion had washed out among the reeds. When Brother Cupido (not yet a brother, of course, but perhaps I had already thus conceived of him in my mind) emerged momentarily, it was directly opposite me, though several yards in from the bank. Almost without reflecting, but with a prayer on my lips, I flung myself forward, without it even occurring to me that I myself had never learned to swim. All I can say is that God Himself must have mightily intervened. As I managed to catch hold of the body churned about in the torrent, my feet found some fastness in all that fervent, fluid mass and I came upright bearing in my arms the now limp body of our brother-to-be. Hands were grasping me from behind, and we were dragged ashore.

It was characteristic of our Father van der Kemp that before proceeding to resuscitate the prostrate man on the bank, the missionary, like some apocalyptic figure, first hauled him back to the edge of the waters, dunked his head into the flood, nearly drowning him a second time, and pronounced upon him the sacramental words of baptism in the name of God, Father, Son and Holy Ghost. Only then did he return the waterlogged man to the bank, where several of us collaborated in administering to him such clumsy but well-meaning attempts at restoration as to bring him back to life.

There was a curious moment when Brother Cupido finally sat up, his face and body still streaming with dirty water, gulped and belched a few times in a most unchristian manner, and forthwith proclaimed his intention to dive back into the river, he being unable to remember anything of the ceremony already performed in our midst. But our Father van der Kemp, shouting at him in an uncommonly peremptory voice, persuaded him that his baptism had indeed taken place and ordered him to hold his peace.

HAVING ENTERED WITH such a demonstration of violence into the brotherhood of the Church, it could be no wonder that Brother Cupido should proceed in like manner with his ministration in the service of the Lord and, later, after he had been ordained, his celebration of the sacraments. I remember an occasion when, already settled in Bethelsdorp, I came upon him vigorously beating up a young Hottentot man who had recently arrived at the mission station and of whom we had great expectations. It was appalling to watch. Although Brother Cupido was considerably smaller, and older, than the other man, whose name was Klaas Links, the attack was so ferocious that his victim was practically beaten to a pulp. Only with the greatest difficulty did I succeed in dragging him off the seemingly lifeless body of the poor young man. Even then it was only by using all my force that he could be prevented from continuing the attack.

After considerable time and effort he finally returned to a state where he could pay heed to my remonstrations and my urgent questioning.

'Why did you such a thing?' I asked.

'Because he refuses to repent his sins and be converted.'

'It is not a thing you can achieve by force,' I admonished him. 'God works in mysterious ways, Brother Cupido, and in His own good time.'

'God cannot abide sin,' he replied. 'This man is like a nail driven into the body of the bleeding Jesus. I cannot allow this.'

'No, Brother,' I pleaded. 'Be patient. Rather go on your knees and pray for him.'

'I have been doing that for a month now and I shall go on doing it. Now I shall wait until he is recovered, and then I shall give him another chance. If he still hardens his heart, I shall beat him again.'

'Brother Cupido, for God's sake! In trying to save this poor man you are placing your own soul at risk through the excesses of your violence.'

'God has spoken to me, Brother Read. I know it is His will that this man must be converted to the faith.'

'Surely not in this manner,' I argued. 'Don't you see you are doing much more harm than good?'

'That is for God to judge.'

'And suppose you kill him?'

'God will see to it that he doesn't die before his soul is saved.'

No amount of arguing could make him see the error of his ways. I resolved to keep a close eye on Brother Cupido, particularly as Klaas Links began to recover. But he outwitted me. Very early one morning, even before our church bell summoned us to prayer, when it was still dark and only the first streaks of blood began to show in the sky, I was awakened by a hellish commotion in a hut nearby. I ran in that direction and came upon Cupido in the process of once again beating young Klaas Links senseless.

Owing to the presence of some other people who had also been awakened by the tumult, we managed to pull Brother Cupido off the body of the hapless man and drag him out of the hut.

This time, in the presence of our Father, I once again tried to reason very urgently with our colleague. He was remorseless, and quietly but most firmly resolved to pursue this violent course of action until such time as his victim repented of his sins and accepted to be redeemed by the blood of Our Lord Jesus Christ.

After a long discussion everybody dispersed, leaving me and our Father van der Kemp alone.

'If Cupido refuses to mend his ways,' I said, deeply saddened by the events, 'we may be left with no choice but to expel him from our flock.'

Father van der Kemp went into a deep reverie, as was his wont. His brooding brow was lowered so darkly, and so tightly drawn, that one could hardly see his eyes.

'You know,' he said at last, with a deep sigh but, I could swear, with an unexpected twinkling of the eyes as well, 'it has been recorded in history that in the days of the Christian king Charlemagne attempts were made to bring the Saxon people into the fold of Christendom. But they refused to be baptised. For thirty-eight years in succession Charlemagne sent expeditions against the Saxons to bring them to their knees. Thousands upon thousands of people were killed. Until at last they submitted and agreed to accept the Word of God.'

'Father, you cannot expect Cupido to keep on attacking this man for thirty-eight years.'

'I trust not. But perhaps we should not interfere unduly with what may well be God's way of going about his work.'

I felt it imprudent to contradict him. And perhaps God was indeed a witness to our conversation. Because just about one month later, after Brother Cupido had once again eschewed our surveillance and beaten the recalcitrant Klaas Links to a moaning heap of tatters and torn flesh, with a shattered nose and blackened eyes and broken ribs and a dislocated arm, the poor young man appeared before us and asked to be baptised. Klaas Links became one of the most ardent believers and one of the most conscientious members of the Bethelsdorp congregation.

THERE HAVE BEEN many other occasions, over the years, when I was struck by the extremes of Cupido's fervour. The first time, as I recall, came less than two months after the memorable day of his baptism, on the long road from Graaff-Reinet to the farm known as Botha's Place, near Fort Frederick in Algoa Bay, where the government had allotted a tract of land to Father van der Kemp for the establishment of a mission station. Ever since his return from the Xhosa people beyond the eastern frontier some years earlier, this had been his dream and he never stopped entreating the authorities to make it happen.

A fair number of our congregation joined the trek, in the hope of finding some place they could call home, after a lifetime spent as strangers in the land they had been wandering in since time immemorial, yet from which the Dutch colonists had been attempting, more and more relentlessly, to expel them. Among these largely destitute and persecuted people Cupido Cockroach and his family could not but strike the observer as exceptional. As the fruit of his own labours as a sawyer, and those of his wife, the soap-boiler Anna Vigilant, he was now the proud owner of his own cart (somewhat rickety, it should be said, but more than serving its purpose), four oxen and a small collection of goats, sheep and cows. He had insisted on accompanying our trek, even though there was little we could offer him as reward. But he scorned the very idea of material gain (his wife, it must be said, was more mercenary in this regard, or perhaps more practical): his eyes, he passionately assured us, being constantly fixed on the cross of Our Lord Jesus.

There were indeed moments when it occurred to me that Cupido's Christian zeal threatened to tax even the near-boundless spiritual resources of our Father van der Kemp, but he refrained from admitting this openly. It was part, I thought, of the cross he himself had chosen to bear in electing to exchange his lucrative career as a military doctor, a scientist and a philosopher for the hazards and tribulations of a life among the deprived of Africa.

We must have been on the road for about ten days when we happened to come past a large cairn erected beside the road as it wound its way through a narrow passage in a range of mountains, the name of which I was not yet familiar with. I had seen such edifices previously (if such they might be called), on the long roads from Cape Town to the interior, and subsequently as I accompanied our Father on his second brief journey to the Xhosas, but had not paid any particular attention to them. They were simply some of the peculiarities one expects in a strange and heathen land. I seemed to recall that they were pointed out to me as structures erected by the Hottentots in honour of some obscure indigenous deity with a near-unpronounceable name; and I believe it was expected of each passer-by from that race to add his own stone to the pile in order to assure a propitious journey.

This cairn was a particularly impressive specimen, towering well above the reach of the tallest among us (which must have been Father van der Kemp himself). But ultimately, surely, there was no need to attach absolute significance to a heap of stones. Consequently, I was particularly surprised at Cupido's reaction as our trajectory took us past this monument. He uttered an exclamation in his native language which in the circumstances I was gratified not to understand, deposited the child he had been carrying in his arms, and dashed towards the pile where, instead of adding to the stones assembled, presumably over centuries, by travellers of his race, he started plucking and tearing them from the heap and casting them away in all directions.

'What are you doing, Brother Cupido?' I enquired.

'These – these are heathen things!' he exploded, in such a rage that he could barely articulate the words. 'They are a blasphemy. They are filthy. They are an insult to God.'

One or two of his companions approached to give him a hand. But Cupido angrily arrested them. He wanted no help, he shouted. This was an obligation laid upon *him* and no one else. To atone, I gathered, for all the wrongs he had committed in the years when he had lived enslaved by the chains of his pagan beliefs.

His wife tried to intervene, laying a hand on his arm to detain him. 'It is not necessary, Cupido.' But he fiercely shook her off and motioned her to retreat.

For the better part of two hours the trek had to tarry, at some safe distance, while Cupido continued to dismantle the entire cairn, stone by stone, hurling them into the bushes and a nearby ravine from where they could not easily be assembled again. Over the years, on many journeys, including the long one to the Cape in 1813 and that last, sad trek beyond the borders of the colony to take him to his final appointed destination in 1815, I saw him repeat this action, with such ferocious energy that it would cause even his calloused hands to blister and chafe.

I know that, particularly in the early years, in the environs of Botha's Place and then around Bethelsdorp where we ultimately settled our mission, Father van der Kemp would gently reason with him to point out that this action was extreme and unnecessary. Provided that in his heart he had turned away from his heathen past, there was no call for dismantling the mere external signs of pagan rituals. But on Cupido this argument made no impression, and his energy never flagged in the execution of this self-imposed vocation.

There was another respect in which his crusade against what had once given meaning to his life was carried to seemingly unwarranted extremities, and that was the enthusiastic dancing and singing that marked the nights of the new moon and the full moon. In this regard, however, he was less successful. These festivals, it would appear, had taken such a hold on the mind and imagination of his people, even those of them who had largely shed their early devotion to superstition, that nothing, but nothing, could make them desist.

Not even Cupido's dire threats, his imprecations and damnations, his outrageous actions. Yet he refused to admit defeat. And after many months of moody contemplation he came up with a remedy I could not but applaud. (Father van der Kemp wryly observed that the solution was not unlike that found, centuries ago, by the Catholic Church in its attempts to stamp out pagan rites in Europe.) He decided that henceforth the dancing and singing could proceed with the same dedication as before, except that Christian psalms would be substituted for the ancient heathen songs. With this everybody seemed content, and our new-moon and full-moon nights at the mission in Bethelsdorp continued, curiously, to be marked by wild indigenous celebrations. Which our Father van der Kemp not only tolerated but, in some unfathomable way, appeared to approve of.

HOW OFTEN OVER the nearly twenty years between what one might term Cupido's accession to grace and my own fall from it have I had occasion to ponder the strange and intimate bond between Father van der Kemp and Cupido. In a somewhat perverse manner, I can now finally bring myself to acknowledge perhaps a tinge of envy in my observation of it. How I would have loved to embrace our missionary as the father he was to Cupido. We were always close, and more and more so as his powers (but not his faculties) waned and he had to keep to his bed for months on end with physical weakness and the pains of rheumatism while I had to take charge of the administration of Botha's Place and later Bethelsdorp. I admired the man and actually, inasmuch as this could be done without succumbing to the temptation of idolatry, worshipped him; I loved him as I have not in all my life loved another person. But in his eyes, I believe and can now admit without rancour, I never was the son to him which our Cupido so unequivocally seemed to be.

That closeness might well have been informed, not only by what their personal histories had in common, but by some remarkable coincidences in their temperament and character, even if at first sight it might seem foolish, if not sinful, to compare a man of our Father's erudition, his nobility of mind, his European sophistication, with someone like Cupido Cockroach, born in poverty and ignorance within a family of indigenes, deprived of education, insight, understanding and opportunity for the greater part of his life, living in squalor, vice and misery until he first saw the light of Christianity. Yet these things, I venture to say, are no more than superficialities. Deep down they must have sensed a link between their shared memories of a depraved and profligate youth devoted to the pursuit of all the indulgences of the flesh, and between their utter devotion, once they had turned towards God, to the interests of the Christian religion, as well as their mutual inclination towards extremes and excesses in the passionate demonstration of their beliefs, their convictions and also their condemnation of whatever to them seemed frivolous, heinous or unworthy.

They were both, it now seems to me, driven by a peculiar and ferocious sense of pride. Not the *vanitas* of the Bible, but a pride derived from unwavering faith. I recall the occasion, soon after our settlement in Bethelsdorp, when having retrieved a ship's bell from a vessel that had run upon the rocks in Algoa Bay, our Father proudly installed it in the steeple of our humble church and duly recorded his sentiments in a letter to the directors of the London Missionary Society in London in these words which I was requested to copy:

He who commands the sea and waves, permitted a ship entering into the Bay to strike upon a rock and to be dashed into pieces; the crew and the cargo were saved, and the sea cast up the ship's bell for our use.

This was one of the few occasions when I dared to voice some mild misgivings about a course of action employed by our Father. How could he believe, I asked as I perused his letter, that God would have caused a ship to run aground only for the sake of providing him with a bell for his little church in the wilderness? Was that not arrogance to the point of blasphemy? Or, at the very least, was it not insufferably naive?

'My son,' the Father said (a form of address which could but poignantly exacerbate my awareness of *not* being a son to him), 'my son, the ways of God are unfathomable and obscure. Who are we to question them? He has provided us with a place of our own in this land of strife and peril and He must have known the importance of ringing His praises in the wilderness with a bell of our own. How can you doubt' – he smiled in benevolent reproach – 'the extremes to which He will go to mark us with the sign of His blessing?'

It was much like Brother Cupido prevailing upon rebellious leaders of his tribe – most notably in Algoa Bay, in that dangerous no man's land between the white colonists and the increasingly restless armies of the Xhosa people, the violent and ever-turbulent Klaas Stuurman, the rowdy ruffian Trompetter, the drunken scoundrel and big-game hunter Boezak – to submit to our preaching since he himself, he insisted, had been chosen by God to overcome a lifetime of blasphemy and transgression for the sake of leading the entire Hottentot nation to redemption.

It was not only pride they had in common. There was the

violent and volatile temper, the contempt for adversaries and
the scornful and dismissive manner in which they treated
these, the often quite reckless assumption that, through their
faith, they were right and others always wrong, the conviction that having themselves battled through the encrustations
of sin before acceding to the truth, they knew better than
anybody else the nature of evil, which entitled them to the
unremitting condemnation of anyone who had not yet seen
the light. (How well I understand this! I know now, too late
perhaps, how much I too, in my eagerness and zeal through
many years to prove to our Father my own assiduity and
unquestioning support and to assure for myself his approval,
might have yielded to the same temptations as Brother
Cupido. Father van der Kemp was quite simply a man so
extraordinary, in his demeanour so saintly, in his effect on
others so forceful, that the stamp of his approval seemed like
the greatest trophy one might wish for, his dismissal or mere
aloofness the most dismal form of rejection.)

But I would be sorely remiss were I not to affirm, as well,
the many other qualities they shared: gentleness, self-sacrifice,
humility, loving kindness. As over the years I saw our Father
weaken and become more gaunt, more emaciated, his frame
more fragile – 'When I first saw the Reverend,' Brother
Cupido once said to me, not long before the old man's death,
'I thought he looked like a blue crane bird; now I think he
looks more like a marabou' – it was not merely the consequence of an ascetic life, but of a gradual hollowing-out and
burning-out from inside, as he cared more and more about
others, and less and less about himself. To the point of
discarding his shirt and wearing only his long frayed and
threadbare coat in all our blistering or freezing seasons, going
about barefoot because he could not bear to be shod while
members of his congregation were too poor to afford shoes.

And Brother Cupido likewise, like a small, poor scarecrow, dwindling to a mere shadow of himself.

Above all, of course, what bound them together was the memory of a youth of excess and unspeakable sin, and a sense of celebration for having been saved from it. How many, many times, did Cupido – in often quite embarrassingly frank terms, I should add – recount his lies and thefts and slanders and fights and bouts of drinking, which grew more and more disproportionate in the retelling; and particularly, as if it afforded him a particular Christian relish, his encounters with women, most shockingly with Anna Vigilant, the person who eventually became his wife, an escapade the fiery and unholy particulars of which I prefer not to reiterate. And how many times did our Father repeat to me, and to whomsoever else might wish (or sometimes not wish) to listen, the events of his own early years. His drinking and carousing, even after he had excelled in military service in Leiden and The Hague, studied in philosophy and the natural sciences in Edinburgh and Middelburg, and qualified as a physician; his unrestrained sexual appetite ('ruled by lust' were his own words); his profligacy and rowdiness; his unruly temper . . . And then the day when it all changed in a single moment of unforeseeable tragedy, when on an outing on the Meuse at Zwijndrecht, on a perfect summer's day at the end of June 1791, a sudden squall capsized the boat in which he was rowing with his wife Stijntje, whom he had practically rescued from the street, and his little daughter Antje, left behind in his care by the married woman with whom he had been having an affair. They were killed, he was saved. And that was the turning point of his life. Previously he had sometimes vacillated about religion. (How well I remember the words in which he told me of the mental distress in which, he said, he had in those dire moments addressed God thus: 'Oh my

Jesus, if I have to trust to Thee alone, I am afraid of being obliged to agree with the Christian doctrine, which has however proved, through repeated investigation, to be a web of absurdities, contradictions and blasphemies!') Now his future had been resolved. Initially, all he knew was that it would be a life devoted to religion, to the Church. But after some time it became clear that the only satisfactory course would be to choose the life of a missionary.

WHAT IS IT that leads men to become missionaries? There cannot be many common denominators. In many respects our Father van der Kemp must have been an exception, in the intensity of his dramatic experience on the road to his own Damascus. For the rest of us in the brotherhood of missionaries the driving forces have undoubtedly been more mundane and devoid of spectacle. In the case of poor Brother van der Lingen a mere glance at his crooked, humpbacked body, or a single utterance in his squeaky voice, must have made it clear – and God knows, I say this without malice, as a simple statement of fact – that he would never have felt at ease in the company of ordinary men and must needs have fled towards the missionary world as his sole sanctuary and refuge. Brother Anderson, whom I later met at Dithakong and to whose care I was forced to entrust Cupido, was – God forgive me – clearly a man driven by the need to exercise authority, something a person of his rather modest endowments could never have demonstrated in a situation inhabited by more forceful and more accomplished men. What about myself? I cannot evade the question, even though I am not always entirely confident of the answer.

Revisiting the memories of my early youth, it now seems to me that I have always been driven by the urge to protect and succour the helpless. How often in my childhood did I try to nurse small hurt birds and animals? – a fledgling with a wing broken by a fall from the nest, a hedgehog savaged by an eager dog, a squirrel wounded by the stone of a wanton boy. I remember particularly the incident with the squirrel, when – no more than ten years old – on my way home to attend to its wound I was pursued by the perpetrator, an ugly little miscreant who used to derive pleasure from bullying all the smaller children in the neighbourhood, and to appear most consummately happy when he could straddle the prostrate body of his victim, rubbing his face in mud or half drowning him in a puddle, refusing to let go before the luckless fellow grovelled before him in tears to acknowledge him as the victor. On this afternoon, the little monster – God have mercy on his soul – overtook and tripped me and tried to prise the squirrel from my grasp. The fight was fierce and rowdy, but did not last long. In the course of it the squirrel was squashed to death. I can still feel the quivering life escaping from that warm and limp little body. I was crying in anger and despair. And in some way as yet inexplicable to me, I found in the heart of my rage the strength to worm myself from the clutches of my adversary, grabbing hold of him by his tousled hair, and starting to hammer his head against the ground until he subsided in sobs, his face streaked with tears and silvery with snot, and began to plead for mercy. Which I then accorded him with a show of grace that surprised myself.

There was another, and possibly decisive, occasion in my adolescence, after I had just begun my apprenticeship as a carpenter, when at a summer fair on the village green of Abridge, where my mother and I lived, I gaped and gawked with everybody else at the animals put up for exhibition. These included a mangy bear with one eye poked out, an exotic little antelope hobbling on three legs, some scruffy monkeys with their thumbs severed, a gaunt camel. There was also a separate stall in front of which a large red banner proclaimed the inmate to be *A wild female from darkest Africa*. The poor creature sat huddled in a bundle of rags in a corner of the stall, cowering and whimpering as abuse and potato peels and rotten apples were hurled at her and the burly, red-faced man in charge of her kept prodding at her tender parts with a long stick to provoke some response. From the brief glimpses I managed to catch, it was not really a grown woman at all but a very young, very skinny black girl with pepper-corn hair and a dirty face. I was sick with abhorrence at the spectacle; yet I could not tear myself away, believing that the moment I turned my back the poor wild creature might be killed. As it turned out, something rather worse happened. When it became clear that the exhibit would stubbornly resist all attempts to elicit some energetic reaction, the trainer, if such he was, tore his broad brown leather belt from his bulging waist and began to belabour mercilessly the filthy young female body before him, encouraged by the shrieking and bellowing of the crowd.

Like all the other children of my generation, I had witnessed public floggings before and even a hanging (although that was without my mother's permission), but this time I could not take it any more. I began to retch and knew I would vomit. Blindly I fled the harrowing scene, tears streaming from my face. I was in such a state when I arrived at our home in Beadle Street that it took a long time before my mother could coax any coherent statement from me. After I had spoken, as I kept on clinging to her, sobbing and crying, she subdued me with icy strength and told me that there was absolutely nothing she could do about it. Cruelty happened in the world, and trying to meddle could only make it worse. I knew that if I had a father, he would have acted differently; but he had left us when I was not yet out of my cradle.

That evening, having foregone supper, I was unable to sleep. I could hear the church bell striking every dark hour. Shortly after midnight, without thinking of putting on any warm clothes over my night shift, I slipped through the window and returned to the fairground, which was now in utter darkness. But I managed to find my way to the row of stalls where the animals had been exhibited. In my mind I had formed a dull resolution to set free all those miserable creatures whose suffering I had witnessed. The camel, the thumbless monkeys, the bear, the little antelope. And the girl from darkest Africa. The animals were still there, each tethered to a pole in its sorry lean-to. Only the last stall, where the girl had been, was empty. My heart was pounding in my chest like one of the exhibition animals tugging at its leash. I could not leave the scene. I found that now that I was put to the test I was too pusillanimous to free the animals. Still I stayed. In my deepest mind I knew that it was not for them I had come, although I dared not admit what my real motive was. Round and round the fairground I wandered until, the fourth or fifth time around, I heard a sound coming from a dilapidated horse-drawn caravan at the far fringe. A moaning, whimpering, weary sound uttered in a childish female voice. Instinctively I knew that it was the girl, the *wild female*.

It was a hot summer night and the door of the caravan stood open. There was a badly smoking lantern inside, spilling its dusty light on the dirty floor. I was almost too scared to investigate, but something stronger than dread lured me to the threshold. I have often wondered since what exactly I could have made out in that treacherous light, and what I superimposed on the scene subsequently. But I am as firmly convinced now as I was on that night that it was the skinny dark girl and her massive, red-faced oppressor, engaged in carnal congress, thrashing about on a pile of filthy bedding in the middle of the floor, among unwashed dishes, scattered clothing and a clutter of domestic utensils. (What did I know of carnal congress then? One should not underestimate the instincts of a child growing up in a backstreet of a country town.) The whole interior was reeking with sweat and indescribable human or animal emissions and effusions.

At some stage the man must have raised himself on his outstretched arms above the keening girl and seen my shadow in the doorway. He bellowed at me. The girl cried out and writhed in the dark. There was no difference between the sounds she uttered then and the whimpering of pain that afternoon.

Like the previous time, I ran, and vomited, and ran again. Leaving all the tethered animals to their fate. And the girl to hers.

It was not yet a conscious decision on my part; but years later I knew that this was the day on which I resolved not to spend the rest of my life in Abridge but to become a missionary and devote my life to rescuing the poor and the oppressed of the world. Which was also, I believe, why Cupido made such a particularly strong impression on me from the day I first encountered him.

CONCERNING MY OWN relationship with Brother Cupido, there was undoubtedly, at the outset, a measure of ambiguity about it. To begin with he was a Hottentot, I was a white man. Which, regrettably, in a land like this, is of some – perhaps decisive – import. Also, although at the time I had not yet been ordained to administer the sacraments (that happy circumstance was not proposed to the London Missionary Society before 1805 and enacted in September of 1806), in Cupido's eyes I formed part of the religious establishment in Graaff-Reinet and was the Reverend van der Kemp's close assistant, whereas he began as a heathen from the wilderness, subsequently to be promoted to a newly converted, eager, but lowly member of the congregation. On the other hand, I was so much younger than he was, being a callow youth of barely twenty-three years old upon my arrival, by which time he must have been – although no one, including himself, could ever be quite sure – at least forty, and experienced in ways of the world of which I could still only, uneasily, dream about.

Also, lacking the gift of languages which our chief missionary so gloriously possessed, it took me some considerable time to master the intricacies and the guttural sounds of the Dutch language, not to mention the Hottentot tongue. (Fortunately, as it turned out, Cupido himself appeared to be more at ease with Dutch than with his mother tongue.)

Yet I dare say that from the beginning there existed some bond of sympathy between us, a readiness to understand and to trust, even at a stage when it could barely find expression except in a mutual beaming of goodwill towards each other. Undoubtedly our shared devotion to woodcraft brought a different, and material, dimension to our collaboration. Working together on the shaping and shaving and joining of various pieces of wood into a sturdy table or a rude chair or a workmanlike bench brought an experience of understanding which afforded us a dimension which I can only call a mutual awareness. An awareness of the life of the wood, of the tree that grew before it became table or bench, of its extension beyond our own lives. Cupido was not merely a practical man but something of an artist. And I discovered in him an affinity with the wood we selected and measured and cut and honed and planed and fitted together which seemed to me an expression of much that neither of us could readily put into words.

Even so, in the beginning at least, it could hardly be described as 'closeness'. This crucial step, I make bold to say, was finally taken in the year of Our Lord 1803, on 20 June to be precise, when I took to wife a young woman of the Hottentot tribe. She was very young at the time, certainly no older than eighteen, and the full inventory of her earthly possessions amounted to two sheepskins and a string of beads to ornament her slender body. If marrying a rich wife could act as a temptation for proving unfaithful to our calling, then I would by the grace of God be preserved from it. Furthermore, I confess that I earnestly believed the decision to take her as my wife might in future safeguard me from the temptations of the flesh which, I can now in my mature years confess, I have from my early youth been prone to. (Even though I am proud to say that I never quite, in those days, fully succumbed to the desire which our Father van der Kemp so openly admits to having experienced in a manner which might have done St Augustine proud; my only all-too-constant surrender occurring in the form of taking my needs in my own hand, as it were, following the lamentable example of Onan.) I could but hope that, poor as she was, my wife would find riches in Christ which neither she nor I was able to define. Her Christian name was, perhaps inevitably, Maria. Her Hottentot name I have never learned to pronounce.

This event, and this choice, provoked endless discussion over many years, at Graaff-Reinet and Botha's Place and Bethelsdorp, later at the Reverend Anderson's station in the place known variously as Lattakoo and Dithakong, and it would seem all over the colony. But I believed then, as I do now, that I could best accomplish my mission by identifying myself completely with my charges and by throwing in my lot with the people I was trying to convert. If this were seen by some to be 'degrading', which I strongly dispute, it could be no more than a temporary ordeal which surely would be amply counterbalanced by the spiritual uplift to follow. And certainly, if any vindication were required, this was provided most impressively when a mere three years later our Father van der Kemp himself, at the advanced age of sixty, took to wife a fourteen-year-old slave girl, Sara, whom he had bought and freed from bondage. (Another year later he also bought, and manumitted, the girl's mother and four siblings for the considerable sum of 3,250 rix-dollars, or £740). By that time my first daughter, named by her mother Soensi Karoossin, had already been baptised, adding a new pearl to the crown of Jesus. (It is gratifying to note here that it was Brother Cupido who insisted on making the child's cradle.)

Even some members of our Hottentot congregation appeared rebuffed by my marriage, and there might have been some among them who would have agreed with poor Brother van der Lingen, the only one among the missionaries who deigned openly to criticise my demeanour. 'What these people expect of us, Brother Read,' he told me in his gentle but censorious voice, 'is to set an example, not to descend to their level. We need to keep their respect. If one day we succeed in elevating them to our level, we shall have reason to rejoice. But that will never happen unless they have someone to look up to.'

Brother Cupido, on the other hand, most enthusiastically applauded my step into matrimony. On the very evening following the ceremony, rather obtrusively just as I was preparing to enter the small wattle-and-daub abode in which my bride was modestly waiting, he stepped into my way to grab hold of my hand as he said, 'Brother Read' (which was how he always addressed me; only Father van der Kemp was 'Reverend' to him), 'Brother Read, today I know the Lord has sent you to us. You are a man of courage and love. I shall praise you in my prayers to the day of my death. The Reverend van der Kemp will be my guide, but you will be my friend.' Followed by much more in the same vein. And then he burst into song.

Even after I had entered the little room Brother Cupido continued to sing outside, very loudly and very enthusiastically. It was so unsettling, I must confess, that only towards morning could my bride and I conclude the nocturnal business we had come together for.

And when I went outside in the early dawn he was there already, waiting for me, clearly prepared, as it soon proved, henceforth to be my shadow on our journey through this vale of tears.

IF TRUTH BE told, he had already begun to show a predilection for what I might call shadowhood as early as on our journey to Algoa Bay. The situation in Graaff-Reinet was by now untenable. Rumours from the Great Fish River region became more and more disturbing, threatening. Warfare in the land of the Xhosa, between the irascible old chief Ndlambe and his young nephew Ngqika, with whom Father van der Kemp had previously, briefly, been stationed, assumed alarming proportions, driving thousands of Xhosa across the border, and causing depredations among the frontier colonists, an increasing number of whom descended on Graaff-Reinet to find security in the proximity of government forces. The Hottentots appeared to be split into two groups with ever-changing loyalties within them: an increasing number, including the Algoa Bay bands of the rather disreputable and treacherous leaders Stuurman, Trompetter and Boezak, joined forces with the invading Xhosa against the whites of the colony, who for a century and a half, since the first arrival of the Dutch, had been the scourge of the indigenous tribes. But many others, particularly those domesticated by permanent or seasonal work with farmers, sought refuge with the whites – most of whom, in turn, did not want to have anything to do with them.

The situation in the little town was heading for a conflagration, especially after the confrontations in and around the village church where I had first observed Brother Cupido. So, when another invitation from the notorious Klaas Stuurman arrived to move to the coast and settle among the Hottentots 'in dire need of religious instruction', as he obsequiously phrased it, and when such a move received the support of the commanding officer of Fort Frederick in Algoa Bay, that seemed to be the obvious solution to our problem.

'The important thing is for the Hottentots to be free,' our Father van der Kemp insisted in our many repeated conversations. 'This used to be their land, Brother. They are accustomed to roaming the plains at will. There is no sense, and no justice, in trying to force them into subservience to the colonists whose only wish is to enslave them. Nor can they expect any justice in an allegiance with the Xhosa, who see no use for them except as buffers to absorb the pressure of whites set on expanding their own territory.'

'But do they *want* to be free?' I once ventured to ask. 'They need protection from someone.'

'Protection, maybe,' he said. 'Not exploitation.'

'How can we prevent exploitation?'

'By assuring them their freedom.'

'But that is a political act, not a religious one.'

'In a place like this there can be no distinction between the two, Brother.'

'Suppose they do not want what we offer?'

'I am not normally a supporter of the Frenchman Rousseau,' he said (and indeed it was the only occasion, as far as I can remember, when he referred openly to any of those dangerous French philosophers who had fomented most of the unrest in the world over the past twenty years and more), 'but in this instance I agree with his remark that there are circumstances in which a people must be *forced* to be free.'

I could not refrain from sighing. But I said, 'How will a move to Algoa Bay help us – help them – to achieve that?'

'It will take us closer to the heart of the troubled region. And it will assist us to be free ourselves. In a place we can call our own, and where those Hottentots who wish to remain apart from the strife of others can live securely in our midst.'

'Where does God come into all this, Father?'

He gave a small, enigmatic smile. 'God is everywhere,' was all he said.

I was not sure that this was really an answer; but one did not readily argue with Father van der Kemp.

And so, on 20 February 1802, almost two months to the day of Brother Cupido's conversion, we set out on the journey to Algoa Bay, accompanied by 109 Hottentots (some of whom deserted along the way, while several others joined our expedition).

Although the journey was not so long, a mere fifteen days or so (nothing compared to that perilous voyage over a decade earlier from England, to Brazil, to Portugal, and at last to the distant Cape), each moment was exhausting and fraught with trepidation about possible attacks from all sides. And yet there was an exhilaration about it, not just because of the prospect of finally moving to a place of our own in this savage land, but about the landscape itself: the harshness of the veld, of scrub and acrid bushes, aloes stretching their dry arms up in what seemed like supplication to an unrelenting sky drained of colour, rough hills and low but forbidding mountain ridges with foreign, as yet nameless vegetation, furtive antelopes darting away at our approach, speckled snakes suddenly rising up and hissing or spitting at us (once killing a cow, once a small child), occasionally a sleek, slinking, ominous figure behind low bushes in the distance, leopard or lynx or lion. And at night, hellish screams and yelpings and arpeggios of laughter echoing against the dark upturned bowl of the sky: only hyenas and jackals, we were assured by Cupido and the others, but sounding for all the world like demons cackling or jeering as they went about their infernal torture, enough to chill the very marrow in one's spine. ('*Out of the depths have I cried unto thee, O Lord,*' read our Father in his stern, unwavering voice beside the huge fire that blazed throughout the night. '*Lord, hear my voice: let thine ears be attentive to the voice of my supplication.*')

And yet, in the midst of one's terror, in the midst of a feeling of being all alone in a strange and distant place – dear God, how far we were from home! – there was an extraordinary, almost exultant, sense of being in a space suspended between heaven and hell, where one's presence, in some wholly inexplicable way, *mattered*. How old and remote Europe seemed from here: old, and remote, and – yes – beautiful, but inexorably sinking, drowning, fading into futility and pastness. While here, in the midst of these sounds of menace and violence and lurking death, here was something different, a timelessness, an awareness of futurity, a still untamed, unpredictable, savage energy, a passion unquenched and unquenchable, a force that might destroy people and lives, but which was life itself, a physical reality, a closeness, an urgency, a rare and unspeakable presence of wonderment and joy.

Through all this, almost literally day and night, Brother Cupido remained by my side like a necessary shadow, leaving me only sporadically to exchange my company for that of our Father. The missionary ensured that religious instruction, and lessons in reading and writing, were not neglected on the road, and several hours each day were diligently devoted to such pursuits. Cupido was as eager to join the lessons as he was to learn more about God and the teaching of the Church; and even before we reached Fort Frederick, where we had been allotted our tract of land at Botha's Place, he was able to write his own name and those of his wife and children.

Anna attended these lessons too, although she was never as forthcoming as her husband. I gathered the impression that she was not so much interested in learning anything from us as in not allowing Cupido out of her sight. Still, in due course, she seemed to gain some particular confidence in me. She undoubtedly held the Father in great respect, but she appeared to be more in awe of him than feeling confident openly to engage him in conversation. With me, on that tedious road, and more especially after our arrival in Algoa Bay, she began to trade stories. For my account of Daniel in the lions' den, she might offer a story about the mantis and the skunk (whom she called a 'mouse-dog'); Jonah in the whale would rate a narrative about a young man who killed a lion, only to find that the dead animal turned into his best friend; and, almost blasphemously, the death of Our Lord Jesus Christ on the cross elicited, unasked, a story about the eland, the ubiquitous mantis and the moon.

Against this background, I suppose, it was inevitable that a year or so later, by which time we had already made our second move, this time to Bethelsdorp, Anna Vigilant came to my room after dark one night, when everybody else, including Father van der Kemp, had already retired, to discuss with me the prospect of her own baptism. It caught me by surprise as Cupido had often imparted to me his anguish at her persistent refusal to follow him into the fold of the Church.

But she was quite frank about it. 'Brother,' she said (an appellation which I found somewhat uncomfortable coming from an unconverted heathen), 'I must go in the water. I want this thing you call baptism.'

'What has made you change your mind?' I asked, only too conscious of her earlier resolute rejection of salvation.

'I want my husband.'

'But you have your husband.'

'You do not understand,' she said impatiently, in her characteristic, formal manner of speaking. 'In all that time when Cupido go with other woman, when he fight and drink and do things, he is still my husband, he come to me, he sleep with me, he is my husband. Now you people of God, you take him away from me. So I must go where he go. You must put me in the water.'

Three months later Father van der Kemp performed the sacrament of baptism on Anna Vigilant and two more children, Anna and Tryntje, born since Cupido's own immersion.

OUR FATHER HAD considered the possibility of effecting the baptism in the sea, it being so close to the site of our mission near Fort Frederick: it was a view we could contemplate every day from where we lived, across a deep narrow valley covered in variegated green vegetation which in winter was set aflame by the fiery red candelabras of the tall aloes. But we had to renounce the idea, as many of our followers were scared of that expanse of water reaching to the horizon and beyond.

How well I remember Brother Cupido's reaction upon first perceiving the sea as we came over the last row of hills before our destination. He stopped in his tracks, carrying as usual one small child on his back and another in his arms. (The eldest boy, Vigilant, was already fourteen years old and had begun to give his father a hand at sawing wood; and little Geertruid was promising to become as adept at boiling soap as her mother.) He uttered an exclamation in his native tongue, and feigned deafness when I requested a translation.

'Is that the sea?' he asked.

'That is it.' Somewhat mischievously I enquired, 'Big enough for you?'

To my surprise, as he scanned that vast ocean from left to right and back again, and from shore to hazy horizon, he said, 'People talk so much about it. I thought it was much, much bigger.' After some reflection, he added, 'Now we shall have enough water for all the cattle.'

'But that water is salty,' I pointed out. 'One cannot drink it.'

'Then why did God make so much, if it is useless?'

I reminded him of the beginning of Creation, when darkness was upon the face of the deep and the Spirit of God moved upon the face of the waters, and God divided the waters and the dry land.

'I see,' he said, evidently bemused, and not appearing entirely persuaded. Then he stared hard at the dark blue ocean again. 'It is alive,' he said, clutching my arm. 'It moves. Will it not come up to us and devour us?'

'If God wills, it will stay down there,' I said.

'I shall have to speak to God about it,' he said, slowly releasing my arm.

'You do that,' I agreed. 'And tonight we can all pray about it.'

He narrowed his eyes again, still staring into the distance. 'Where does it go to?' he asked. 'Once it gets there where we can no longer see it: where does it go to then? Where does it stop?'

'It stops,' I suggested, somewhat guilty about my distortion of geography, 'where I come from. It stops at Europe and at England.'

'You come from the other side?'

I nodded my agreement. And thought again: how remote that other world, that 'other side', had become. Almost: how irrelevant. What mattered was *this* here, *this* now. There was a discovery of freedom in it. But also, curiously, the deep ultramarine, almost black wash in the distance, where sea met sky, brought a shiver to the spine, as if it were something to be feared, and even in its absence an ominous presence not to be denied.

HOW STRANGE, UNCANNY, it seemed that the distant Europe could continue to affect our lives so urgently. Not long after our arrival at Botha's Place we learned that a peace treaty had been signed at Amiens between France and England, in terms of which the Cape would be restored to Holland, now renamed the Batavian Republic. The British garrison was to be withdrawn from Fort Frederick, leaving us to the mercy of the opposing forces.

The situation was dire. From the east, more and more desperate Xhosas were streaming across the Great Fish River;

in the immediate vicinity of the fort a commando of colonists were preparing for attack. The Cape governor sailed to Algoa Bay to discuss our uncertain future; since Father van der Kemp could not at that time be moved from his bed, the governor came all the way to Botha's Place. He was anxious to move the entire station to Cape Town without delay, but our Father adamantly refused. God had brought us there, he said; God would look after us. At least, the governor entreated him, we should move into the fort as soon as it had been vacated by the garrison. But once again our Father rejected the proposal, arguing that this would be a cowardly thing to do. Moreover, there was not room enough for all our faithful followers, and to leave some behind would be an act of betrayal with which he could not wound his conscience.

I wholeheartedly supported this position. Yet no one could deny the heavy burden of trepidation and responsibility and, above all perhaps, uncertainty placed upon us. Over the past few years, in spite of all the threats against us, we could rely on the support of a sympathetic British government in the Cape. What was to happen when the Dutch returned? We had seen enough of the hostile attitude of the colonists in the frontier area to fear for the future.

A number of our Hottentot followers were ready to flee. But it was Cupido who, with a single helper, a recent convert, Samson, moved in among them and persuaded them to stay – by pleading with them, threatening them, beating up a few of the most rebellious, and finally exhorting them to start singing together, so energetically that no sleep was possible for any soul at the station from dusk to the following dawn.

The governor prepared to leave, and the inhabitants of our station at Botha's Place returned to their homes. I was confident that Cupido's enthusiasm would preserve them from any further thoughts of desertion – and as it turned out, my faith was justified. After the others had left, I remained behind for a few more days to take delivery of a generous gift the governor had offered us from the garrison's supplies: including a large quantity of rice, several casks of salted meat, a fair number of sheep, oxen and cows, three wagons, a fish net, a corn mill, two corn sieves, and a smith's bellows (which prompted me in due course to establish a fully equipped smithy at the mission).

However, the precarious nature of our situation was soon brought home when barely a week after the governor's departure, our mission was attacked by a troop of armed Hottentots in the deep of the night. All our endeavours to persuade them to an amicable agreement were in vain; their only response was to fire at us with their muskets.

Brother Cupido, tearing himself away from our entreating hands, approached them in the dark and started talking to them in a friendly manner. This was greeted by a chorus of abusive shouts, to this effect: Look, here comes a peacemaker! Kill him, shoot him!

'For God's sake, Brother Cupido,' I shouted after him, ready to follow him beyond the fringe of the light cast by our fires, but I was restrained by many hands. (Our Father was still confined to his bed in pain and quiet anguish.)

Then followed a new burst of shooting. I heard Cupido cry out. The next moment he managed to come hobbling back to us, having received, as it turned out, a bullet in the left leg. He was immediately taken away to Father van der Kemp's quarters where the good doctor, himself in pain, could attend to his wound, assisted by some of the women, including the young girl who was subsequently to become my wife. Even today I remember the scene in that smoke-filled hut, its only furniture consisting of two narrow beds of sheepskin stretched across poles, a simple table and two small benches. Father van der Kemp — already old beyond his years — lay under a few karosses, as those animal skins, roughly sewn together, are called in these climes, clad in no more than a coarse linen shirt, a blue kersey jacket and trousers. His bald but nobly chiselled head rested on a wooden block covered in hide; his intelligent features bore testimony to sorrow and to the exigencies of his precarious life. Around him, their heads turbaned and the bundles of their bodies wrapped in rags and tatters, dusted by the sad light of the single oil lamp, the women came and went in their bustling ministrations to the wounded Cupido.

At that stage we abandoned all attempts to fight back against the enemy forces in the dark. We could only hope that the marauders would be content to leave with our cattle. Yet it soon appeared that they were bent on killing us all. To that end they made use of our cattle in the way, I learned later from Father van der Kemp, they must have apprehended from the Xhosa: rounding up the cattle in front of them as a vast shield, they made an assault on our meagre dwellings.

But Providence had so ordained that only a day before I had gathered some planks newly sawn by Brother Cupido and laid them down in the passage between our house and the one next to it. The cattle took fright at these, and refusing to cross over them, they veered to the side, exposing the attackers in the rear. Our people, being in the utmost danger and compelled by the need for self-defence, started firing blindly without even attempting to take aim, on account of the dark. But the hand of God directed a ball in such a way that the chief of the troop was wounded in the thigh, by which an artery was severed, and the violent effusion of blood within a few minutes put an end to his life, whereupon the whole troop fled.

The following morning the dead body was found and

identified by some of our congregants as that of Andries, brother of the very Klaas Stuurman who had been instrumental in persuading us to trek to Algoa Bay.

THIS EVENT HAD an unexpected consequence. A few of our men had been dispatched to convey the news to Klaas Stuurman, whom we knew to be encamped some distance to the other side of the fort, at the mouth of a small stream. We were preparing for a major assault on the mission to avenge the death of the chief's brother. Instead, our two emissaries returned towards evening – there was a particularly spectacular sunset, the whole sky streaked in gaudy colours, which Anna Vigilant interpreted as an omen of impending slaughter – accompanied by a small detachment of Stuurman's men, dressed in European clothes (but barefoot), wearing great broad-brimmed hats, all of them armed with muskets. They drove before them a small group of long-horned cattle.

As our Father was still confined to his bed in agony, it fell upon me to receive the visitors. Following his urgent admonition, I left my own gun behind, if not without trepidation; and having instructed most of our deacons and elders to wait in their dwellings, armed to the teeth should anything untoward occur, I endeavoured to stride out with a great show of confidence, as I imagined our Father would have done (and as, in fact, I had seen him do on that memorable occasion in Graaff-Reinet). Quite unexpectedly, and entirely unbidden, Brother Cupido made his appearance at my side, hobbling rather painfully on his injured leg. It was too late to send him back; and even had I attempted to do so I am sure he would have refused. And in all frankness I must confess that his presence did shore up my own deficient courage.

The delegation halted a hundred yards or so from our

church, where I went to meet them, both arms outstretched and with my hands turned up to demonstrate my good intentions. To my immense relief, they responded in like manner.

They addressed me in quite fluent Dutch, and I was preparing to reply in the same language, of which I had by then a reasonable command; but to my surprise Brother Cupido intervened, announcing that he would act as interpreter. Without waiting for consent from either the emissaries or myself, he opened the discussion with a long peroration in the Hottentot tongue, which he then very laconically summarised for me in a mere sentence or two. Thereupon the negotiations began. Stuurman's emissaries requested that the body of the dead man be handed to them for burial. I had no objection to that. What most surprised me was the very profuse manner in which they apologised on behalf of the deceased, explaining that it had all been a terrible mistake: our proximity to the fort had led them to believe that we were allied to the military forces of the colony. I made it clear, through Cupido, that we were more than happy to treat the sorry event as a misunderstanding and that we were looking forward to continued amicable relations in future.

My fairly brief message was conveyed by Cupido in another peroration delivered in most dramatic and histrionic fashion, his version continuing for at least three or four times the length of my own; and I must say, our interlocutors appeared most impressed, even somewhat timorous, upon our assurances of good intentions.

The discussion was concluded with a ceremonious exchange of gifts: the Stuurman people offered us the six oxen they had brought, while I made the customary presentation of tobacco and even a small quantity of brandy; with some hesitation I felt obliged to turn down their quite brazen request for gunpowder.

The men went off in the deepening dusk, carrying upon their shoulders the body, wrapped in a green blanket. I felt most relieved at the unexpectedly peaceful turn of events, which I immediately went to communicate to Father van der Kemp. It was not before the following day that the event was placed in a new perspective when I thanked Brother Cupido for his intervention and enquired, more or less in passing, what had gone into his passionate rendering of my final message of peace. Only then, with a very broad smile, did he explain to me that what he had issued to the visitors had not been a declaration of peaceful intent but a dire warning: during the attack, he had told them, it was so dark that no one could see what was happening, which meant that the death of Andries Stuurman had not been caused by our gunfire at all. It had been our God who had personally intervened to project the ball and smite the heathen; and should their tribe ever again venture to attack us, he had warned them, the same God would return to pursue them to the ends of the earth and strike down every man, woman, child, cow and goat among them. *It is a fearful thing*, he had quoted from Scripture, *to fall into the hands of the living God*.

I deemed it prudent not to transmit this intelligence to our Father van der Kemp.

THERE WAS ALSO the question of the late Andries Stuurman's musket. In some inexplicable manner it was lost in the confusion of that night. And when the delegation arrived to retrieve the dead man's body and they enquired about it, nobody had seen it anywhere. With that, the matter rested. But it must have been about a month later when, returning from the beach where I had said my prayers, I came upon Brother Cupido sitting on his haunches in the dense bushes along the slope leading up to the fort, assembling a musket he had taken apart. All the pieces were spread out on a square of canvas, and in the process of reassembling them he oiled each one separately and meticulously before restoring it to its place in the mechanism. What particularly struck me about the weapon was a silver star that had been affixed to the side of the barrel, and which Cupido stroked with a special show of what I can only call 'affection'. Almost, if I dare say so, in the way a man might sensuously caress the cheek of his beloved. He looked up at my approach, but did not seem unduly perturbed by my presence.

'And this?' I asked in surprise. 'Where did you get this gun?'

'It belonged to that Andries Stuurman,' he said quite frankly.

'But everybody was looking for it after the attack. It was nowhere to be found.'

'It came to me,' he said calmly.

'You were not even there when it happened,' I said. 'You were with Father van der Kemp, attended to by the women.'

He shrugged. 'It came to me later,' he said. 'I think God meant me to have it, because I was wounded in the attack.' He pointed down to his still bandaged upper leg.

'You will have to surrender it,' I told him, as sternly as I could. 'You know Father van der Kemp does not want arms lying about at the mission.'

'It is not lying about, I am looking after it.'

'But it does not belong to you, Brother Cupido.'

'God sent it to me. He clearly does not want me to be unarmed in the face of our heathen enemies.'

'We must trust Him to defend us.'

'He placed it in my hands for our defence, Brother Read. I cannot go against the will of the Lord. Nor should you.' (He did not phrase it so elegantly, but I tried afterwards, in my diary, which I am here transcribing, to capture the gist of our conversation.)

'Stuurman promised never to trouble us again.'

'There may be others. We must always pray and be prepared, Brother Read.'


BOTH OF US, as it turned out, were right. We were not bothered by Stuurman's people again; in fact, praise God, we managed to do some rewarding missionary work in their midst. But there were other groups of marauders that brought no end of complications to our lives; and the farmers in the frontier territory did cause us serious harm through raids, threats and undermining action of every kind which, in due course, compelled us, in spite of our early objection, to move our little settlement into the fort. It must be no less than astounding, in the circumstances, that we continued to persevere in our missionary work (adding no fewer than twenty new converts to our flock), our preaching of the Word being accompanied by the power of His Spirit, and His holy arm revealing itself more and more. Apart from this, we provided instruction in various crafts, as well as in reading and writing to the increasing number of Hottentots flocking to us for assistance, comfort and protection.

These lessons caused particular aggravation to the farmers in the area, who protested that this would merely make these people more 'unruly', and that being the offspring of Canaan, son of Ham, they had been cursed with perpetual servitude to the whites elected by God.

So insidious was the hostility of the colonists that as soon as we had been ensconced in the fort, they razed the settlement at Botha's Place to the ground, burning down every little hut and cottage.

With our Father van der Kemp still mostly incapacitated by illness and in no fit state to do more than conduct the voluminous correspondence which I had to copy on his behalf, I made more and more use of Brother Cupido and his colleague, Brother Samson, a man of placid goodwill and a kind of stolid, bovine innocence, to conduct the morning and evening services. Much of the correspondence was with the new masters of the colony, because following the conditions of the Peace of Amiens the Cape had now indeed become Dutch again. Fortunately many of our fears about collusion between the colonists and the new government were soon allayed, and by the middle of 1803 we were at last allotted our own tract of land – albeit a most barren and unprepossessing property, almost wholly devoid of vegetation, with an alarming insufficiency of water, fiercely hot in summer and exposed to the rigours of severe cold in winter. But at least it was ours, and at last we had a place we could not again be dispossessed of. From his fine resources of irony and wisdom our Father chose to name it Bethelsdorp, after the sanctuary established by Jacob when he was salvaged from the strange gods in whose midst he had dwelled.

IT WAS HARD work to establish the new mission station. We had to build a new church, of reeds and clay, to serve as a school too, with wings to accommodate our Father and myself, and a number of small dwellings for our congregation. (Any more permanent structures had to be postponed until we had more certainty about our future.) As the doctor's health started improving again, a sure sign that God's blessing was upon the place, he courageously planted the beginnings of an orchard – oranges, apples, quinces, peaches – while I occupied myself with a vegetable garden. We had some help from our followers, but regrettably they were seldom to be relied on to persevere with any undertaking started invariably with great enthusiasm and in high spirits, much preferring, it seemed, to idle about in the sun of winter or the shade of summer, as they benevolently and with languid interest observed us, their shepherds, at work. Yet they were most assiduous in attending our school, and could sing in church for many hours; which, I tried to persuade myself, proved a goodwill that was much needed in our world, still beset on all sides by threats and real dangers from wandering tribesmen and armed colonists alike.

Brother Cupido could always be relied on in situations of emergency, even though the wound in his thigh was slow to heal, and festered several times, leaving him with a permanent limp.

'It is to be like my wife,' he would remark in a rare jocular spirit. 'Now she does not feel so much alone.'

He was always at hand when she boiled her soap, and occasionally they would leave the mission station for several days on his small wagon to collect *ganna* bushes that were required for the lye she used. But once, I recall, they returned from the recently established district of Uitenhage, the wagon empty and their mood visibly downcast. When I questioned him, he was evasive at first, but in the end broke his resentful silence to report an encounter with a colonist on whose farm they had tried to collect *ganna*. Although they had gone to the trouble of first obtaining a written pass from the landdrost of the new district, a requirement only recently imposed on any Hottentot wishing to move from one place to another, the farmer had approached them with his musket and told them in no uncertain terms to vacate his farm, or they would both be shot and killed. When Cupido had shown him the pass, the man had torn it into strips, saying, 'I don't care a damn about the landdrost. He has no say anywhere outside his little drostdy.'

'It will take time for people to get used to these things,' I tried to comfort him. 'And there are other places to collect your *ganna*.'

He shook his head despondently. 'I don't understand what is happening, Brother Read,' he said. 'Why is there so much fighting all around us? The Boers, the Hottentots, the Xhosa, everybody. All of them wanting to kill one another. Where is the Kingdom of God?'

'It is in our hearts, Brother Cupido,' I tried to reason.

'No!' he objected with unexpected vehemence. 'We need it everywhere. And we need it now. Every day I preach to our people to tell them about God and how He will provide for us and protect us. But I see nothing of it. If they are hungry, where is God to give them food? If enemies attack us, this is what happens.' He slapped his crooked thigh, wincing with the unexpected pain.

'We will have our reward in heaven,' I assured him. 'The more we suffer on earth, the greater our reward will be.'

'Yes, I know that. But that is not enough for a hungry man. It is not enough for a woman who loses her child. It is not enough for that child. My people are suffering badly, Brother Read.'

'That is what faith is for.' There was a hollow feeling in my stomach, and in my mind. Then I had an inspiration. 'Look at our Father: he had everything a man could wish for. An abundance of food, a good house, a wife, friends, riches, power. People listened to him, they looked up to him. But he gave it all up to come and live here with us, to be hungry with us, to be in pain with us. Because he knows we will all reap the fruit of our suffering one day.'

He grunted. After a while he said, 'Perhaps the man is mad.'

'Perhaps we are all mad,' I said lightly. 'But maybe the world needs madmen like us. Who knows, if the world is saved one day, it will be because we have been there.'

'Do you really believe that?'

'Yes, I do.' Almost against my will I added, much more softly, 'I have got to, Brother Cupido. Because otherwise . . .' After a pause I continued: 'Don't you see? I need *you* to help *me* believe.'

It was not premeditated. Only in speaking the words I discovered my thoughts. And I know I was right even in the most simple and direct sense. My success as a missionary, my very being as a missionary, depended on making converts. Among these, Brother Cupido was, so far, the most important. If he began to doubt his own mission, everything I had done, everything I believed, my frightful journey across the seas to come to this remote place – dazzling in the light of the sun, yet suffused with a mystery I could not fathom, a kind of darkness – my very self, would have been in vain and would lose its meaning. Quite simply, I needed this small, crooked, limping man in order to know who I was.

Brother Cupido listened to me, and appeared to ponder my remarks. Then he shook his head very slowly. 'I still wish we could *see* something of that Kingdom of God,' he said. 'My people need it. What they are suffering is not only in the head or in the heart. It is in the body. We have enemies. We go hungry. We need help.'

'This is the way God tries those who have faith in Him,' I said.

'Perhaps,' Brother Cupido said grimly, 'that is why He has so few friends.' He got up with a sigh. 'I shall have to speak to God about it,' he said.

He walked away, into the sun. It was shining directly in my eyes, so I could only see his slight, angular silhouette –

resembling some stick insect, a grasshopper or a harvester cricket or a mantis perhaps – as it dwindled into the distance, a small cloud of dust surrounding his head like a halo. A most curious impression, as if he did not so much move towards the sun as right into it. Until he disappeared in the blinding blaze.

HE DID CONFER with God as he had promised. I happened to come upon him not long after our conversation, one morning when he was repairing his wagon some distance downhill from the mission, in a clump of euphorbias with their strangely prehistoric aspect, as if I were suddenly transported to an altogether different time and space. Hearing him talk quite loudly, I assumed he was speaking to one of the other congregants, but there was no responding voice; and as I approached through the trees I could see that he was all by himself. He had his back to me, so it was easy to move closer unnoticed; moreover, I heard him using my name, so naturally my curiosity was aroused.

He was talking to God. Not praying, but talking as one would to another person, with disconcerting familiarity, even with a tone of disapproval or admonition in his voice.

'. . . spoke to Brother Read about it, but I'm not sure he quite understands. It cannot go on like this. I'm sorry, God, but I have spoken to You about this before and You don't seem to be paying any attention to me. I know You have many things to do, but this is important. You brought me to this place and You wanted me to be Your child, and I have gone through a lot on account of You, so I think You owe me something. Now there is this thing about the farmer who wanted to shoot me and Anna off his farm. I have been abused by many people in this world, I can take it. But it is unfair to Anna. She was only collecting some *ganna* for her soap, and You know she makes the best soap in the land. But how can You expect her to do her work properly if You won't let her have *ganna*? And it is unfair to me too. Because I am acting in Your service and in Your name. So if I am threatened with a gun, *You* are the one who is insulted. What will these farmers think of You if You cannot even stand up for Yourself? They're a bad lot and it is time You started doing something about it, otherwise no one will have any respect for You. I don't want to have to talk to You about it again.'

At this point I judged it prudent to withdraw.

Since then there were other occasions when I could overhear Brother Cupido's conversations with God. But for obvious reasons such opportunities were rare. The slightest hint of my approach would silence him. As it happened, however, the conversations were superseded by another form of communication. As his skills in reading and writing improved, which they quite impressively did, he took to writing letters to God. These he invariably entrusted to me for transmission: he never asked how I did it; evidently his faith in me was sufficient to assume that I would know what route to follow. Believing that our Father might frown on such an activity, I decided, not without some anxious soul-searching, not to alert him to the correspondence. The letters were few and far between. Clearly they were taken so seriously by Brother Cupido that only the most pressing circumstances would propel him into writing. But for various reasons they were always particularly precious to me.

On one of the first of these occasions a commando of Boers raided the mission station in an endeavour, they explained quite brutally, to detain Hottentots suspected of murder, stock theft and other crimes. They were careful not to interfere with the missionaries themselves, as even the new Batavian government in the Cape had made it clear that we were to be left unhindered in the pursuit of our religious duties; but the members of our congregation were ever-vulnerable to such depredations. Even when no incriminating evidence was found, the Boers would be sure to ply their targets with alcohol in one form or the other, knowing the weakness of the Hottentots in this regard. And once they were inebriated, misdemeanours or acts of violence were almost inevitable, which would warrant a return of the commando. Alternatively, members of our congregation would be enticed from the mission with lurid temptations of promiscuity or promises of lucrative work (which never materialised, but resulted in vagrancy and created new oppor-tunities for arrest). On this particular occasion, which came shortly after my marriage to Maria, three of our most prom-ising catechism candidates were taken away on allegations of theft, which were palpably false but left us powerless to inter-vene.

After the commando had left with their captives, who were dragged behind their horses (at an easy pace for as long as they remained within our sight; but we knew from terrible experience that they would break into a gallop as soon as they were obscured by the first ridge or cluster of bushes, to arrive at their destination trailing only the tragic remains in the dust), Brother Cupido withdrew to the schoolroom, which was then vacant. And after a few hours he brought me the following letter, tightly folded and tied up with a very thin thong:

dear and estemed Revrend God I think You were not
hear today or You wud have interfeared to stop the boers
that took of zacharias and daniel and mathew our frends
and members of our churh who we all are now and

who are Your chuldren like I am now You must be tiered sometime and need a rest I understand that but You must chose a beter time we needed You hear to stop the mudrers so that is why I am teling You about it to stop them and to send a boult of Your litning to kill them all very ded even befor they rich graf rennet Revrend God we depend on You to help us if You can not help us were do You think we can go to how can we go on trusting You from Your derest brother cupido cockrch

In another letter, less dramatic but no less urgent, he raises the problem of one of the severe droughts that withered our crops and completely dried up the stream that was our only source of running water:

> dear and estemed Revrend God it is dry the peple are dying the cattle are dying we need rain in the old days Tsuigoab used to send Heitsi Eibib to bring us rain so now it is Your duty if You care about us at all from Your most loveable brother cupido cockrch

On this occasion, I should place on record, the rains came almost immediately, so copiously that much of the mission washed away and a number of huts were swept down to the Sunday's River and ended up in the sea. Which duly chastened my derest and most loveable Brother Cupido and may have been the reason why in his correspondence with God he never referred to meteorological matters again.

Those were difficult times we lived through at the new mission station. But I also had problems of my own to contend with, some of them very personal indeed. Following my wedding,

I think I can say that, as I had hoped and prayed, it blunted the edge of my carnal cravings. But there was another problem which I could never have foreseen and which hitherto I have not confided to anyone, least of all, and for obvious reasons, to our Father van der Kemp. It was this: that whenever I proceeded to embrace my wife in the manner expected of husband and wife, I found that in my mind's eye I saw before me that other, poor, dusky female person of the fairground, a vision still so vivid after all those years that it felt, every time, as if she were there in my arms. And I do not know whether this could be construed as redemption or damnation, which seem to be closer together than I had ever imagined. Nor can I tell whether this was what, ultimately, drove me to the terrible sin that has now resulted in my suspension from the Church, which is the only thing of true value I have known in my life.

MOST OF THE PROBLEMS at Bethelsdorp continued to be caused by farmers driven from their homes by Xhosa invaders and venting their frustration on wandering little bands of Hottentots. The restoration of the Cape to Dutch control made these attackers even bolder than before, in the belief that the new government would side with them. This often happened, mainly because the Batavians did not wish to offend their distant kinsmen; but they were sometimes sympathetic to our cause as well, although in their comments on Bethelsdorp they were continuously scathing in an often patently unfair manner. Which, in turn, made our Father van der Kemp more intransigent, his redoubtable opposition founded on what, in a letter to the governor which I was asked to copy, he described as our sole and God-ordained duty: the urgent need to work among 'the helpless heathen, who hitherto have been left without the means of grace'.

We were dealt an unexpected blow when a ship, the brig *John*, bringing us desperately needed supplies (including a printing press, bellows for our forge, a whole consignment of books our Father had ordered, and my own allowance of 150 rix-dollars) went down in a storm off Cape Agulhas. But praise be to God that the ship bringing us this news had at least a fresh supply of corn on board, so that after several months of deprivation we could eat bread again, instead of resorting to our usual substitute for the Eucharist, a sticky concoction of baked dried pears.

Certainly, all was not disheartening or hurtful. Our congregation continued to grow through some thirty new converts, among them my young wife and the villainous Hottentot leader Boezak; these were followed, soon after, by a young black boy, David, the son of the Xhosa chief Tshatshu, as well as by my first-born daughter, since it was my ardent wish that this first fruit of my marriage might early be rescued by grace from the power of Satan and the dominion of sin.

Inspired by such clear signs of God's blessing, my preaching on Sundays became, if I dare in all humility say so myself, increasingly inspired. I do not think it amiss to mention that there was some benevolent rivalry between Brother Cupido and myself; but of course I had the advantage of conducting the breaking of the bread and the pouring of the wine, whereas he could not as yet proceed beyond preaching. So enthusiastic was the response from the congregation that more often than not my voice, never of a particularly resounding quality, was drowned by the sobbing and crying of the congregation, most obviously during the Lord's Supper.

For a long time we had been looking forward to a visit by the Batavian government's representative, Commissary-General de Mist, and his young scribe, Dr Lichtenstein, as we fervently believed that their personal acquaintance with our mission would convince them of the justness of our cause against the colonists. Also, we learned that our Father and de Mist had known each other in their youth in Leiden, which might make for a more hearty understanding than we had at first anticipated. To my own deep disappointment, however, the contrary seemed to happen. Upon their first meeting with our Father in Algoa Bay, at which I assisted, I was deeply moved by the poignancy of the scene when in the hottest part of the morning our Father approached, seated on a bare plank across the front part of a wagon drawn by four meagre oxen, without a hat, his venerable bald head exposed to the merciless rays of the summer sun. Tall, gaunt, austere, yet venerable, he was dressed, as always, in a threadbare black coat, waistcoat and breeches, without shirt, neckcloth or stockings, and leather sandals bound upon his feet in the manner of the Hottentots.

They had a heart-warming conversation, and when the commissary-general returned the visit the following day by coming to Bethelsdorp, I believed that he had been converted to our cause. But de Mist's demeanour was decidedly reserved on this occasion; and it should not be difficult to imagine my discomfort and dejection when, much later, I read in Dr Lichtenstein's account of his voyage the following comments on our poor but blessed mission:

It is scarcely possible to describe the wretched situation in which this establishment appeared to us. On a wide plain, without a tree, almost without water fit to drink, are scattered forty or fifty little huts, so low that a man cannot stand upright in them. In the midst is a small clay-hut thatched with straw, which goes by the name of a church, and close by some smaller huts of the same materials for the missionaries. All are so wretchedly built, and are kept with so little care and attention, that they have a perfectly ruinous appearance. For a great way around, not a bush is to be seen, for what there might have been originally, has so long ago been used for firewood: the ground is perfectly naked and hard-trodden down, nowhere the least trace of human industry: wherever the eye is cast, nothing is presented but lean, ragged or naked figures, with indolent sleepy countenances . . .

His own hut is totally destitute of comfort, even of any approach to neatness, and is perfectly consistent with the negligence of earthly cares which he preaches. He would certainly have done much better to have inspired his Hottentots with some taste for the refinements of civilisation, rather than to have levelled himself with them, and adopted the habits of negligence and filth.

From this he draws the sad conclusion:

Van der Kemp is of little value as a missionary, partly because he is a mere enthusiast, and too much absorbed in the idea of conversion, partly because he is too learned, that is to say, too little acquainted with the common concerns of life, to turn the attention even of a raw Hottentot to them.

On the very day of the visit, it happened that our Father, in resolutely joyous temper, happily conducted an inspection of the station with me, concluding at the end of our round: 'Do you not agree, Brother Read, that these quarters offer an excellent occasion to practise oneself in struggling with adversity, suffering, poverty, cares and deprivation?' And before I could attempt a reply, he continued, 'It is now the fourth day, is it not, that we have to go without bread, which as you know is no exception. I do not possess a single pair of shoes. When it rains, I get soaked in my own house. But God gives us more joy than the godless and blesses us with goods that easily make us forget our small worldly delights.'

He was indeed incorrigible. Even writing down these words now, so much later, I am dumbfounded by the way in which at the time we looked past the tawdry reality before us to keep our eyes on the great truth shining through them; and the presence of our Father lent an illumination to the most drab facts of our existence as one felt the glow of true inspiration emanating from him.

But it was still all so temporary. Within a disconcertingly short time news came that the Cape was once more to change hands and be restored to Britain, which could not but cast everything into renewed turmoil, even if the prospect of being under British rule again was heartening to our spirits. In the midst of it, presumably as a result of continued pressure exerted on the authorities by the discontented farmers, Father van der Kemp and myself were summoned to Cape Town to work out a new arrangement for our continued missionary exertions. I could not but suspect that the move should be construed as a strong sign of disapproval, if not of censure. And initially our circumstances at the Cape were indeed deeply alarming; to such a degree that we were obliged to consider the possibility of having to leave the country altogether and begin anew elsewhere. Fortunately, in the end, the international situation was resolved in favour of England and everything turned out reasonably well. At least we were allowed to continue, which the new British government in the colony soon confirmed. But it was distressing, to say the least, temporarily to have to abandon Bethelsdorp to the care of others – two new missionaries who happened to be visiting, as well as, of course, the fiery inspiration of Brother Cupido and the placid ministrations of Brother Samson – for several months.

What I remember especially about our leave-taking was an incident that in itself had nothing to do with religion (although in retrospect it may indeed have been profoundly religious). On the eve of our departure Brother Cupido and I were taking a walk in the veld to discuss the practical administration of the place in our absence, when suddenly, as we approached a small and unstable fountain that came trickling from the bed of a dry stream and where the women often went to draw water, he grasped my arm to hold me back. I saw, a mere six or seven paces from us, directly against the sinking sun, a large snake rearing up in menace, its slithery black forked tongue darting in and out of its mouth, its beady black eyes shining with a venom accumulated since the time of Genesis.

'Look, Brother,' Cupido whispered. 'Can you see the jewel on its head?'

I could not immediately discern what he had seen, but admittedly the last strong rays of the sun glinted off the scaly flat head in such a way as briefly to resemble a diadem perched up there.

'Do not move,' he hissed at me.

'What shall we do?' I asked in alarm. 'We have nothing with which to defend ourselves.'

To my dismay he said a very strange thing indeed: 'The snake is only there if you wish to see it.'

'What do you mean?' I said, taking a cautious step backwards.

'This is something my wife has taught me,' he whispered. 'It is just another way of saying that we have faith in God.'

'Do you think the snake knows that?' I could not help but ask.

'Brother Read,' he said very gently, 'look at me.'

'What?'

'Just look at me.'

Barely able to avert my eyes from the snake I looked at him. To my own shame I must admit that I was quaking with fear.

Brother Cupido stared straight into my eyes for a moment.

Then, to my amazement, he announced, 'The snake is no longer there.'

I could not believe my ears. 'What do you mean?' I asked.

'Look. He is gone.'

I turned my head to take another look. There was no sign of the snake.

'Is this some kind of heathen magic?' I demanded sternly, but still shaking.

'I willed it to go,' he said calmly, as if this was the most natural thing in the world, adding after a moment, 'I mean I asked God to will it to go.'

Somehow I knew then, with a strange, other-worldly peace settling in my mind, that our mission would come to no harm while we were away. I could rely on the two new missionaries who were to have control of the station in our absence, Brothers Tromp and Ullbricht (soon to be assisted by the arrival of yet another, Brother Erasmus Smit); but more importantly, I placed an absolute trust in Brother Cupido.

AMONG THE MANY things that befell us in Cape Town, where we arrived after a tortuous journey of five weeks, was a most grievous event: the death of my wife's brother October, not from natural causes but by execution. With two others, we learned, he had deserted from Bethelsdorp in our absence, only to be apprehended in Wynberg and sentenced to death on charges of having murdered a family of colonists. This was heartbreaking news. But when we began making enquiries the case became alarmingly murky. To begin with, neither our Father nor I, nor in fact my wife, October's own sister, was allowed to visit the men in prison. In the end we had to approach another missionary, Brother Kohrhammer, who happened to be in town, to gain access to the men and prepare them for the gallows. The account we gained in this round-about way was no clearer than the several versions provided by the judicial authorities. All we could establish was that there had been an argument with our Brother Cupido at Bethelsdorp, the particulars of which remained obscure, and as a result they had decided to leave the station in the hope of catching up with us in Cape Town. On a farm near Swellendam where they stopped to ask for food, they were apprehended as vagrants, locked up overnight in a stable and in the morning were set upon by the farmer and several of his neighbours, who had been summoned, and nearly flogged to death. It would seem that at nightfall they returned to the farm to exact their revenge in a most heinous manner.

According to Brother Kohrhammer the landdrost had disal-lowed their evidence about the flogging on the basis of being 'irrelevant', while allowing the dead farmer's neighbours to testify about a musket found with the condemned men, all knowledge of which they strenuously denied in the land-drost's court. Yet I should add something that most painfully upset me, which is that to Brother Kohrhammer they confessed that they had stolen this musket from Cupido's hut prior to leaving Bethelsdorp. It struck me like a dagger in the stomach, not only because it immeasurably complicated the case, but that in a way beyond my reasoning the fact appeared to implicate me personally, honing and refining the guilt that had lodged in my intestines. Furthermore, there could be no doubt about it at all, as Brother Kohrhammer reported that at the trial the deceased farmer's neighbours had described in great particulars the appearance of the musket, which bore on the side of the barrel a silver star.

Our Father attempted to send a message to Governor Janssens to have the case reviewed, but he could not be reached; I could only surmise that this should be viewed as a consequence of a recent acrimonious letter from Janssens to Father van der Kemp about his alleged 'unreasonable hostility' towards the colonists and his persistent strong protection of the Hottentots in the belief that this was 'the only way of averting God's revenge on this godless country'. By the time the governor did grant him an audience it was too late for intervention as the men had already been executed. At least, Brother Kohrhammer assured us, the three men had died trusting in the Saviour.

I should say here, with a tortured conscience, that my wife Maria received the news with a most unsettling demonstration of grief. She did not weep – not silently, not even loudly. She howled. It was like hearing some wild animal trapped in a whirlpool of pain too great for expression. She tore off her clothes, then flew at me and tried to reduce my own garments to shreds. When I restrained her, she began to run about in the room we rented from a most pious woman, the widow Hendrina Pieterse, who lived just off the Boerenplein, breaking everything she could lay her hands on – a chair, a small washstand, a pitcher and ewer. It was a most shocking and unnerving sight to behold; and all the while she continued to howl like a wolf at the moon. Even our Father was brought to the scene from his room adjacent to ours, and together, after considerable effort, we managed to subdue her and to make her lie down. But at intervals throughout the following night she would jump up and start howling and attacking me again with a ferocity difficult to believe. Even after all the intervening years I hesitate to say so openly, but it was as if a thin veneer of civilisation and religion had been stripped from her, exposing an uncouth and savage creature below the skin which appalled and deeply saddened me.

Much of our anguish, both hers and mine, was due to the very little we knew about the true events leading to the execution of her brother. But we knew that we would have to wait for our return to Bethelsdorp to clear up the remaining confusion about the entire sorry affair, and in due course my wife learned to curb the violence of her emotions, though she remained withdrawn into a sullen silence for a long time to follow.

However, there was one direct consequence of the devastating event which might be said to be positive, and this assumed the form of a resolution that shaped itself in my mind and which upon discussion with Father van der Kemp found in him a most energetic ally, namely, immediately upon our return, to commence an exhaustive research throughout the entire frontier territory into abuses and atrocities visited by colonists upon the Hottentots. Even if this endeavour were to take years, we would ensure that October's death had not been in vain. This evil had already persisted for too long and spread too wide. Now was the time for us to exact just retribution. The mills of God might grind slowly, but in the end I had faith that they would grind exceeding sure. It was, at least, a cause to which I knew I could wholeheartedly commit myself, a cause larger than my paltry individual life, lending a direction and a profound significance to all my missionary exertions hitherto. And I had already resolved whom to employ as my deputy to collect and collate on my behalf whatever information could be brought to light, and in whatever manner. It would – and could – be no one but Brother Cupido.

As soon as we set foot in Bethelsdorp again, following the cessation of hostilities between Britain and Holland which brought to a long-awaited term our eventful sojourn in the Cape, and leaving Father van der Kemp to confer with the missionaries Tromp, Ullbricht and Smit, I sought Brother Cupido out, to enquire, not only in general terms about all that had occurred in our absence, but most pertinently about the late October and his two accomplices.

The matter of their quarrel was readily explained. It seemed that as soon as our Father and I had left for the distant Cape, October had laid claim to my humble little hut on the grounds that he was my wife's brother. Cupido had strongly resisted, obviously because the nature of the bond between us had instilled proprietary feelings in his breast, and also because he assumed that occupying my abode would reinforce his authority in my absence. October had taken offence at this and within days the matter had grown beyond all proportion, so that it had come as no surprise to anybody at the mission to see him and his two friends go – allegedly to find us and report the whole affair. (It transpired, in fact, that Cupido's parting words to them had been: 'Go, hurry, and find out for yourself whose side he is on.' Which, in view of all that had happened since, was particularly dolorous to me.)

At that stage I broached the matter that had lain most heavily on my mind.

'And the musket?' I asked him, point-blank.

Cupido feigned innocence. 'What musket?'

'Your musket. The one that belonged to Andries Stuurman and which you appropriated. The one October had with him when they showed up on the farm at Swellendam, and which led to murder and execution.'

'I had nothing to do with it,' said Cupido. 'The musket is here.'

I breathed in deeply. 'Do you care to show it to me, Brother?'

He promptly turned round, crouched at his heap of bedding in the corner and extracted from it the musket, bearing on the side the distinctive silver star which I promptly recognised from the previous time I had seen him clean and assemble it in the bushes.

He said nothing, nor did I.

THERE IS ONE other event from our excursion to Cape Town to be recorded, but whether it was for better or for worse I confess I can still not say with complete sincerity. It concerns an action by Father van der Kemp to which I have previously alluded, namely his decision to buy, and set free, at a price of fifty rix-dollars apiece, two female slaves, Dorenda of Bengal and a fourteen-year-old girl, allegedly the daughter of a Muslim priest, of Malagasy birth, known as Sara of the Cape, whom he took back to Bethelsdorp with us and subsequently registered as Sara Janse, upon the occasion in 1806 of his formally taking her as his wife. A year later she presented him with their first child, followed by three more in the course of the next four years, which would suggest that the good man's missionary position embraced a surprising variety of exertions. Truly, God moves in mysterious ways.

To the head office of the LMS in London he dictated to me a letter to be written on his behalf, in which he expressed the hope 'that in this step I have consulted and followed the will of God, and that this alliance will not prove a stumbling block to me in my missionary work, my present wife being fully resolved to accompany me wherever it shall please God to send me'.

OUR ENDEAVOURS TO collect evidence about the maltreatment of Hottentots by colonists became a nightmarish journey to hell; yet the more we uncovered, the more indispensable it became to continue. The first testimony acquired by Brother Cupido, when he was on a journey to the Kasouga River to gather a load of wood on his wagon, came from an elderly man known as Januarie (it is a common phenomenon in the colony for farmers to call the Hottentots or slaves who work for them by the name of the month of their birth or acquisition), on the farm Rietboschlaagte. According to Januarie his young son Booi had been a herdsman in the employ of the farmer Barend Theron. One day Booi had been sent to the veld with the farmer's sons Peet and Dries to guard the cattle as they were grazing near the river. It was December, and the heat was unbearable; towards the middle of the day the two white boys went down to the water for a swim, in spite of stern commands to the contrary by their father, and while they were cavorting in the shallow water, their clothes strewn on some boulders at the edge, where they had left their father's musket, a small band of Xhosa men emerged from the thickets and started driving away the cattle. Booi shouted at them, but they flung a volley of assegais in his direction, one of which pierced the fleshy part of the boy's left arm. The farmer's sons came scurrying from the river to retrieve the musket, but ran off into the bushes when an eruption of shouting from the Xhosas made them realise that they had been detected. Naked as they were, and impotent to intervene, the boys had no choice but to leave their clothes and the musket for the marauders to collect, and to wait until the enemy had left the scene before returning, dejected and dismayed, to the farmstead to face the wrath of their father.

Knowing him to be a tempestuous and unreasonable man, they concocted a story to the effect that the attackers had set upon them during their vigil, and that in spite of fierce resistance by the boys (resulting in several Xhosa being shot dead), they had eventually been overwhelmed, stripped of their clothing and deprived of their weapon, whereupon the attackers had fled, carrying with them the bodies of their dead comrades.

'We could still have beaten them,' explained the elder of the two sons in a flourish of invention, 'but Booi stopped us. We could see that he was friends with the Xhosas, and we think he probably arranged with them beforehand to attack us. You know what these treacherous Hottentots are like.'

How this could have happened if Booi had been the only one to sustain an assegai wound, no one cared to explain.

Barend Theron had already suffered in previous raids in which his brother and another of his sons had been killed, and flew into such a rage upon hearing the story fabricated by Peet and Dries, that no attempt was made to verify it. He rounded up some of his neighbours to go in pursuit of the robbers, but it was too late.

Upon his return the next day, after a night in the saddle, the farmer and his neighbours turned on young Booi, whose wound had still not been attended to, and flogged him to death.

Old Januarie's protests fell on deaf ears, and when he went to lodge a complaint with Landdrost Cuyler of Uitenhage, a squat, short-tempered man with a reputation for siding with the colonists and loathing Hottentots and most especially missionaries, the poor old man received a flogging from the landdrost's assistants by way of warning, before being sent off to trudge back the three exhausting days to the farm on the Kasouga, where in retribution for his exertions he was flogged again.

The second statement collected by Cupido, on one of his regular travels through the area to collect *ganna* for his wife, concerned a prominent colonist from the Swartkops River in Algoa Bay, Martha Johanna Ferreira, widely known as 'angry Martha', who lived with her husband and ten children on her brother-in-law's farm. She was accused by some of her Hottentot labourers of having set fire to the hut of a Hottentot woman, Rachel, who was burned to death amid her meagre possessions; a relative of the deceased, a young boy known as Hendrik, had become another victim of the same merciless woman who in a fit of rage had allegedly thrust his feet in a cauldron of boiling water, as a result of which he had lost several of his toes.

Cupido's third case, gleaned on a roundabout journey to Graaff-Reinet where he went to sell a large load of soap recently manufactured by Anna Vigilant, was based on an all too common complaint: a middle-aged Hottentot man, known derogatorily as Voertsek, had announced upon the completion of his year's contract with the farmer Hermanus Maritz from Bruintjieshoogte his resolve to leave the farm. However, the farmer had then pointed out that having accumulated so much debt during his indenture he would not be permitted to leave until he had discharged everything he owed; after an angry altercation in which Voertsek had been beaten with a wooden pole to within an inch of his life, he had been allowed to leave after all – but Hermanus Maritz insisted on keeping his wife and three children in his thrall. Knowing the violent temper of his master, Voertsek believed it was only a matter of time before they would be killed. But once again, when he travelled to Uitenhage to request redress from Landdrost Cuyler, he was badly beaten and sent on his way. Two days before his encounter with Brother Cupido he had received word from Bruintjieshoogte that one of his children, then aged four, had indeed been bludgeoned to death by the farmer's wife.

I cannot rehearse again the entire dreary accumulation of statements, allegations and accusations. It was almost too much to bear the first time round, and there have been so many vain repetitions since then. It took us five years to compile the catalogue and could, I suppose, have gone on for much longer. Whereas in the early stages of our inquest Brother Cupido and others had travelled far and wide to collect the testimonies, soon the complainants started coming to us of their own accord, to register their joint and several ordeals, including well over a hundred instances of murder in the district of Uitenhage alone. More and more of those who otherwise were accustomed to join the Xhosas or unite themselves in the woods to seek redress were now flocking to Bethelsdorp in hope of finding sanctuary and succour with us. The time had come to act.

Father van der Kemp's early attempts to translate these accounts into practical measures failed dismally. Landdrost Cuyler, as might have been expected, contemptuously dismissed everything out of hand, demonstrating the most obnoxious behaviour imaginable and not hesitating openly to insult the saintly, elderly man to his face. Attempts to approach the governor appointed to the Cape after the colony had reverted to British rule, the Earl of Caledon, met with equal bluntness. Only when in exasperation I dared to write a letter directly to our authorities in London was the matter taken up. As it happened, the letter was widely published abroad, and in due course the new governor at the Cape, Sir John Cradock, received direct instruction from Lord Liverpool to institute a full inquiry.

Father van der Kemp and I were summoned to Cape Town. It was a hazardous journey. Even the elements seemed to conspire against us, and crossing the swollen Gourits River we certainly would have drowned had God not intervened to help us ashore, bedraggled and exhausted. At that time our Father's health was already so frail that I feared for his life. And well I might, as it pleased the God of Heaven and Earth to gather the reverend old man to His bosom, attended by his distraught young widow who was far advanced into pregnancy with her fourth child, in the sad, sad month of December, 1811, after a series of small apoplexies, while we were still lodged at the Cape.

The only words of comfort I could turn to in that time of obscurity and incomprehension were in the second Book of Samuel: *Know ye not that there is a prince and a great man fallen this day in Israel?* But words – even, I confess, the words of Holy Writ – were of little comfort in those dark days. Our Father was dead. That was the stark and simple fact with which we now had to learn to live.

And upon my solitary return to Bethelsdorp there was another death to be apprised of. In our absence, Cupido Cockroach's industrious wife, Anna Vigilant, had also quietly left this world.

IT WAS DIFFICULT to learn from Brother Cupido exactly how it had happened. There was an unaccustomed, savage look in his eyes as he spoke to me about it, and his account was incoherent; that madness which I had sensed in him from the very beginning lay simmering just beneath the surface of his mind. All I could eventually construe from his ramblings, and that truly did not make much sense to me, was that she had become more and more tired towards the end. A list-lessness had taken hold of her. Upon hearing from us, in one of our sporadic letters from the Cape to report on our progress with the investigation, Anna had apparently said, 'It will all come to nothing, Cupido. You may be a man of God today but you are still a Hottentot. Those people are white. We have no chance against them.'

'Father van der Kemp and Brother Read are also white,' he had remonstrated in indignation. 'In God's eyes there is no white or black, Anna.'

'He is their God,' she answered in a flat, lifeless voice, as he reported it to me. 'In the end, when everything else is taken away from us, that is all that matters. Whose side are we on? Black or white?'

'God's side,' he insisted, quite angrily.

'Their God,' she said again. 'He is not my Tkaggen. He is not your. Tsui-Goab. He can never be on our side.'

Then, on the last night he had seen her alive, Anna had called him to her bed, it seems, and had said something exceeding strange. I am trying to reconstruct it in my mind, the way he said it: *Tonight I'm going to dream very far, Cupido. You may not see me again.*

He did not understand what she meant; nor, quite evidently, did I.

He had spent that night outside, beyond the confines of our mission station, looking up at the stars, rehearsing their Hottentot names in his mind. But for that, everything in him seemed empty.

*Tonight I'm going to dream very far, Cupido.*

Over and over.

In the morning, when he returned to their hut, Anna was gone. (Where were the children? I don't know. He never said. He chose never to speak about it again.) There was literally no trace of her: no footprints in the dust, no sign that she had taken anything with her.

'I remembered my mother then,' he told me cryptically.

'What about your mother?' I asked him.

'Just my mother.'

That was all he was prepared to say.

YET THERE WAS an unexpected sequel to our abbreviated conversation. Some time later, it might have been a week or more, Brother Cupido brought me another of his letters to God. This one was almost blasphemous, in spite of the customary respectful opening:

> dear and estemed Reverend God You made a bad misteak this time and You must now it otherwise things will stay rong in the world first You tuk our father when he was far away in a strange place ful of ennemies now You come to take away my anna Reverend God this is not fare all her life she tride to be good she made the best sope in the hole land that washed the witest much witer than sin can be washed I know she did not always belief in You but how can You blame her she was a bushman but in her deep heart she was a tru beliefer she beliefed in the stones and the water and the sky and the stars and the eland and the holy mantis and everything was to her just god god god she made no differens people and animules and stones and stars she coud talk to them

all she was a good woman she coud make sparks come
out from her at that time when it happened I thot it
was my fireflies but it had nothing to do with me it was
her it was Anna and I think those were reel stars coming
from her for twenty years I live with a star and now
You take her away You know what I wud like to say tonit
is for gaunab to take You and to put You in his blak
heaven but I now I cannot do that for You have Your
own hell for us and I wish You coud go there Yourself
just to feel what it is like for I am in that hell tonit and
if only once only once You coud walk on that milky way
of live ashes and burn Your feet You will understand this
pain that is in me tonit God. I am sorry for Anna and
I am sorry for all the rong I did in my life I wish You
coud take me to be with her for I dont want to live if
she is gone and I dont even now where she is gone to
it is not fare is all I can say tonit it is not fare and my
heart is sore from Your dearest sorroful brother cupido
cocruch

AFTER ALL THE YEARS of preparation, our indefatigable efforts
to bring to book the colonists accused of atrocities committed
against their Hottentot servants debouched in the lamentable
court proceedings widely known since then as the Black
Circuit, which started soon after our Father's death. It is
history now and still too painful for further elaboration. Not
a single colonist was found guilty of murder. A number of
them received light sentences for minor misdemeanours. But
the experience remained shrouded in ambiguity. The
colonists, predictably, interpreted it as a victory over the 'evil'
perpetrated by Hottentots and missionaries alike; few
conceded that behind the verdict lurked a shadow of suspicion which no court finding could dispel. Those of us who

*knew* what was happening in the outlying districts every day of the year, who had seen with our own eyes the bruises and the wounds, the broken limbs, the tortured bodies of the victims, could never forget what we had witnessed. In good faith we had procured and produced our evidence, but we had lacked the judicial skill to present it to the far-from-dispassionate scrutiny of a colonial court of law. Of course we could not have remained silent, ever, in the face of so much evil. But we might have been more cautious in bearing testimony against those we ourselves had found guilty long before we knew enough. We might have been less arrogant in our pursuit of truth and justice, more humble before God. Perhaps we had not sufficiently heeded the dangers of exaggeration and inflation in the minds of people who had been driven beyond endurance. And so it came as a moment of awful devastation finally to read the verdict of the learned judges:

If the informers, Messrs van der Kemp and Read, had taken the trouble to have gone into a summary and impartial investigation of the different stories related to them, many of those complaints which have made so much noise, as well within as without the colony, must have been considered by themselves in imagination only, and consequently neither the Government nor the Court of Justice would have been troubled by them.

We had indeed erred in a number of cases. For instance, 'Angry Martha' Ferreira, it was argued in court, had never set fire to the hut of the woman who had died in the blaze: on the contrary, she had tended the woman with potions and compresses during her illness and had left a candle with her to comfort her in the dark, which the invalid had accidentally knocked over in the night, causing the dilapidated little place to catch fire. The young boy Hendrik had lost his way in the veld in the middle of winter and had been brought to the woman's home nearly frozen to death; she had brought him round by placing him in a tub of hot water, and had then treated him with warm wine, oatmeal poultices and a concoction of boiled wild figs. As a consequence, his life had been saved, although he had indeed lost a few toes. The court, perhaps with reason, had decided to take Martha Ferreira's word rather than that of the boy or of other labourers. But once one has been alerted to the almost constantly recurring forms of abuse, punishment and torture in our colony, followed by lies and concealment and collusion among relatives and neighbours, sleep does not come easy at night.

Yet, what it all amounts to, in the bluntest possible terms, is that we lost. Not because the verdict went against us. But because by having our testimonies rejected we failed those many helpless men, women and children who had come to us for help, as a last refuge against deprivation and terror and suffering simply because they were black; they had trusted us, they had risked their meagre well-being and perhaps their lives by confessing to us. They had come to us for bread and we had given them stones instead. This had happened in spite of our best intentions and the best of our abilities. But these had demonstrably not been good enough.

And today, these years later, I am beginning to think that perhaps our Hottentots were not the only ones we failed, their cause not the only one we unwittingly betrayed. We also failed the colonists of the country. It is inconceivably hard to admit this today, but it must be said. We failed them. Even those among them who had been cruel and vicious, murderers, abusers, rapists, out of fear – fear of what they could not comprehend about their dark and dangerous land, this land which I know can also be dazzling with light, and generous, and grand. We did not look beyond their reign of terror inspired by fear, and so we overlooked the simple fact that they were human too, suffering too, and ignorant too – of us, of the indigenous peoples, of their own inadequacies and prejudices, and ultimately filled with that ungodly fear, fear of the land itself.

Where did we go astray? By being intent too much on the body and the world, not enough on the spirit, on the Word?

Whatever it was, what should have been celebration has become lamentation. We have lost. My God. We have lost so much because we have betrayed so much. In fighting against the weakness of others we became trapped within our own human weakness, blocking the way to so much *more* that we might have been. They might not have *wanted* to be mean or cruel. Just as surely as we did not want to be cruel. We did not *want* to fail. But we did. And now we have lost. God have mercy on our souls.

BROTHER CUPIDO'S PREOCCUPATION with the Word became more and more intense, as his proficiency in reading and writing improved and we employed him increasingly in preaching sermons on Sundays. These began as simple passages from Scripture, but of his own accord, and sometimes in spite of clear instructions to the contrary, he just could not restrict himself to reading and felt impelled to add some observations of his own at the end. It was somewhat like an etching to which a title is added; and gradually the titles expand and become more comprehensive (if occasionally less comprehensible), until they overtake the picture in importance and develop into entire works of literature in their own right.

It also led to wholly unforeseen excesses and convolutions. The most exorbitant, and also the most fantastic, came to light on a late Sunday afternoon when I chanced upon Brother Cupido some distance away from the mission in a small kloof overgrown with euphorbias, aloes and blue plumbagos (which I had by then laboriously begun to identify). It was a year or so after Anna Vigilant's death, and he was sitting with his Bible on his knees, tilted at an angle to catch the last deep yellow rays of the setting sun. Following his wife's death I had obtained the Bible from our office in Cape Town, with the specific purpose of offering it to Brother Cupido as a source of solace after his recent loss. What struck me on this occasion was how thin the great volume on his knees had become. Between the heavy covers of the great Dutch State Bible with their brass clasps and embossed gold lettering there was only a spare wad of pages left, nothing like the hefty tome I had presented to him barely a year before.

He had not seen me approach as he was so engrossed in what he was doing, so I stopped in some perplexity to observe him. He was reading aloud to himself, following with one finger the words on the big page, as if each were an insect he had to crush before moving on to the next. I remember it was a chapter from St Paul's epistle to the Romans. The reading came quite smoothly by now, but there were still words he stumbled over, which he would then scrutinise with pinched brows, and volubly repeat, before proceeding. At the end of the page he turned it over and continued from the top of the next. I do not know what transfixed me so, but I could not persuade myself to go any closer and interrupt his concentration.

When he reached the end of this page, just as I was preparing at last to step forward and address him, he performed a most stupendous action. He tore out the page of which he had just read recto and verso, crumpled it, and proceeded to stuff it into his mouth.

Both fascinated and horrified, I exclaimed, 'Brother Cupido!'

He looked up, startled, snapping the great book shut, then shook his head and continued to masticate for a good while before, with slightly bulging eyes and quite considerable effort, he swallowed.

By this time I was kneeling in the dust in front of him.

'Brother Cupido,' I repeated in complete consternation. 'What is happening? What are you doing?'

'I am consuming the Word of God,' he said in his sermon-ising voice, seemingly unperturbed.

'But . . .' I was at a loss for words. 'It is a *new* Bible, Brother!' I stammered stupidly, as if that made all the differ-ence.

He shrugged.

'Why are you doing that?' I insisted, in a much more peremptory voice than I customarily adopt.

'There is so much that I still do not understand, Brother Read,' he explained patiently, as if I were a child to be taught something of importance. 'So I decided I must eat it and swallow it to absorb it in my body. Only then will the Word of God be fully part of me. Then no one can ever take it from me again. Is it not so?'

'But you have devoured nearly the whole Bible.'

'I still have Corinthians to go. Then Galatians. Then Ephesians. Then –'

'I know, I know,' I interrupted. 'But surely this is not the way to go about it.'

'I spoke to God,' he said, 'and that is what He told me.' His mouth was drawn into a very stubborn line.

After a long time he turned to look at me again. And

without any prompting, as if he were preaching not to me but to the euphorbias, the plumbago bushes, a tortoise purposefully ambling past, the few tall aloes, he began to recite:

'*In the beginning was the Word, and the Word was with God, and the Word was God. The same was in the beginning with God. All things were made by him; and without him was not any thing made that was made. In him was life; and the life was the light of men. And the light shineth in darkness; and the darkness comprehended it not.*'

There was something eerie about the scene, as if I were not seeing it but dreaming it. And curiously perhaps, I felt my own faith restored.

AFTER THE BLACK Circuit there was a noticeable decline in the number of people who flocked to us at Bethelsdorp. It was perhaps a sign of the tension on the frontier beginning slowly to ease up. But undoubtedly many potential congregants were also turned away through losing trust in us. Also, we had to contend with bad droughts which made mere physical survival difficult. And yet in some respects the mission also flourished as we began deliberately to improve our facilities by building some new and sturdier houses and setting up various small industries: the weaving of mats and baskets, shoemaking, tanning sheepskins, cooperage, carpentry, lime burning. Sometime before the Black Circuit I had helped Brother Ullbricht to set up a windmill and a watermill, even if it remained a concern that except for the rainy season there would never be sufficient water for grinding. It was Brother Cupido who insisted that we persevere. It might be God's way of testing us, he insisted. If the mill was ready and the rains stayed away, it could merely be a temporary setback; but if the rains came and there was no mill, it would be an indictment for a lack of faith, which was much more serious.

And so in some ways, yes, we suffered, while in others we might be said to have prospered, or at least to have survived. Certainly, after the long trial and its regrettable outcome, survival in itself was already of significance. Yet I felt as if, personally, I was wandering through a no man's land. Ever since the death of our Father van der Kemp I was aware of a numbness in me, a dazed feeling, exacerbated by Anna Vigilant's passing, and then by the long-winded trial moving towards its depressing conclusion. Today, without the aid of my diaries, which I have now disposed of, I have no clear recollection of the time that elapsed between events.

I felt myself in a kind of limbo. I recalled a few lines which our Father would sometimes recite from the *Inferno* by the poet Dante which he had read in his youth. (My own reading, I readily admit, has never been particularly extensive. Many may see me as an ignorant man. But it is hard, and ever harder, to see my way through the wilderness.) The words I am thinking of now have something to do with lost souls in limbo, two lovers, I seem to recall, if such thoughts are not sinful, who 'hand in hand on the dark wind drifting go'. There I was on my own dark wind, with no hand to grasp, without aim or direction, perhaps, at least upon occasion, without hope. Were it not for Brother Cupido, I am not sure I would have traversed that benighted period.

The turning point came unexpectedly, as such things tend to happen (and even then, so often, we do not recognise them when they do come to pass), in 1813, when an envoy from the LMS in London, the Reverend John Campbell, was sent to inspect our mission stations in the colony and beyond. He had to be fetched from Cape Town. In normal circumstances it would have been incumbent upon me to undertake the journey, but in those distressing times it was inconceivable for me to absent myself from Bethelsdorp. Everything might just fall apart. And so, after earnest consultation with God and discussions with my colleagues, it was decided to dispatch Brother Cupido on my own wagon. Apart from any other consideration it might help, I thought, to extract himself from the gloom that had settled on him since the death of his wife.

As it turned out, it was to be a decisive moment in his life.

'My heart will go with you,' I told him on the day I took my leave of him, pressing his frail and awkward insect body to my own. And in a most unexpected way this was exactly what happened.

On some of my own journeys, as most particularly on that fateful last passage to Cape Town travelling with our late lamented Father van der Kemp inexorably towards disappointment and death, I might be said to have been abstracted or even absent, my thoughts being so occupied with other matters as to be almost oblivious to the material facts of the voyage, the space we were travelling through. But on this occasion, although physically absent from what occurred from day to day, I felt so intimately implicated in every inch of Brother Cupido's way (as if, it once occurred to me, I had become one of the Bible pages he had ingested) that I lived in complete and minute awareness of it. I knew little of the actualities of the enterprise, though some particulars, especially of the return, were subsequently relayed to me by Brother Campbell and others, or I deduced from letters to God remitted to me for delivery after Cupido's return to Bethelsdorp (revealing, now, a surprising improvement in orthography and syntax, and a newly found predilection for capital letters). But the intelligence of our progress was vivid: as if images from the previous journey, the registering of which I was not even conscious of at the time, now inserted themselves into the present, charged with an almost unbearable acuity.

These ranged from panoramic landscapes – an immediacy of rich vegetation on slopes to either side of the wagon which gradually became mountains, and then receded to left and right in deep purples and fierce blues, then softening to mauve and lilac, to the faintest and most delicate blue, as the plains began to billow and undulate in hills and ridges and valleys and indentations – to the tiniest particulars: a small bright tortoise here, the silvery parchment of a skin shed by a vanished snake, swarms of birds teeming in vast family nests, iridescent long-beaked sunbirds and cheeky honey birds, mottled partridges darting through dry grass, guinea fowl scattering in the scrub, the forlorn death cries of the ibises they call hadedas in these parts, scarlet or yellow-and-black weaver birds in trees reaching across along a narrow watercourse, long-legged secretary birds proceeding with their studied air of self-importance, a family of meerkats attacking a yellow snake, the cry of an eagle high overhead, vultures drawing narrowing spirals in a sky bleached of all colour as they descend on the carcass of an antelope or, once, a camelopard left behind by lions or leopards, the scuttling of an unworldly, scaly *ietermagô* digging into an antheap, dung beetles scurrying about the droppings of buffalo or wildebeest (once, undoubtedly, an elephant), a small bright green mantis embossed on a twig, long lines of ants etched along the cracked surface of a dried-up river bed, on a few rare occasions a glimpse of a majestic eland.

It was the latter that brought back snatches of tales told by Brother Cupido, handed down from generation to generation of his people, or of Anna Vigilant's. I remembered what he had told me of her beliefs about the Bushmen's world of shades and ancestors: of sacred spaces opening up (but visible only to the alert, and the initiated) in dried tree stumps or among the red flint rocks of a ridge or a koppie, where one might travel from the visible world into the invisible, from the present into a remote and timeless past, or where beings from that other world might erupt into our own. And as he travelled along — as *we* travelled along — I could imagine these arid plains transformed into a cornucopia of vegetation, exotic fruits and potent plants and tortuous roots which screamed like human beings when you extracted them; and see those other beings populating the empty space around. Hundreds, thousands, millions of them, all the forgotten and now resuscitated dead, since the beginning of the earth when the sons of God went in unto the daughters of men, to bring forth people and people and people. All the dead of this vast land in solemn procession, transparent with antiquity, returning to reclaim possession of their earth which we had laid waste with our hunting and our wars and our depredations and devastations in our urge to expand, to become ever more powerful, ever more arrogant — while trampling underfoot not only the generations of the past but all their spirits and ghosts and revenants and gods; and not only their gods, but *our* God, our Father insulted and dishonoured and abused by our crude possession of the creation that had once been His. That great word of the Beginning still reverberated in my mind: *Be fruitful, and multiply, and replenish the earth, and subdue it, and have dominion over the fish of the sea, and over the fowl of the air, and over every living thing that moveth upon the earth.* My God, my God, what have we done in the name of that dominion and for the sake of that subjugation? All those countless dead, now rising up to nod their heads at

us and shake their fists at us in silent sorrow and accusa-
tion. Not just the hundreds we had failed in the course of
our Black Circuit, but the innumerable dead laid waste in
this vast space, where slowly our footprints are being filled
with caved-in sand and then blown away by the winds of
heaven. What of all that endless past had survived? What
would survive of *us*, now trundling across the desolate
spaces of this beautiful land towards what uncertain future?
Oh my God, my God, what have we done?

THERE IS ONE of my earlier voyages I remember very well
– not overland, but across the sea: that voyage from England
to Brazil to Portugal, then back to England, and on to the
Cape, in one frail wave-tossed ship after the other. What I
remember most vividly is not the marvels of the crossing
(silvery flying fish that seemed to come from another kind
of space altogether, and returned to it after the brief resplen-
dent flash of their passing to remind us of a world beyond
our own; three or four times the sudden, silent surging of a
whale from below, Leviathan from the unplumbed deep; the
impossible ink-black blue of the ocean; the proximity of the
stars at night, the masthead dancing among the constella-
tions), nor the horrors attendant upon it (the bouts of sick-
ness that caused five or six, then fifteen, then twenty-five
men to die in convulsions, to be buried at sea in stitched-up
canvases; the terrible screaming of slaves tossed overboard
in a sudden storm which made it necessary to rid the ship
of ballast), but the more mundane yet unbearable noise caused
by the animals transported on board to supply our need of
fresh meat: the grunting and squealing of pigs, the bleating
of sheep, the lowing and bellowing of cattle, the crowing and
cackling of chickens, the gobbling of turkeys – a cacophony

that went on day and night in that veritable ark. Which made me think of Father Noah during his forty days and nights which must have been beyond all imagining. No wonder that at the end of the aimless voyage the first thing he could do was to drink himself into a stupor.

This journey had its own complement of sheep and cattle and fowls and ducks, but it was bearable, sometimes even reassuring or amusing (and they could always be replenished en route as one progressed from farm to farm, from one mountain range to the next, until the last wide plains fanned open ahead and one could perceive the blue mass of the Table Mountain at the other end, marking the end of land and the beginning of the seas that stretch to the frigid extremities of the earth).

Dear and Esteemed Reverent God, I wish to Thank You for the Ride on this Wagon belonging to my Brother Read that broht me to this Place Cape Town to fetch the New Brother Campbell come to inspec all our Missuns. That make me Remember so well my long ago Ride with the man Mister Servaas Ziervogel on his Two Wagons. Perhaps you forgot that Ride by now it was Long Ago and you must be Old as You live from Before the time of the World but I shall never forget it as Long as I live becose of the many Things that man Mister Ziervogel toht and showd me on the Way the Mirores espesly for I think Mirores are the wonderfulest Things you Created in Your Creashn. It was so Sad that in the Klein Karoo in the Rooiberge where we met the man calld Izaac Levinsohn on his way from the Great Fish River he told us that Poor Mister Ziervogel was killd four heres ago on the other Side of the Keiskamma River by Xhsa people who stole his Two Wagons now I Wonder what happened to all his mirores somewhere deep in the Land all of them with My Face on them. Perhaps it is what You Wanted Reverent God to spred Your Word unto the Heathn. And I Thank You for the opptunity You give me on this Ride to Prepare my Soul for meeting with our New Brother Campbell becose all along the way I coud preche to the peple. I preched at Boschfontein and in the Kouga Mountains and at Kransberg, I preched in the Kammanassie Mountain and at Rooiheuwel and Onrust and even in the Touwsberg, I preched in the Waboomsberge and the Fonteintjiesberg and the Kwadouwsberg, and I preched in the Waaihoek and on Blomfontein and Wolwedans and Klipheuwel, and then in the Tygerberg and now here in Cape Town. And all the way I prepare my Sole for you and the New Reverend. Evywhere we come I brake down the stone heaps of Heitsi Eibib to show that I am now on the Side of God even if it make my heart a little bit sore because of evything My Mother told me but now I kno it is a sin and an Abomnition in the Site of the Lord my God up there in Heven where You sit. It must be close to where Tsui Goab livs and I must ask you Reverent God plese to give him my greetings if you See him and Tell him I am doing my Best for You and for Him with all my Lov I send you Reverent God from your derest and most lovly servant Brother Cupido Cockrch.

A mere two or three days' journey from our mission station on the return journey Brother Cupido composed another letter comprising his impressions on the Reverend John Campbell and their shared travels which, as it soon transpired, were only the beginning of a voyage which would soon involve me as well, transporting us well beyond the frontiers of our colony to that distant place where he now commands his own mission station while I live in the daily contemplation of my sin.

Dearest and Most Esteemed Reverend God, Once again I sit down to Commnicate to you the Ride on the Wagon of Brother Read which is now almost over to tell you that I met in Cape Town the New Reverent John Campbell who You have not Met yet becose he is not Yet in Bethelsdorp. So I wish to tell you that I find him a Good Man a bit short in the Legs and somewhat Fat but he will soon loose that if he comes to share our Live. Also his two eyes do not look in the same directn at the same time but I think that helps him to see more like a chamelon so he will be good to inspect all our missuns he will not miss any thing. He has a Kind Dispostn and tries to share his Food with all of us on the Wagon evry Day which is the sine of a Man of God. He also trust me with everything which is Another sine of God I must test the Rivers on our way and tell him if we must hurry on or wait or go the long way round also he does not argew when I make a decisn as when we had to make trek of twelve ours without a stop but it was necesry to get the oxen to a better place in time and he believd me. So I can trust Brother Campbell too and we spoke a lot on the trek not just about his busnes at Bethelsdorp and in the colny but much much further even across the Great River they call the Gariep and where peple live in places with Strange Names that I want to see befor I die you know Reverent my mother said I must walk far in the World so perhaps meeting this New Reverent he will lead me wher you Want me to go. There is not much I can do now in Bethelsdorp

any more becose Anna is dead and I spose it was Your
Will but I told You before and I am Sure You kno it too
even if You are to Prode to Say so but I forgiv you from
my Bottom even if it was the Stupdest Thing you ever
did in Your Live. A man must chersh a gode woman
when he sees her as I kno I chershed her from that niht
she made the sparks fly it was the Best Niht I have lovd
in my Live. This I tell You becose You ask us to be Onest
and this is My Onest Word, from your dearest and most
Chershd Obedient Servant Cupido Cockrch.

I MUST RESUME my account of Brother Cupido's return with
Brother Campbell in March of that year, 1813. At this
moment I am too perturbed by the memory of that Letter
to God and Brother Cupido's comments upon his love for
Anna Vigilant which bring home again to me the melancholy,
indeed the horror (if it is not a sin to term 'horror' something which was so beautiful), of my own transgression. I
have no interest in writing here the account of my own life,
which is indeed why I have also destroyed my diaries, only
to gather some random recollections of the part of it I was
privileged to share with Brother Cupido Cockroach, in order
to find, I think, coherence in my existence, which has been
shattered. Only by doing this can I have any hope of finding
some direction in it, some new hope, which may lead me to
doing something worthwhile again to the glory of God in
atonement for my sin. For this is the darkness I contend with:
that in my youth I had consciously renounced a life of my
own in order to devote it to the service of others, those very
others to whom through my own misdemeanour I have now
become a stumbling block.

And even that is in doubt. Was it truly to others that I
wished to dedicate myself or was I propelled to the pursuit

of an image of lewdness I had cherished in my bosom ever since that day when I had seen the wretched black girl cowering in fear and pain, and that night when I had witnessed the spasms of her carnal congress with her wicked master with whom I have in my mind throughout my life exchanged places?

It is compounded by this irony, which derives from the brief period after their return from the Cape, and before I set out with Brother Campbell and Cupido to visit the outlying mission stations of the LMS in order to inspect them and formulate recommendations on their future development (a project for which, after our Father van der Kemp's death, I was regarded as incompetent – even though no one would say so to my face; but I am not stupid, even though I may be a fool). Brother Cupido had so successfully concluded his mission to the Cape that I wished now to contribute to the advancement of his career. He was no longer a young man and looked in fact much older than his years, consequently I resolved to have him promoted to an elder in the church. To ensure that there would be no suggestion of favouritism I promoted another man with him, a most dutiful and conscientious elderly man, the half-blood Andries Pretorius (known in these parts as a 'Bastard', which, however, is no denigration, merely a designation).

This was, I should mention, a particularly difficult time for me. In Cupido's absence to the Cape it was an ordeal for me to manage the mission without any assistance; on many occasions I had to admit to myself that if our masters in London really endeavoured in the mission of Brother Campbell to convey their disapproval of my own abilities, they may indeed have been right. But there was a much more personal side to my increasing feeling of worthlessness too. I hesitate to publicise it, but it is part of my burden, and part of my pain. Ever since the execution of her brother October during our visit to Cape Town in 1811, my dear wife, whom I swear I have always held in the highest regard, had withdrawn from me what is known as her conjugal favours (even though the sacrament refers to duties and obligations). This had condemned me to a curbing of even those few private pleasures, sinful as they might yet have been, in my life. (Not, dear God, that I wish to complain. It is all my own fault. But it was hard. It was very hard. I am, I believe, by nature a passionate man.)

Once or twice I had ventured to broach this in private conversation with Brother Cupido, as I may yet relate, but I did not find it proper, or even worthy, to intimate too much. For some reason I felt more at ease discussing family matters with Cupido's fellow elder, that benevolent man Andries Pretorius. And as it happened, Brother Pretorius had a daughter of nubile years, Sabina, an uncommonly beautiful young woman. I resisted. I prayed day and night. I resisted for years, for which I praise God. It helped to be away from Bethelsdorp during that long, long journey with my brothers Campbell and Cupido (whom in due course I had promoted to the status of missionary) which took us beyond the borders of the colony and determined Cupido's fate. But after our return, and once he had been dispatched on his own mission, and out of my life – as I shall relate in due course – I could not bear it any longer. I continued to pray, but it was to no avail. The flesh was too weak. I suppose I could have sent Brother Pretorius and his family elsewhere, to Graaff-Reinet or wherever, but how could I inflict such a drastic intervention on all their lives merely to remove temptation from my own? It appeared indeed like a challenge God had placed in my way. I had to prove the fibre of my Christian conviction, and the fabric of my whole life, by proving that I could resist.

I tried to return, in every sense of the word, to my own wife Maria; a few times, I am ashamed to say, I even forced myself on her. (And every time, every time there was behind my closed eyes the memory of that other, abused young woman from deepest Africa.) But in the end we sinned. *I* sinned. For a few months, I am ashamed, and not ashamed, to say we knew bliss. Was that the only small corner of Paradise I experienced in my life? Then God willed it that Sabina should fall pregnant. His punishment, clear for all to see. (But why punish *her*? Is that fair and just? These questions mark the measure of my fall, the extent of my blasphemy and my sin.) Only then were they banished to Graaff-Reinet. And I to hell. Or purgatory, at least.

One slender consolation is that Brother Cupido was no longer there at the time, at Bethelsdorp, to witness it. But it is worth considering that if he *had* been there it might not have happened in the first place.

I MUST RETURN TO the business at hand. Brother Campbell brought a favourable report on Cupido's behaviour and demeanour during their month-long journey from Cape Town. He could, he said, during the journey leave the full management of the trek to our trustworthy brother, to whom he appreciatively referred as 'our travelling director'. As for his character, on the basis of his treatment of the attendants of our wagon and the oxen in his care, and his preaching to every person they encountered along the way, whether singly or in groups, Brother Campbell described him as 'a humane Hottentot'.

He did note a tendency of which I, too, had been aware from the beginning, and that was Cupido's habit of going off on his own for some time every day or every other day, staying away for perhaps an hour or so, occasionally for up to half a day. Questioned about it, he would merely shrug and explain that he had gone off 'to pray in the bushes'; in the face of such pious devotions Brother Campbell concluded that it was better not to pry too closely. I tried to explain to him some of the eccentricities of our brother, but as I myself had not always understood them it was not an easy task and had to be abandoned. The man, I must concede even today, was a mystery and an unfathomable compilation of contradictions, most particularly in his concept and exercise of Christian worship; but of his sincerity and utter conviction there could never be any doubt whatsoever, even if many construed it, as I myself sometimes did, as madness. I often thought, and still do as I think back, that if more of us could have the rock-fast conviction of his faith, the world might have been a better place.

Under other circumstances our closeness might have been unusual, and difficult to sustain; but in the bleak surroundings of Bethelsdorp he often was, particularly after the demise of our Father, the only person I could genuinely unburden my heart to. There was one occasion to which I have already briefly referred, soon after his return from the Cape with Brother Campbell, when our discussion turned to his celibacy since the death of his wife, and my relationship with Maria.

'I miss my Anna every day and every night of my life,' he admitted. 'But now God has decided to take her away, so I must accept it. In the beginning it was very hard, and I spoke bitterly to Him. I thought it was a mistake. But it is not for me to harden my heart against Him. And He knows best. Can I say I am a lonely man now that she is gone? Yes, I am lonely. But are you not lonely? Is everybody not lonely? Is that not the way God made us? You can sit right next to somebody, as I am sitting here next to you, and I can still be lonely.

I can lie with a woman in my arms and still be lonely. Is that not so? And then there is this thing too: what I have of her deep inside me, where I also keep the Word that I ate, no man can ever take away from me. So how can I complain?'

'Yes, I saw you and Anna together. I know you have good memories.'

'You do not need memories, Brother,' he said. 'You still have your wife beside you.'

'She is beside me,' I said, 'but is she really *with* me?'

'That is not for me to say.'

'Perhaps the flesh is too much with me,' I said, almost in a whisper, after a long time. It felt almost sacrilegious to share this with him, with anyone. 'I know we aspire to the life of the spirit. But the very fact that she is *there* keeps her flesh before me.'

'Have you never made sparks with a woman?' he suddenly asked.

I could not give him a direct answer, but I could feel my face flush very hot.

Only after some time, fumbling, I cleared my throat and said, 'We should not speak about such things.'

'God made a man and He made a woman. Did He not make sparks too?'

'Yes, but they are shameful.'

'If God made them,' he said, 'how can they be shameful?'

'God wants us to aspire to the things of the spirit.'

'Does the spirit not live in a body then?'

'The body is just a poor earthen vessel,' I argued, more with myself than with him.

'But then he filled that clay pot with dreams,' he persisted. 'That was what Anna always said. And now, even if she is dead, I still have her words. And her dreams. I must look after her dreams the way I looked after my Baas's sheep when

I was a child. And I can only keep them if my clay pot is treated well.'

Again I was silent.

'When I was very small,' he suddenly started again, 'I went outside our hut one night to piss, and the stars were so close above my head that I plucked one and took it to my mother.'

'Was she happy with it?'

'No, she sent me out again to put it back.'

'Why are you telling me this?'

'I don't know. Mostly I think I say what God puts in my head. If you don't understand, it is not your fault. If God wants you to understand He will make it happen.'

'Perhaps,' I said after another silence, 'your mother knew that the right place for a star is in the sky. We cannot try to keep it inside a hut where it can be smothered and die.' There was a tiny feeling of triumph in me as I added, 'Perhaps that is true of the spirit and the body too.'

'A star is not a spirit,' he said patiently. 'A star is a star. It is more like an eland or a mantis or the moon than a spirit.'

'But you believe in the spirit,' I argued. 'Otherwise you would not have had yourself baptised.'

'Yes,' he said, it seemed blithely. 'Of course I believe in the spirit. But also in the star. And in the clay pot where I keep my dreams.'

How often did I recall his words in the years that followed, especially in the darkness that came upon me after I had transgressed with Sabina Pretorius. And I am still not sure that I quite understand them.

BROTHER ULLBRICHT, THE new missionary at our station, had followed our Father van der Kemp's example and my own (God have mercy upon him) and taken to wife a young

Hottentot girl. So Bethelsdorp was now, we trusted, in good hands, and I was free to accompany Brother Campbell and various others, including Brother Cupido, on the long voyage of inspection that was to take us beyond the confines of the colony, to pave the way for the future of our enterprise among the heathen.

It was an amazing journey, exhausting and at times dangerous, but it instilled in me a new sense of awe for the vastness of the continent in which we find ourselves. I believe it also brought me a deeper understanding of Brother Cupido. In those remote climes – barren and yet not barren – one came to see it through our brother's eyes and be made aware of the manifold minutiae in which life can express itself: an ever renewed discovery of riches in indigenous peoples, animals, birds, insects, plants, even rocks and stones. I had heard of some of the accounts of the naturalist and traveller Burchell who had recently passed through those parts and on whose trail we trekked through the previously untrodden Bushmanland (untrodden, that is, of course, by the feet of white men like him, and me), and these accounts had to some extent prepared my mind for the discoveries that awaited us.

It was an illuminating experience to cross the wide, shimmering expanse of the great but (at that time of the year) not very deep Gariep River, for so long regarded as the frontier of the known world, on the far side of which demons and strange races were reputed to have lived; to us, the other side seemed very much like a continuation of what we had perceived before, an endless, dry, flat, gently undulating expanse, sporadically interrupted by ridges or low, flinty mountain ranges, and with acacias, some of them growing to a great size, as the main vegetation. On these plains we often came across small herds of quaggas, of springbok, or of wildebeest, those curious animals which partake of the horse, the ox, the stag and the antelope. From time to time there were signs of predators as well, including lions. This landscape, like a vast parchment unfolding as we progressed, and on which our imprint must have served as a primitive form of writing, continued until we reached, near the confluence of the Gariep and another large river, the tiny mission station of Klaarwater, no more than a collection of small round Hottentot huts surrounding a larger construction of reeds which served as church and schoolroom. We met there the missionary in charge of the station, Brother Anderson, a stocky and somewhat surly man who afforded us hospitality but not much conviviality; even Brother Campbell, usually so cheerful and uncomplaining, appeared to be somewhat taken aback by his lack of generosity. His assistant, the affable but evidently sickly Brother Lambert Janz, made a much more pleasant impression. So did the local Griqua captain, Adam Kok, who insisted on leading us on a hippopotamus hunt along the river.

In the immediate vicinity of Klaarwater I encountered a great variety of birds, some quite unbelievably beautiful, and exorbitantly colourful in those largely drab surroundings. There were few insects, mostly nondescript; but in the thatch of the church Brother Cupido recognised on the Sunday morning, when he was invited to offer a sermon there, a very small green mantis, which appeared to perturb him greatly. So much, in fact, that after staring at the insect as if petrified, he suddenly turned on his heel to flee from the church, leaving it to me to conduct the service.

I was hoping to discuss the matter with him afterwards, but for quite some time he very studiously avoided being drawn into a discussion of the subject.

From Klaarwater we covered a considerable distance across the great plains of Lattakoo, also known by some as

Dithakong, where nothing but the distant horizon bounded our prospect, excepting behind us, where the blue summits of the Kamhanni Mountains near the Kruman rose to break the evenness of the line. The soil was in most parts sandy and of a very rich colour. In my mind, the scraggy little station of the Matchappee tribe at Dithakong, a mere scattering of feeble little reed huts on the merciless plain, will for ever be imprinted as 'the place of stones': dry dust covering the spare earth which lies like a carcass stripped of its skin, marked by whitish ridges of stone and ragged dongas cut into the earth, presumably by torrential rains in seasons beyond human memory. There was a dry river bed, its course marked with large blue rocks, which some of the local people assured us might run with angry water for a day or two in a time of abundant flooding, but no more. Above this meagre course stretched a long ridge with what we were told were the vestiges of ancient Hottentot fortresses; but this, I confess, judging by the actual building standards and propensities of these people, appeared to me more the product of wishful thinking and wild fantasy than anything else. A most unprepossessing place set in a harsh and even malevolent landscape not meant for human occupation. As we stood there looking about, a small red dust devil came whirling along the river bed towards us, churning dry white grass, twigs, thorns and shreds of bark into the air. To my surprise, Brother Cupido became terrified at this sight. He immediately ran to our wagon, retrieved from it a small barrel of water and splashed the precious liquid (more precious by far, in those conditions, than wine or brandy) on the ground right in the path of the approaching whirlwind.

'*Sarês, sarês,*' he shouted, casting the empty barrel aside and running back to the wagon to take refuge on it, cowering under a canvas.

Even more amazed than I had been at his reaction to the dust devil, I observed this curious but unimpressive phenomenon of nature dissipate as it approached the dark stain of water on the ground, disappearing entirely before it reached the spot.

'How could you have done a thing like that?' I berated him later. 'What if we die of thirst in this place?'

'Better to die of thirst than to be taken by that thing,' he grumbled.

'But why, Brother? What is the matter?'

'It is *sarês*,' he said, avoiding my eyes.

'What is *sarês*?' I pressed him.

'The Devil.'

That was all I could get out of him, however urgently I attempted to coax something coherent and meaningful from him.

'You are talking like the heathen you once were,' I admonished him. 'You are a Christian now.'

'The Devil is still the Devil.'

He would not budge from that, and in the end I had to abandon the attempt.

Fortunately for us, the loss of the water was not serious. A mere day's trek from there we reached a spot on the Kruman where there was a deep pool, reputed by the local people to be so deep that no one had ever discovered the bottom yet. It was surrounded by the most lush vegetation imaginable, and it did not seem too far-fetched when a young man from the local mission assured us, with a great show of conviction, that this was where Paradise had once been. He even showed us a boulder which, he asserted, was the rock struck by Moses with his staff to cause a spring to gush out. There was indeed something Old Testament-like about that region, which made it hard to treat our young informant too harshly.

And still our journey continued – westward, along the Gariep to Namaqualand, before at last returning along the bleak coastline to the Cape, and then on the final month of the trek back to Bethelsdorp.

On this last leg of our travels there was one incident which I cannot omit from my narration. It happened on the farm of the colonist Johannes Coetzer near Piquet Berg off the west coast. We arrived there just before nightfall, in inclement weather. There was a howling wind, driving the rain nearly horizontally into our faces as we stopped to ask permission to outspan. When the farmer learned that there were missionaries in our party, we were promptly invited to come inside. The house was rather larger than the farmsteads we had become accustomed to: built of dressed stone, square and quite formidable in the large yard protected by a number of shady trees, and flanked by several ample outbuildings – a shed, stables, sties, a chicken run.

We were invited to partake of dinner with the family, which consisted of quite a collection: the farmer and his wife, seventeen children, a grandmother and an uncle. From our party there were Brother Campbell and myself, and indeed Brother Cupido: the moment Mr Coetzer learned that he was my assistant, he was pressed to join us. It was the first time our brother was invited to dine at the table of a Dutch farmer. He was quite moved by the experience, I could see. And in exchange I proposed, after the huge meal, that he lead us in prayer. I am not sure that it was altogether well advised, as it took him the better part of two hours to work his way through an extensive reading from the Scriptures, followed by a long and most enthusiastic commentary upon the reading, a quite rambling but nevertheless inspiring prayer, and a robust singing of hymns in which, as might be expected, Brother Cupido outsung us all. At the end of it every member of the family was visibly moved and his own face was streaked with tears. In the dull yellow glare of the lamplight it struck me for the first time how old he had become.

I BELIEVE IT WAS his performance on this occasion which inspired Brother Campbell soon afterwards to request at a meeting of missionaries from all over the country in Graaff-Reinet that my proposal be accepted for Brother Cupido, with five other men, to be appointed as missionaries in order to extend our efforts at reaching out into the wilderness of Africa beyond the frontiers of the colony which we had so recently visited.

God must have approved of the initiative, as only a few months later there was an urgent message from Brother Anderson at Klaarwater, calling upon Brother Cupido to betake himself back to that village to fill the place of Brother Lambert Janz who, it transpired, had recently died.

After the rather unprepossessing impression Klaarwater had made on us during the journey (although at least it was less desolate than Dithakong), I did not really expect Brother Cupido to demonstrate any positive feelings about the call. But much to my surprise he reacted with unbridled enthusiasm, evidently believing that the mere fact the call had been sent meant that God Himself had inspired it. When I tried to discuss the impediments attached to such a move, he quite curtly reminded me of St Paul's vision in the place called Troas, as described in the Acts chapter 16 verse 9: *There stood a man of Macedonia, and prayed him, saying, Come over into Macedonia, and help us. And after he had seen the vision, immediately we endeavoured to go into Macedonia, assuredly gathering that the Lord had called us for to preach the gospel unto them.*

'So how can I not go?' demanded Brother Cupido. 'This call comes from God Himself.'

I still tried to make him appreciate the risk attached to such a response, but could make no headway against his passionate conviction. And even though, like Brother Campbell and myself, Cupido had been less than impressed by Brother Anderson's surliness at Klaarwater, he now dismissed it as being of no consequence. God had called him, he had no choice but to go.

There was but a single factor about the occasion that cast something of a pall over his prospects. 'It is that mantis,' he ventured to explain when finally pressed.

'What mantis?' I enquired.

'Don't you remember the mantis in the thatch of the church at Klaarwater?'

I had to think hard to recall it; at last, still perplexed, I nodded.

'A mantis in the veld is a good thing,' he said, avoiding my eyes. 'My mother used to say it was Heitsi-Eibib himself.'

'Then why did this one unsettle you so?'

'Because it was *inside*. A mantis, like a star, must not come indoors. It makes bad things happen.'

'It is just superstition, Brother Cupido,' I remonstrated. 'You are a Christian now.'

'That is what I am trying to tell myself,' he said, subdued. 'But one never knows.' Adding after a moment, 'It may even be God's way of testing me.'

He declined to be drawn on it again, and thenceforth our preparations continued unimpeded.

With something of a heavy heart I wrote to Brother Anderson to inform him of our decision, and also sent off a letter to the governor in Cape Town asking permission for Brother Cupido to leave the colony on the Lord's business.

The reply arrived without undue delay, whereupon several of us assisted our dear brother to prepare the departure. I took it upon myself to equip him for the undertaking. A small wagon he had of his own, but a thorough repair would have to be put to the Society's account.

He had one last request. He wanted a new Bible to take with him into the wilderness. Truth be told, I was somewhat reluctant at first, bearing in mind what had happened to the previous one. But to him it made perfect sense.

'I need a Bible to preach from,' he said. 'If I hold it in my hands and read from it, the words out there in the book will speak to the words inside me to make the people stronger.'

There was little I could say to refute this. And certainly it made sense for a missionary in the deep interior to have a Bible. So in the end I offered him my own, with a firm admonishment not to consume it like the first.

Now that all obstacles had been cleared away and Brother Cupido demonstrated such enthusiasm, my own misgivings began to give way to a new surge of optimism. Undoubtedly the Lord was preparing him for a great work. For the previous months he had been in rotation with us in giving public instruction and generally proved to be so affected during his performances that on every occasion his face was shimmering with tears.

On 18 April 1815 the two of us left on the newly repaired wagon for Graaff-Reinet, from where he was to proceed to his new post. I remember with what pride he recalled that upon arriving at Algoa Bay, some thirteen years before, he had possessed four oxen and a cart: now he had no fewer than ten oxen and a wagon. The future, he assured me as he began to muster his courage once more, could not but further improve his standing in the world.

\*　　\*　　\*

BUT THERE WAS along the way, and before we had even reached Graaff-Reinet, a single mishap of little import in itself, but to which Brother Cupido appeared to attach a significance out of all proportion to the event: as we were unloading the wagon in the late afternoon of the third day to prepare for the evening meal, our brother stumbled over a sinewy root and dropped the package he had been carrying: a mirror wrapped in black crape. Its impact upon the ground was such that it shattered into an exorbitant number of very small shards.

It still pains me to report that the misadventure caused him to break into tears. He dropped to his knees and started crying quite inconsolably, and nothing I could say in my attempts to persuade him that a mere material object should not be the occasion of such distress had any effect whatsoever. I believe he did not sleep at all that night, sitting some distance away from the fire, staring into the dark, uttering no sound apart from heaving a deep sigh from time to time. Throughout most of the following day he remained speechless, seated on the back of the wagon as if engrossed in the veld receding behind us, fading from a motley of colours into a uniform greyish ochre. In one hand he clutched a single insignificant shard of the mirror, as if grimly bent on transporting it with him into the unknown, unknowable future which, for once, seemed unmatched by his faith. Clearly there was behind the fact of the small event a tract of hopelessness, and a capacity for suffering, beyond my grasp.

During the following days I tried to engage him in conversation about the occurrence, but he remained evasive. For some time I even thought that he might decide to turn back and renounce his decision to accept the call to Klaarwater.

'Brother,' I said at last, when all else seemed to fail us, 'let us pray.'

Compared to the almost exuberant abandon with which he usually embraced such opportunities, he seemed, again, more resigned than eager or anxious. I called upon all my reserves of faith and zeal to lay his case before the Lord; and after a long time, in what was rather a display of dumb and dull resignation than conviction of any kind, he appeared to settle into the inevitable. All he said, when we finally rose from our knees, was, 'I was in that mirror, Brother Read. Now I left myself behind. What will happen to me?'

It was this simple remark that brought back to me memories of the innumerable occasions over the previous years when I had found him, in his hut or in some thicket in the veld, with the mirror set up before him, addressing it as if it were a guest, a friend, a confidant. I had often considered broaching the subject with him, apprehensive as I was about a shade of idolatry in what almost amounted to his worship of the artefact; but always I had refrained, feeling that such a step would be an unforgivable intrusion, would violate not just a privacy but an intimacy which it was not my business or my privilege to share. I still could not fathom it; even now as I write, I must confess that it lies beyond my grasp. There are moments when I think: if I could have reached to the bottom of this, I might, finally, have understood something about the man. But it obstinately eluded me; still does. And I have to live with the terrible suspicion that it may be more a failure or a deficiency in myself than a mystery or a delusion in him.

As FOR ME, in writing down all these reminiscences, forcing myself to face everything that has happened to him, to me, to us, I think – I hope – I am groping towards a measure of understanding of what we have lived through, as well as of the course which may yet lie ahead. He was so confident about his call, and about continuing and persevering on his way. For his sake too I cannot now give up. In spite of the valley of the shadow of death I have been traversing lately, through my own humiliation and disgrace and suffering, I shall go on. I shall go to some distant part of our colony – not to flee, like Jonah, from my duty, or from my memories, but to find a place where there is more need of me, a place where the challenge will be greater, and life undoubtedly much harder, in order to turn so much darkness into light. I cannot tell if I shall succeed, I have been such a weak man heretofore. But I must try. Not least because, in a way I cannot as yet fathom, I believe I owe it to Brother Cupido – that spindly little man who has shown me a glimpse of the true faith, even if to others it so often seemed like madness.

I SAW HIM ONCE again, towards the end of the following year. Shortly before that I had received a distressing letter from him about the not entirely unforeseeable souring of his relations with Brother Anderson, which had come about in a decidedly unpleasant fashion, if I may say so. On the same wagon from the deep interior arrived another letter, from Brother Anderson himself, to cast a somewhat different light on the matter.

It seemed that within days of his arrival at Klaarwater our brother had begun in his customary unrestrained manner to apply himself to the souls and the emotions of his new congregation. He would commence at about nine o'clock in the evening with a singing party, going round to all the houses singing until everybody joined, and then continuing until morning. Though some sang, others evidently talked and laughed, the whole exercise opening, as Brother Anderson chose to phrase it, 'a door for uncleanness and immorality, also an encouragement to indolence in the daytime'. He had nothing against the singing, he insisted, 'but why must it be done at night?'

In Brother Cupido's letter he pointed out that he had simply followed the same approach which had proved so successful in Bethelsdorp, adding that he could not be persuaded to insult God by bowing to instructions which went contrary to the Christian spirit of charity and generosity.

What perturbed me was the concluding lines from Brother Anderson's letter:

'I do not wish to be accused of prejudice against Cupido, but I must emphasise that I had much to do to put a stop to these outrageous practices.'

Those were drastic words. Clearly the time had come for me to intervene. I embarked on the arduous journey with a heavy heart, not having any intimation at all of what might lie ahead.

News of my approach must have preceded me, for upon my arrival at the junction of the Gariep and the Hei-Gariep (the one the Bushmen call the Cuoa and colonists the Vaal) I spied Cupido and others on the opposite bank. They immediately came towards me through the river, hanging on to the tails of their oxen. It truly was a joyful meeting to us all.

During my ensuing sojourn at Klaarwater I learned that in spite of the obstacles of language he had been preaching diligently to the Kora and the Griqua people in that district, making use as far as possible of interpreters; but because of the strained relations with Brother Anderson he was deeply unhappy. After a brief enquiry I decided that the only manner in which to resolve the tension would be to transfer Brother Cupido to Dithakong, where he could henceforth act on his own without interference.

The work would be strenuous, as I reckoned there were

six to eight hundred Kora all told in the vast region where he would be active, but he saw that as no problem. It was more worrisome to learn, soon afterwards, that our Directors were expecting him to achieve in two years what it seemed one might more realistically accomplish in ten. No person can form an idea of the difficulty of introducing the Gospel and civilisation among a barbarous people but those who experience it. The Corannas of Malapietze are at present wandering, and there will be some difficulty in collecting them. It was worrying too to remind myself that he did not know their language. But surely the indigenous languages of the continent must all be related. I compelled myself to believe that all would yet be well. He had faith, had he not?

Above all, such was Cupido's relief at being removed from the proximity of Father Anderson, that nothing I said could diminish his enthusiasm.

There might have been an added reason for this, as I learned, not without some misgiving, that he had recently been married to a Hottentot woman from Father Anderson's congregation and that a son had already been born to them. In fact, during my visit he requested me to baptise the infant. I tried earnestly to engage him in conversation about this whole matter, remembering only too well what he had so adamantly affirmed on the occasion of our last discussion on the issue of matrimony and women, but he eluded all attempts to corner him. It was only when I was preparing to leave again on my wagon that he came up to me and handed me another letter he had written to God and which, as so often before, he entreated me to deliver.

And then I left. In many respects I felt reassured about him at that moment which I presume one might call the climax of his life, as a missionary in charge of his own station in the deep interior. 'This is where I want to be, Brother Read,' he had assured me when I had tried to voice some final misgivings. 'I belong here with the stones. God shall turn them into bread.' He had such faith in Him. He also had – how well I remembered that – the Word, quite literally, inside him. There was something indomitable about the little man. Then why was there such a feeling of sad premonition in me too? As if I – or perhaps not I, but our Mission Society – were shedding him there in the wilderness, turning our backs on him, leaving him to his fate, to Africa? I shall never forget the last glimpse I had of him as I looked back through the hood of the wagon, his frail and by now aged body like a sliver of dried biltong, with his head bowed and the sun beating down on it so fiercely that it seemed a radiance was emitted from his small round skull. Smaller and smaller he became in the distance, obscured by the red dust churned up by the trampling oxen and by our wheels, smaller and ever smaller, dwindling to insignificance, to the size of an insect.

All the provision I had to leave with him was a single sheep, trusting that for the rest the Corannas would provide for him. But then, at least, he had his wagon, did he not? And his wife. And his new small son. And, of course, the Word.

Dearest and most esteemed Reverent God, I must xplain to you other wise You will never be Sure. Brother Read brouht me here to this place where there is almost nothing, just the thorn trees and the dry grass and the Stones. And the peple most of them far away but I have my Wagon I can travel and find them where they are and together we shall Praise the Lord. I take with me my little piece of miror everywhere I go to show the

peple the lovliness of God. I have a new Wife too who
I must introduce to You because You may be suprised
to see her here after I told you so many times I am
Happy to live alone after you let Anna go away. But
that was because I really believed it was so. In
Bethelsdorp I had all my Work to do and there was
many peple all the time but in a Far place like this there
is mostly only silence. So when I was at Klaarwater
with that Stupid Brother Anderson forgive me for
saying so but he is stupid then I met Katryn a young
woman and she has life in her. She is not the kind of
woman to make Sparks fly but I am not loking for that
I had my Anna and also there are many kinds of sparks.
But what I thouht was this that Sant Paul you know
Sant Paul he said so clearly I say therefore to the unmarried and widows it is good for them if they abide even
as I but if they cannot Contain let them Marry for it
is better to marry than to burn. If we burn in this place
we shall burn together and from the Sun not from the
Flesh. Also this place is near the River with the Deep
Water where the peple say the Paradise was long ago
so I think of how You came to this Place and said Let
us make Man in our Image after our Likenes and let
them have Dominon over the Fish of the sea and over
the Foul of the air and over the Cattle and over all the
Earth and over every Creeping thing that creepeth upon
the earth so God created Man in his own Image and
God saw that it was good. But you kno God the lone-
lyness that get to a Man in a Place like this and that is
why you said it is not good that the man should be
alone I will make him an help meet for him. And you
knew better than Sant Paul because why You was there
First. That is why I am here now and my wife Katryn

nex to me and we shall make the wilderness bloom
and Brother Anderson can go to hell but I tell You I
shall be here with my little bit of miror and all my
Love your ever Obedint lovly child Cupido Cockrch.

# THREE

## 1 8 1 5 –?

## Dithakong

# I

# The Place of Stones

THREE THINGS, Brother Cupido would think at his outspan in Dithakong, three things mark this tract of land as a place like no other. One is the oryx, the gemsbok, that raises its horns against the white sky. Another is the camel thorn, the *kameeldoring*, with its hard wood and its stringy bark, its yellow puffs, its pods like human ears, and the birds that nest in its branches, and the shade its umbrella provides for whatever has need of pause and refreshment, and the flames that rise from its trunk if after its death you need fire against the predators and the grey-feet spirits of the dead who wander about in the night. And the third thing of this place is the bedrock of blue jonas stone, the oldest stone in the world, according to those who know (and particularly those who don't), as this was the stone first created by Tsui-Goab, before he made people and snakes, followed much later by the other animals.

At the very end, after people and snakes and animals and wind and stars have all gone, only stone will remain. In the beginning the footprints of human beings lay among the rocks. But we know that for every person there is a wind which has been made just for that man or woman. This wind follows you like your shadow. And when you die one day, your wind comes softly to blow across your tracks and cover them with sand. Afterwards it goes on blowing your story through the world to make sure that distant people will pick it up. But one day, after time itself has blown away, there will be no one in that timelessness to know that you once left your footprints there.

Scripture, it is true, tells the story differently. But gradually, as a result of the long stay at Dithakong, and the drought, and the hunger, and the open spaces around him, Cupido comes to think, as Anna Vigilant told him long ago, that perhaps it does not matter so much if Tsui-Goab says one thing and Tkaggen another, the Lord God something else again. For all he knows, there may be other gods in other places. One cannot listen to them all. One cannot even know all their names. And while you don't know, perhaps all you can do is to keep your ears open for what the stone itself has to say.

This is how he explains it to his new wife Katryn too. She is different from Anna Vigilant, and she isn't San either, but it is good to have her with him. And here, according to the Word, they can now be fruitful and fill the earth. Even though he is no longer young, and done with the things of a child.

The people of this region seem hospitable enough. But poor. It still remains to be seen how well they can look after a missionary. Brother Read has assured him that they would have nothing to worry about: from what he was told, they will want for nothing. Moreover, the Society in Cape Town will be sending them provisions at regular intervals. And then there is still his stipend. This has not been fixed yet, but according to Brother Read it will not be less than a hundred rix-dollars a year.

'And then I can probably go on sawing wood too,' he tells Katryn. 'I could even do some trading.'

'Where will you get things to trade?'

'Just wait. We will soon find out what is most in demand here.'

'You are a missionary now, Cupido,' she reprimands him. 'There will hardly be time for other things.'

'In this place I won't have a big congregation to keep me busy,' he argues. 'Six to eight hundred all told was what Brother Read said. You heard him.'

'But they don't all live in the same place, Cupido. They are spread out from horizon to horizon.'

'I have a wagon, look at it. I have come a long way in my life. And I'm going much further, I tell you. The two of us together. With the help of the Lord.'

'We shall need Him. These Kora people can be difficult. You don't even know their language.'

'I'll manage. And you can help, you can speak the language.'

'Not much. And the Kora can be obstreperous, I tell you.' She narrows her eyes as if to stare right through him. 'Do you know what their name means? "Kora".'

'Isn't it just a name?'

'No, Cupido. It means *Judgement*. As in Judgement Day.'

'A good name. Because those who do not want to listen to me will be judged. I shall strike them with the judgement of the Lord.'

'What if *you* are the one to be judged?'

'I trust in God, Katryn. We are in His hand.'

'Watch out that He doesn't let us slip through His fingers. No one will even know about it.'

'Don't be lacking in faith. Together with God and the Kora we'll turn this desert into a paradise.'

'It would have been better if they had put us down in Kuruman. They have water and greenery there.'

'We were brought here with a purpose. In this place we are far beyond all frontiers and boundaries. We're on the edge of everything that is beyond. This is how God wants to try us.'

'That is what I'm worried about. Look at that sky.'

She motions. The sun has just set. The sky is black and blue as if it has been badly beaten in the face.

'We're just at the beginning,' he insists.

'Of what?'

'Of everything.'

'This place looks more than nothing, Cupido.'

'Go and call our congregation,' he says. 'It is time for the evening service. Tonight we can sing for a long time. Here is no one to bother us, and we can bother no one.'

With a small sigh she obeys. The singing softens her own heart too. That is what first drew her to him.

It applies to the members of his congregation too. Only a handful. Perhaps eighty, perhaps a hundred. But it is a start.

From time to time others come, but some of the brothers and sisters have already moved away. The Kora are not people who like to stay in one place, they keep moving on, this way and that, following the wind or the stars or the rain. Which means that Cupido also has to keep on moving, to herd them together like a flock of sheep. This he enjoys. Ever since his childhood he has been dreaming of living like this. Waiting for the day when he would leave on the wings of an eagle. An *arend* sent specially for him. Whenever he begins to talk about that Katryn knows there is a long conversation ahead. Invariably he would fetch his big Bible to read to her, chapter and verse. From Deuteronomy: *He found him in a desert land, and in the waste howling wilderness; he led him about, he instructed him, he kept him as the apple of his eye. As an eagle stirreth up her nest, fluttereth over her young, spreadeth abroad her wings, taketh them, beareth them on her wings: So the Lord alone did lead him* . . . Or from the Psalms, or from Ezekiel: *Thus saith the Lord God: A great eagle with great wings, longwinged, full of feathers, which had divers colours, came unto Lebanon, and took the highest branch of the cedar* . . . And afterwards they would sing together, and he would preach to her. About how, one day, he would fly away with that eagle, just wait. Into the whole wide world to convert the heathen to the greater glory of God. Not so? Use the talents the Lord God has given you and do not bury them in a cloth, says the Word. The Word in his hands, the Word in his stomach.

From time to time they also receive visitors from elsewhere. Church people from Kuruman or Lattakoo, or even from as far afield as Namaqualand. And then, once, the two wagons all the way from the Cape, just imagine. Two wagons with sixteen oxen apiece, accompanied by eight men on horseback. And a host of Hottentots, some on mules, most on foot. They are grey with exhaustion, and this is only the beginning of their journey.

'We heard there was a mission station in this place,' says the leader of the group to Cupido. An enormous man with a broad-rimmed hat and a wild black beard, carrying an impatient crop in his huge hand. 'Where can I find him?'

'You have found him now,' says Cupido with a broad, welcoming smile.

'Miserable place,' the man says, openly antagonistic. 'Well, where is he?'

'I am the missionary.'

'Look, man.' From the jerky movements of the crop one can see that there is thunder in the offing; it wriggles about like a snake in the dry grass. 'I don't think you understand me properly. I'm looking for the missionary. Now go and call your baas.'

'I am the missionary of the London Missionary Society,' says Cupido, adopting an attitude out of keeping with his rather dishevelled appearance. 'Ordained by the Brothers Read and Campbell, in Graaff-Reinet. In June of the year of Our Lord 1814.'

The huge man changes his grip on the crop. For a moment he seems on the point of attacking the insignificant person in front of him. Then, unexpectedly, a gaping red hole opens in his black beard. 'We shall see, my little Hottentot,' he says. It sounds like a peal of thunder in a dark blue cloud in the distance. 'Let us outspan first. Then we can talk.'

'Welcome in the name of the Father, the Son, and the Holy Ghost,' says Cupido.

For a moment it is, again, difficult to predict how the bearded man will respond. Once again he growls deep in his throat, then turns back to his men to start giving orders for the evening. His many helpers spread out in all directions in search of firewood.

When everything is ready, the big man returns to Cupido, wielding once again his busy little crop.

'I suppose you've got something for us to eat?' he says.

Brother Cupido feels a large hand grasping him where it hurts. 'What kind of food did you have in mind?' he asks cautiously.

'A sheep or something.'

'*Ai*,' he moans. In his mind he calculates what he has. But he sighs and says, 'God told us to love our neighbour. We don't have much. But what we have we shall share with love.'

Soon after the wether has been caught and slaughtered – the very sheep Brother Read gave him at their parting – Katryn comes to corner him.

'What is this with the sheep?' she asks.

'The people must eat, Katryn.' But he avoids her eyes.

'They got enough food of their own.'

'How do you know?'

'Because I had a look. One of the wagons is loaded with meat. Ostrich, giraffe, gemsbok, hartebeest, wildebeest, zebra, you name it. What do they want with our little sheep?'

'God told us to share with our neighbour.'

'What makes them our neighbours? They're a lot of good-for-nothings. We'll have nothing left when they are through with us.'

'Don't talk like that, Katryn. Cast your bread upon the water, says the Book.'

'There's no water here.'

'The Lord will provide.'

'The Lord will take from us even what we don't have.'

'We are gathering a treasure in heaven.'

'What use is heaven to us? We live *here*.'

She is sounding more and more like Anna, he thinks. But he persists, 'Now you're sinning in your thoughts, Katryn.'

'It isn't sinful to want to stay alive. We have a child to think about. And another one that's swelling inside me.'

'We shall prosper and be rich in this place to which He has brought us.'

'I'll believe that when I see it. If you go on sharing with others what we don't even have for ourselves, we'll soon be as poor as meerkats.'

'All we need is faith.'

'We'll need more than faith.'

He sighs heavily. 'Come, we must take care of these people. We have a duty.'

'*You* may have a duty,' says Katryn. 'Not I.'

'You are my wife,' he says emphatically.

She shrugs. 'All right then. I'm coming. But give them an earful of the Word first. Perhaps that will shame them.'

Just before supper Cupido goes to fetch his Bible, installs himself on the front seat of his wagon and opens the book on his thin knees. In the beginning there is a muted murmuring of gossip and mockery among the men, but as he proceeds to read in his big voice they become subdued.

During the prayer one can hear an ant crawl. Then comes the singing. It rings out under the stars as if the sky had been turned upside down like a large basin to amplify the sound into an almighty roar. And as they sing, the moon detaches itself from the horizon and starts floating upward like an ox-bladder.

From then on the men treat Brother Cupido with respect. And when the food is dished out he and his family find themselves treated to an abundance of venison such as they have never partaken of before.

As the night grows older the men's tongues are loosened. They start talking about the long hunt ahead, and Brother Cupido trembles with enthusiasm. Their talk brings back his own early years, from the time he and Heitsi-Eibib roamed the plains together, the day he killed the lion with a stare, the day the elephant prepared to trample him and then collapsed in its tracks, all the days when there was no other hunter to match him in the wild, when strangers came from all over the colony to hire him as their huntsman. It is as if an old fire that has long since subsided into grey and barely glowing embers are suddenly stirring in a breath of wind, breaking into a feeble flickering, then into dancing flames. There is an urge in him to join in the talk, but he holds back. This is no longer permitted. His life now belongs to the Lord. He has made his choice, he should keep to it. Though God knows how hard it is. He frowns in urgent concentration, listening with such intensity as if he would lure a lion from a patch of thorn bushes.

This is the third year the band of hunters are off into the wild like this, they tell him. Previously their journeys veered more towards Namaqualand; this year they are eager to move in a different direction. They are prepared to shoot whatever comes in their way. Whatever is too much for the bearers to handle or to load on the wagons, they will simply leave behind. For they are the kings of the hunt, are they not, and wherever they pass the veld must be littered with the white bones of their passage. As a sign for those who are to follow later. The sky will be black with vultures, the nights will resound with the cackling and screaming of scavengers. Antelope, zebra, wildebeest, giraffes, tigers (this is their word) and wolves (their terminology again), lions, hippopotamuses, rhinoceros. And then, above all: elephants.

Two years earlier, one of the hunters says, they chased a herd of elephants into a swamp where they got stuck in the mud, and fifty-seven were killed in one morning. Pity that most were cows and calves, so there wasn't much ivory; but what the hell. For a hunter an elephant is an elephant, and what counts is the kill.

The bearded man gets quite carried away by his own narrative; he is trembling with what seems like a fever, glowing in the light of the fire like a huge ember.

'There is nothing in God's whole creation I love more than an elephant,' he exclaims, too excited to remain seated any longer. He climbs on the huge trunk of a fallen *kameeldoring* to address them. 'It is the most beautiful thing God has ever made. The most beautiful, the most noble, the greatest. One stands in awe before it. If it raises its trunk and throws dust into the air and starts waving its big ears, trumpeting as if the Day of Judgement has arrived, there is no other creature that is a match for an elephant. I love him and respect him as a brother, as a father, as a great-great-grandfather. Look, there may be people who believe that gold, or diamonds, or a beautiful woman is the most desirable thing on earth, but let me tell you: there is nothing like an elephant. If I find his tracks crossing my way, I swear to God – even if I am on a trading trip, not hunting at all, I cannot have a moment's rest before I have followed that elephant and killed him. Even if it takes days. What am I saying? Even if takes weeks or months. It is just too much for me. That is how I love an elephant.'

After this astounding declaration of love there is a long, very black silence – they are all trapped in the hollow hand of the night, below the moon – before anyone else dares to say a word.

Then, very slowly, the conversation begins to flow again. Now they are talking about the hunting ground they are heading for. This is where Cupido can abandon himself to the names and names. It is like the old days when he was on that journey with the trader Servaas Ziervogel: and the names are, if possible, even more alluring and strange, names with which one can dream an endless road that opens into the wilderness. The way Anna Vigilant would have done if she were here tonight. He cannot tell whether he will remember them correctly, or in the right order: perhaps they never existed in any order. But that doesn't matter. They are names. Names of places beyond all he knows or ever could have dreamed of.

There are Ghanzi and the Tebraveld
there are the deep well at Tkams and the region of
   Otjimpolo
there are Damaraland and the Kunene
and every now and then there is mention of
   Okavango and the lake at Ngami
as well as Kgalagadi and the Chella Mountains
and Lebebe and Omabonde
and the Okawabga River and Andara and Humpata
the Honey River and Mossamedes
and Lubango and Benguela

and Ekundju and Humbe and Ondanguena and
   Kuamati
there are shinboro and the Caculuva River

and once Brother Cupido is properly warmed up, he is ready
to add from his memories of that long-ago trader:

Samarkand and Sumatra
   Vladivostok and Nizhni-Novgorod
and the Great Bear and Orion with his girdle and the
Southern Cross
and, for all one can tell, Saturn and Uranus
and the New Jerusalem with its streets of gold inlaid
with opals, pearls, emeralds,
with rubies and jasper and seven gates and angels
ascending and descending

God above, what untold and untellable splendours still lie
ahead for these wagons and these men? What – he dares to
think in this dark hollow of the night-without-end – still lies
ahead for *him*?

# 2

# Here and There and Everywhere

AFTER THE WAGONS and the people have left again – thank God they wouldn't tarry any longer, the hunting grounds were waiting – Cupido starts working on his own little wagon. From now on, he has decided, he will serve his congregation from the wagon. If the Kora will not come to him, then – by God – he will go to them.

There is an ancient fire burning inside him, a fire like a thorn bush that refuses to be consumed. This is their place now, this stretch of almost limitless land; here they will flourish.

It isn't easy, he soon discovers. The first problem is the language. There is only a small scattering of Kora who can understand him, and of what *they* speak he cannot make out much. Fortunately Katryn can interpret here and there, having grown up in these parts. But it isn't long before she corners him:

'Cupido, you got to learn their language. There is no other way.'

'I am too old for such things,' he says, shaking his head of greying hair. 'My mind gets all mixed up with the words.' But his eyes soon brighten again. 'I'm sure it doesn't really matter. God will make sure that they understand. Even if He has to split into fiery tongues to make them listen.'

'Those days are past,' she reminds him in her down-to-earth way.

'In the meantime you must stand in and interpret for us.'

'I'm not made for talking,' she says. 'That is not what I said yes for when I took you as my husband.'

'The ways of the Lord are not our ways,' he says calmly. 'We can only follow where He leads.'

From time to time, as in the old days, the roads take him past cairns erected for Heitsi-Eibib. Then he dutifully reins in the oxen and dismantles the whole mound and throws away the stones. 'Heathen stuff,' he mumbles. Yet, if one watches closely, one may discover that he no longer performs this duty with quite the same passion as in the days following his conversion. It may be because his back is getting stiff with the passing years. And after their first few trips Katryn begins to notice that he would occasionally drive past a cairn without stopping. She deliberately refrains from asking about it, but after a while he finds it necessary to explain anyway:

'One cannot spend all one's time throwing away stones,' he mumbles gruffly. 'It's too tiring. I think I need my strength for better things. If God really wants to get rid of the stones He will do it in His own way.'

She wisely decides not to reply. As the new child grows inside her, she agrees that he should save his strength for worthier things.

Whenever they outspan on the road, drawing ever wider circles in the barren land, people materialise from behind stones and thorn trees and come to listen. Nobody really knows where they come from. They are like flying ants after a rainstorm: one moment there is nothing, the next the whole world is quivering and rustling with their presence, as in the very beginning when Tsui-Goab called forth people from the stones. Then Brother Cupido preaches a sermon while they stand listening with open mouths, because this man knows how to spread the Word: his voice would start in a whisper, then gradually build up to rolls of thunder, rising and diving like a bird in flight, one moment a mountain eagle in the dizzy heights of heaven, then a swallow darting just above the plain; often he speaks until he himself bursts out crying, drawing copious tears from his audience too, even when they cannot understand a word he is saying.

Afterwards Katryn would admit, 'God must be truly with you, Cupido. I don't know how you do it, but you even turn *me* into a believer just by listening to you.'

Throughout that vast region of sand and stone they trek. First in a northerly direction, to places like Bothitong and Magwagwe and Logageneng and Tokolwane and Paropeng; then in the very opposite direction, often lured purely by the names:

Vlermuislaagte and Makukukwe
Gemsbok, Bloubospan
and on to Heuningkrans or Honey Cliff, to Pramberg
    or Tit Mountain
to Denkbeeld, which means Image
and Grootgewaag, or Risked-a-Lot
to Vuilnek, Dirty-Neck, and Omvrede, Peace-All-
    Round
to Dammetjie and Titiespoort
and Jakkalsrus and Miershoopholte
and from there to Diepdruppels, Deep-Drops, and
    Vyboom, Fig Tree
and Geduld, Patience

until he can write all their names on the map inside his hand. Each one has its memory stamped on his mind: this is where the right-front ox went lame, this is where the team leader was scared by a bustard and sprained his ankle, this is where the child had the squitters, here they found the sweetest honey imaginable in a black-hook thorn bush from a bees' nest a nondescript little bird had pointed out, there it got so dry that he had to piss in his own hand to have some moisture, there the wagon's hood was so badly torn that they had to replace it with a couple of oxhides, there more than thirteen people appeared from among a cluster of wild pomegranate bushes to listen to his sermon, only to steal two of their oxen while they were sleeping after the service, here one of the rear wheels broke, there Katryn's new child was born, and there he died . . .

Circles and lines criss-crossing through the land, going everywhere, going nowhere. Still he has to fight the urge simply to go right on, not to turn back again at all, to see where it will take him, right through Africa, through the world, wherever there have been people, and then beyond. To the far side of beyond.

Once it almost happens by itself. He is sitting on the front seat as the oxen placidly go their way. His eyes are not peering ahead as usual, but looking up. High above the earth the speck of a bird draws a thin line through the pale sky, up and up, until it is almost too far to see with the naked eye. An eagle. An *arend*. And Brother Cupido's heart turns light in his body, he himself becomes lighter and lighter, he feels himself beginning to levitate, floating on the thermals of the empty sky, on and on, in the wake of the eagle. Until Katryn complains from behind, under the hood:

'Have we not passed our turn-off long ago? Where are you going? This way we shall never get home again.'

With a sigh he turns the wagon round. Perhaps one day, he thinks. Perhaps one day. His *arend* is sure to come, the one his mother spoke of. For the time being it is back to Dithakong. Always back. And every time they outspan there are fewer Kora people left to come home to.

# 3

# A Letter from Heaven

WHETHER IT IS Katryn's nagging (since the death of the child she has become a weight on his mind), or whether it is just because there is so much time to think in this emptiness, Brother Cupido cannot tell. But worry is beginning to fray his equanimity. About the dwindling of his congregation, like a flock of sheep under the depredations of jackals or lynxes or nameless creatures of the night. It is not the declining numbers as such that concern him, but the fact that there are ever fewer people available to take care of him and his family. From the day they were deposited in this place, the arrangement with the Society, as Brother Read conveyed it to him, has been that the congregation would take charge of him and spread its protective eagle's wings over him. If there are no Kora left, who will look after them? The few who remain are destitute like himself. Some of them in fact are turning to *him* for help. Now they all have to scour the stony kopies and ridges together in search of *veldkos*. A tortoise here, there a tsamma, or an edible root, or a wild plum, sometimes a hare or — praise the Lord! — a duiker. It keeps one going, but one becomes so skinny it feels as if your navel is chafing your spine.

He cannot understand what has become of the provisions and the stipend the Society is supposed to provide. Brother Read has been so adamant about it. At least a hundred rix-dollars a year – *at least* a hundred, he said – and a sheep or even an ox at regular intervals, some flour and sugar and coffee, even a span of tobacco, and oddments of clothing now and then. Yet so far: nothing. Honest to God, nothing. This is what the Word says: *Man shall not live by bread alone, but by every word that proceedeth out of the mouth of God.* But he has already stuffed himself with the Word; a crust of bread will not be amiss.

Always back to the Word for comfort and reassurance: *I will lift up mine eyes unto the hills, from whence cometh my help.* Not much here in the line of hills, only rough and rocky outcrops, and yet they are also God's handiwork, are they not? But there is no sign of help. With his own eyes Brother Cupido can see the child become thinner and thinner, more and more of a little stick insect like his father, only the little pot-belly is getting rounder, and the eyes are covered with milky membranes, and on his upper lip the snot crusts grow hard.

That is when Brother Cupido takes out his precious writing things. The neat little chest he made in Bethelsdorp long ago, when he was still learning to write. A clutch of quills he has picked up in the veld and sharpened: wild duck, wild goose, secretary bird, all of them made by God. Powdered ink which he sparingly mixes with a few drops of water, and which is running out alarmingly. A cherished pile of clean white sheets of paper which he laboriously covers, one by one, with his large, spindly writing.

*Dearly beloved Brother Read, I sit myself down to tell you* . . .

Or sometimes: *Our Honoured and deeply respected Brother John Campbell* . . .

And when he finds himself in an extremity, which seems to be happening more and more these days: *Dearly beloved and Most Honourable Revrend God* . . .

These letters have to be carefully stowed until there is an opportunity to travel to Kuruman or to approach somebody from there, so that they can be dispatched from that station. He knows it may take months, possibly a year or more, before they will reach a destination, Cape Town or Bethelsdorp, but God doesn't care about time.

Occasionally there is news from outside, not in a letter but reported by someone coming from afar: such and such has died, such-and-such has gone back to England, somebody else has arrived, through the infinite mercy of God the labour in His vineyard is continuing, pray for us.

Pray for me too, Brother Cupido says to himself.

'They don't hear you,' Katryn comments. 'We're too far away. No mercy can reach us here.'

'No, we just got to wait,' he assures her. 'Remember, if it goes bad with the body, we still have the Word.'

'The Word won't give us food and clothes. The Word couldn't stop death taking my child either,' she says sullenly.

Brother Cupido holds firm: '*Watch and pray, that ye enter not into temptation. God will provide.*'

And then he pens another letter to Brother Read. A long letter this time, to explain at length everything that has been damming up inside him, and everything Katryn has been complaining about. Because now things are truly bad, even if he has to admit it himself. No fewer than eight of his precious white pages he devotes to this letter. There isn't much left between him and ultimate silence.

But no answer comes. Instead of that, there is alarming news blown by the wind about his brother missionary. That he committed adultery with Sabina, the daughter of the church elder Andries Pretorius. That he has been dismissed from his position. That his future is to be decided by Brother Campbell, assisted by a new missionary who has recently arrived from England, Brother Moffat, who has come to head the station at Kuruman.

He writes a heart-rending letter to the new reverend. It is mostly Katryn who dictates to him; only here and there does he have to temper the tone. About how long they have been in this place now. Two years. Longer. And since that first sheep they have not received anything else. That his people are starving. That there is no money coming in. But much more important than money: no provisions. Please send help, most Honourable, Respected Revrend!

And then, one day, a letter comes. It is a *smous* on a long narrow wagon who brings it. He isn't sure who has sent it: as far as he knows it has been passed on from one hand to another. For all he knows, he grins, it might come all the way from heaven: just look at the lovely blue envelope.

Brother Cupido takes the letter. He leaves the *smous* standing where they met. What he needs now above all else is to be alone in the veld with his letter.

The day is still and fearsomely hot. The stones lie strewn about the way God must have flung them on an early day of creation when He lost His temper and tried to kill the damned serpent. *It shall bruise thy head, and thou shalt bruise his heel.*

He keeps looking back. No one should see him here. This is something utterly private between him, and his letter. And between them and the Lord God.

When he is quite sure that there is nobody near, he sits down on a jonas stone. He straightens the letter on his high, knobbly knees. Trying to rid it of all the creases of months and maybe years of travelling. All distance is suspended. It is as if he were standing in front of God Himself. He slides one horny thumbnail under the lacquer seal and begins meticulously to loosen it, bit by bit. He has time.

When at long last it is removed, he folds the letter open and once again smoothes it.

Now he will know. At long last, after the endless waiting, all will be revealed. And his life will change for good.

First he inclines his head and closes his eyes. To ask for the blessing of the Lord on this day and this message. That it may be to His greater glory.

He looks up and allows his eyes to wander across the landscape. The tract of land which has now become his responsibility. At last it all feels worthwhile. He can feel God's hand on him.

But he has forgotten about the Devil.

From nowhere, in that bare landscape where one can see for many days in every direction, a whirlwind makes its appearance. The child of the Devil, *sarês*. He sees it approach across the plains, almost transparent, starting as no more than a little cloud of dust and dried grass, twigs, thorns, husks, dead insects, the desiccated limb of a mantis, presumably devoured by the female after mating. It comes closer, grows larger, turns denser and darker. He sits paralysed. He has no water with him to pour out in its path. He does not even have a drop of piss in him.

*Sarês* comes whirling straight at him, grasps at the tatters of his clothes, rattles his knees. Grabs the letter from his hands. Hurls it high up in the air, churns it out of sight. Until there is nothing left to be seen. Only light, trembling with heat. As if it has never happened.

The letter from heaven has been taken from him, for ever.

# 4

## A Curse

FOR A WHILE Brother Cupido avoids Katryn, knowing she is
bound to enquire about the letter, and he cannot immediately face the reproach in her eyes. But it isn't possible to
stay out of her way for long – she sees to that – and as soon
as she finds an occasion, that very evening beside the fire
where they are eating their meagre veld food, swallowed
down with small gulps of water, she asks point-blank:

'What did that letter say?'

'What letter?'

'The letter that came with the *smous* wagon.'

'The Lord giveth and the Lord taketh away.'

'What does that mean?'

He sighs. It is no use trying to hide anything from her. He
tells her about the whirlwind.

'It was *sarês*,' she says without hesitating.

He remains silent for a long time, then nods. 'I thought
so too.'

'So you never read it?'

He shakes his head.

'Do you at least know where it came from?'

He shakes his head again.

'Now we'll never know,' she says in a tone of resignation.

'If God wants us to know, He will send a message.'

'How can you go on believing?'

'What else can I do, Katryn?'

'You must send another message to that new missionary they talking about. What's his name? The one at Kuruman. Isn't it Moffat?'

'Yes, Moffat. I already sent four messages.' He shrugs. 'He must be a very busy man.'

'He is too important for you, that's what he is.'

'They say he is still very young.'

'Little piss-can. A snothead.'

'You mustn't say such things about a man of God, Katryn.'

'He doesn't act like a man of God. He could have come to see you long ago. You been with the Society much longer than he. He was still sucking his mother's teat when you were already a missionary.'

'He will come when the time is right.'

This makes her angry. 'You think the time will ever be right? Must I tell you why he is not coming? Because he is from England. He is too white for our kind. We are brown as stones.'

'It's a sin to say such things.'

'I say things the way they are.'

'I am a missionary, baptised in the Sunday's River, called by God.'

'But the river will never wash you white, Cupido. Get that into your head.'

'It's not that.'

'What else? I tell you, if you were white he'd have been here long ago. If you were white you would have had your money long ago. If you were white they would have looked after us. Food and clothes and everything.' She spits on the ground. 'Even the Kora don't respect you. They only believe a white man. You're too much like them.'

'That is not the way Brother Read taught us.'

'Not all of them are like Brother Read. Their God is white.'

'No, Katryn!' Honest to God, he thinks, if that had been permitted he would have raised his hand against her today. 'A child of the Lord cannot say such things.'

'I don't want to be a white God's child.'

'You were baptised.'

'A splash of water doesn't make me white. I wish he'd drowned me. Then I wouldn't have been sitting on this godforsaken plain today.'

'Katryn, Katryn.' He feels like crying. 'Don't be like that, man. We must walk together, all the way, for God's sake, please. Otherwise what will become of us?'

'What *has* become of us?' she goes on with rare obstinacy. 'Look what we had when we came here. Look what we got now.'

'That is not important. You must keep your eyes on the Lord.'

'You keep looking up at Him and you step in a turd.'

'Oh, Katryn.'

'Yes, Cupido.'

How many of those conversations have there been? It is like a man preparing to go into deep water and taking his clothes off bit by bit until he is as naked as your finger. Then, suddenly, there is no water.

And Katryn becomes more and more recalcitrant. Soon she is no longer prepared to go out on the wagon with him when he leaves on his preaching trips: she chooses to stay where she is. With the children. The little one that has begun to walk and the new baby at her breast.

He keeps on drawing his lines and circles in the endless veld. In due course he travels with only two oxen, leaving the others behind to rest them. He himself is light enough; and most of the time he doesn't even ride on the wagon but walks alongside the oxen. With the diminutive team leader in front.

Before every journey he still takes his place on the front seat and opens the Bible. More from habit and superstition than anything else the few remaining people at the mission form a thin little circle to listen to him. Most of them do not understand what Brother Cupido is reading, but at least they still come. In deathly silence they listen to him. Even the stones and the thorn bushes and the few wild pomegranate bushes keep their silence.

The same Psalm every time: *My help cometh from the Lord, which made heaven and earth. He will not suffer thy foot to be moved; he that keepeth thee will not slumber. The Lord shall preserve thy going out and thy coming in from this time forth, and even for evermore.*

And then he would go off on the ever more rickety little wagon. This way to Nokaneng and Ga-Ramatale and Magobeng; then in the opposite direction to Dwaalhoek and Duine. And it isn't far from there, at the Losberg Plain, just as they come down the Koranna Mountain, that the wagon stumbles for the last time in its tracks and comes to a standstill, its rear axle smashed.

It has happened before, at shorter and shorter intervals, that they had problems. A rim, a hub, the draught-pole, the cross-beam, a few spokes or yokes. But those he could repair, his hands could find a remedy. As if the wagon were an invalid that just wanted one to know about its ailments; and if you didn't pay enough attention it would get more and more obstreperous. But this time is worse. The wagon has been struck in its very core. And this is the end. Cupido tells the little team leader to stand among the limestone ridges and begins to pray. Passionately, as he knows so well. Until his face is smeared with tears, the only moisture in the landscape.

Come down and help me today, Lord-God, he says. I have always kept Your commandments, haven't I? Now it's time You did something for *me*. And anyway, I'm not asking it for myself but to spread Your word. So help me!

But God must be occupied elsewhere. For three days they stand there in the merciless sun before a thin grey thong of a man comes past on a mule. He agrees to go for help. Another two days before he comes back with a couple of helpers. Together they set the axle between two splints the way one would set a broken leg. But that will only see them home: there is no life left in that axle. They have to take it very, very slowly, hobbling along. Two weeks before they see the wretched little group of huts at Dithakong huddled together among the *swarthaak* thorns, like a small flock of sheep beside a dried-up waterhole.

'I thought you were never coming back,' Katryn says listlessly.

'If it depended on God I would still have been out there,' says Brother Cupido with rare bitterness in his parched voice. 'We had to make do on our own.'

'You should have come before. Most of the people have gone. They said they couldn't just sit here, waiting to die.'

'How many are left?'

'Fourteen.'

'That's better than nothing. With fourteen believers we can still move that ridge to the sea.'

'It would be better to move the sea to the ridge. Or a river. Or even a well. We're dying of thirst in this place.'

'Just give me time to fix the wagon.'

But this time it doesn't work. It is as if the wagon itself has given up hope. When he has the axle repaired one of the front wheels breaks. Not just crippled: it falls apart, leaving only a small bundle of splintered wood fragments. A month for a new wheel. Then the second one breaks. The wagon is finished.

That is when Brother Cupido summons his family and his congregation. By that time eight of the fourteen are left. He lifts the big Bible high above his head in his rickety arms, then bends over and places the book in the dust at his feet. Extends an arm to the wagon. His whole body is trembling with fury. And then he intones in a voice such as even the most trusted members of his congregation would never have thought possible.

'You, wagon!'

He stops, too far gone to resume without a pause.

'You, wagon!' the congregation chants, as if they have been given precise liturgical instructions.

'In the name of God, Father, Son and Holy Ghost . . .'

'In the name of God, Father, Son and Holy Ghost . . .'

'. . . I place the curse of Heaven and Hell upon you.'

'. . . I place the curse of Heaven and Hell upon you.'

Now he is really moving into full stride:

'I curse you in your rim and your hub, and in your spokes and your axles, I curse you in your front seat and your dashboard and your spine and your draught-pole, I curse you in your tar-bucket and your axle-pin straps.

'I curse you that you will never again know the mercy and loving kindness of rain or dew, but that you will shrivel up and crack in sunlight and moonlight until there is nothing left of you and you are consumed by ants and spiders and wasps and flies and bluebottles in the veld.

'I curse you that you will be struck with croup and consumption and blackwater and heartburn and menstruation pains.

'I curse you to beyond the ends of the earth, and to the deepest depths of the pool of fire and brimstone.

'I curse you to become the seat of the Whore of Babylon who will consume you in the flames of a slow fire.

'I curse you . . .'

Brother Cupido gasps for breath, his face glistening with sweat, his eyes bloodshot. He cannot think of anything else, anything more terrible or annihilating to add. Exhausted, staggering, with a moan in his throat that sounds like a sob, he concludes:

'And I wish you *die!*'

That night three more of his Kora abscond. Now there are only five people left at the mission, apart from Brother Cupido and his family:

— a deaf man who is also blind in one eye from which pus continually leaks

— two elderly sisters, both soft in the head

— a young cripple who has been an orphan since birth

— and one ancient man who can no longer walk.

# 5

# The End of the Mission Station

NOTHING AND NOBODY can prevent Brother Cupido from continuing to preach. From the old bleached skeleton of a sheep in the veld he retrieves a ram's horn, with which he summons, three times a day – at sunrise, at midday and at sunset – the last of the faithful to prayers. Strictly speaking, there is no need for the horn, as his family and the five remaining members of his congregation are never far away: they tend to keep to the spare shade of the wild pomegranates and the blackthorn, close to the single camel thorn where he holds his services; but just in case a stranger should find himself in the vicinity – runaway, visitor, deserter – the horn may lure him to prayer. God's great work has to continue, whether there is an audience or not. Moreover, he argues, if his call is loud enough, if he speaks with enough vigour, God may well call forth an entirely new congregation from the veld: among the stones and shrubs and rare trees, among the dwindling numbers of veld creatures, there may well be some who yet prove receptive. Because in the very beginning of the world there was no distinction between man and animal and stone and tree: they all spoke the same language and understood each other. So it may indeed happen again.

All he has to do is to keep the faith. He just *has* to. Otherwise, what will become of him? Everybody is looking up to him. He *has* to. And that inspires him to preach more and more fervently, to pray with ever more conviction, to sing with more and more abandon. Especially when Katryn is about.

Only he knows that it is really himself he is trying to convince.

When he isn't involved in the business of the church, he wanders in the veld on his own. Just as, previously, he travelled about in his wagon, he now makes his rounds on foot, coming to know intimately every outspan, every shrub and rock, every bleached skeleton, every white bone or black curved horn. He goes about attentive to their many voices. Because he can hear them speak. There are voices everywhere. Innumerable voices. The voice of God – unless it is Tsui-Goab's – speaking through every tree and stone and particle of dust or dry blade of grass or insect, and at night the stars and the moon.

On her own Katryn also speaks to the moon. She no longer remembers what the missionaries told her: she is returning to sources and origins. To the moon she sings:

> *Tsui-Goab, I greet you!*
> *Give us an abundance of honey*
> *Give us grass for our sheep*
> *Give us enough milk . . .*

Once, when she becomes aware of another's presence, she looks up and finds Brother Cupido watching her.

Now he is going to berate her, she knows. She has transgressed. He will never forgive her for turning so openly against his God.

But he just stares at her for a while. Then turns round and wanders off to the night. What she will remember is the sadness in his face, those few moments he stood looking at her in the light of the fire. A desolation that reaches beyond this outspan and the moon and the stars. To something she does not really know. Perhaps he doesn't either.

When they speak again, it is not about her song that night, but about the other things that come up between them so often these days.

'I can see you no longer believe me, Katryn,' he says with this new sadness in his voice.

'It is not that I don't believe you, Cupido,' she protests. 'It is that *nobody* believes you.'

'They got to!' he says angrily. 'They cannot harden their hearts to the Word.'

'Perhaps the Word is no longer enough. Not in this place.'

'No, it's not that. It is this thing I told you the other day: that they *cannot* believe you, whatever you say. Because to them you will never be a real missionary. You are not white.'

'There is so much I still want to do!' he explodes. 'If only they would give me a chance.'

'They won't. Because they cannot.'

'Must I give up then?' he asks. His thin shoulders are sagging as if there were no bone in them. 'How can I do that? Some of us *must* go on believing, no matter how hard it is.'

'And if it doesn't help any more?'

'Even then. Most especially if it's useless. Because it is for their sake that I believe. If I don't, then what will become of the world?'

'They think you're mad. So what's the use?'

'I cannot answer you. All I know is that if I stop, everything will fall apart. Not just for myself, but for them too. I must be here to stand between them and . . .'

'And what?' she asks.

He shrugs. 'I don't know myself, Katryn. Just something else. Something that has no name.'

'If you can't give it a name then it doesn't matter. *You* are the one who always spoke about the word. So what has happened? Have you lost the word?'

'Maybe the word is not enough any more.'

'What else is there then?'

'Perhaps what is important is only what there are no words for.'

'You're talking shit now, Cupido.'

And then the child begins to cry – it is crying more and more, it seems – and that is the end of their talk.

But it resumes, again and again. Becoming worse all the time. Until the word stops for them too and Katryn becomes like a stone in his presence, her back turned to him in sullenness and mute rage.

For a while. A while during which four of his five remaining church members also abscond. Even the crippled boy. Now only the old man remains, the one who *cannot* walk.

Even that does not bring Brother Cupido's preaching to an end. Since the dry old man cannot move, he has no choice but to sit and listen. And when Brother Cupido has done with him, he returns to his solitary rounds in the veld, to preach to rock and tree and bone. From time to time he squats beside a patch of sand and scribbles with a twig on the ground. It is the only writing material left to him, straight from the hand of God. In the flat box at their outspan there is only one of the beautiful white pages left, but that one he keeps, even though he does not yet know to what purpose. Just in case. He has to be prepared in case the Lord chooses to come to him. In the meantime he will spend his days here in the veld, writing in the sand or on the trunks of trees, or speaking to the stones or to the solitary camel thorn that has no choice but to stand listening, with its many pods of ears.

Sometimes he stays out in the veld for days without coming

home, living on whatever he can scrape together: a tsamma, perhaps a lizard, or if he is very lucky a handful of wild honey, a locust or two. God is still good. *Praise the Lord, my soul.*

There are times when he gets dizzy, after a few days without food or drink. Then he stumbles over his own feet and lies squirming in the dust. It is like Anna, years ago, in her trances of dreaming. If Katryn comes upon him like that, she gets scared that he may die. But he angrily pushes her off. This is God's way of talking to him, he says. He may seem dead, but his head is still wide awake. And it is while lying there, prone, that he goes on his farthest walks: all the roads his wagon can no longer travel, and which his feet have to stay away from because his work keeps him here. But in his head he can walk where he wants to, to all the places Servaas Ziervogel spoke about so many years ago, and Brother Read and the Reverend van der Kemp, and those hunters the other day; all those places and the names of many others that come to him without anyone knowing where they have been hatched: names like Haskrnmy, and Zwglno, and Khowrtz, and Skrtahmpi. Names so strange that no tongue can pronounce them but which ring in his head like bells, church bells, big and small. And on these journeys in his head he can walk without ever getting tired, and without his body growing old or weak, walk and walk until his feet disappear below him: and when he looks down he can see that his whole body is covered with feathers, that his arms have changed into wings, that he is transformed into an eagle, a great *arend*, and that now he can fly as he has dreamed since his early childhood, over all the rocky ridges and the distant blue ranges, over Gamohaan and the Skurweberge and the Nuuweveldsberge, over the whole of Africa, over the world, without ever stopping to rest, he, Brother Cupido Cockroach, child of God.

'You talking too much, Cupido,' Katryn says. 'Come with me, you got to lie down.'

'If I am silent the stones will cry out.'

She, too, begins to wonder whether he may be mad.

And she is worried about her children. Both are starving, she can see. And what else can she expect? What is there left to eat?

'You must send another message to the Reverend at Kuruman,' she urges.

'He is like God,' he insists. 'He will come when the time is right. This is the Society's way of testing us. And God's way too. Once we can get through this thing, everything will change. You'll see. If he comes, he will bring a whole wagonload of food. And a flock of sheep. That was what they promised us when they sent us here, and they are men of God, they won't lie. Then the Kora will also come back, because food will make their faith strong. It is hard for a hungry man to believe. We just have to go on, Katryn.'

She does not bother to answer. She only shakes her head.

Until one early morning he wakes up to find her bustling about in the little lean-to shelter.

'What are you doing?' he asks, his head reeling, as he finds it hard to sleep at night.

'I'm going,' she says. It is the first time in weeks that she has answered.

'Where?'

'I'm going back to Klaarwater. The place they now call Griquatown. I'm taking the children with me.'

'What is there at Klaarwater which isn't here?'

She gives an ugly laugh. 'Life,' she says.

'But God is here.'

'Then it is time I go away from here and kick the dust in His face.'

'You cannot leave me here alone,' he says in sudden panic.

'You can come with me,' she relents. 'It is for you to say. But I'm not staying any longer. I cannot let my children die.'

He says nothing, but he crouches beside the bedding to grope for something under the kaross.

'What are you doing now?' asks Katryn.

'I want you to take this with you,' he mumbles, embarrassed, holding out to her the small, bright fragment of mirror he brought with him all the way from Bethelsdorp. It is only a shard, but it is something.

'What must I do with this?' she asks, suspicious.

'It is all there is left of me,' he explains, pressing it into her hand.

She wants to ask and argue, but she can see in his face that it will be better not to speak now.

'Thank you, Cupido,' she says, thrusting it into her small bundle.

He bends over and picks up the eldest child.

'Come then,' he says.

'You coming too?' she asks, taken by surprise.

'No. You know I cannot. But I shall walk with you for a day. Otherwise the children will get too heavy for you.'

They walk without talking, from sunrise to sunset. All day long a miserable wind keeps blowing. Then he lies down with her, the children next to them. The moon comes up, then the stars appear. Not one of them sleeps. She holds his hand, that is all.

Until daybreak. Then she gets up and ties the kaross round her; it is the only clothing she still has. The children are naked. He helps her to pick them up: the baby on her back, the elder one on her hip. He stands looking after them as they go. She doesn't look back once. Smaller and smaller she becomes, until she disappears completely. The wind is still blowing through the emptiness. When he looks down he can see that it has obliterated her footprints.

Only then does he turn round and start walking on the long road back.

From time to time, when he reaches a sandy patch, he squats on his haunches, scrapes a small smooth square on the sand, picks up a twig and starts writing. He no longer knows whom he is writing to. But it is his last tenuous grasp on words.

When he reaches Dithakong at nightfall it is quiet. Not the kind of silence that speaks of sleeping people, but a silence with no life in it.

He goes to look behind his ragged little shelter of dry branches, where the almost-dead old man used to lie. But there is nobody.

He stands up and starts calling through cupped hands: 'Grandpa!' Then listens for a while before he calls again: 'Grandpa!'

No sound in reply.

He goes back round the shelter and picks up his ram's horn, walks a few paces into the veld under the open sky, and begins to blow. It sounds like an ox bellowing, a mighty beast that fills the whole emptiness with its reverberating sound.

Only the silence responds. The stars remain unmoved.

Should he try to pluck one of them again tonight? Would it help?

But they are too high. When he was small, he could reach there. But no longer.

Once more he bellows like a dying animal.

It remains quiet.

The old man will not come back again. He knows that now. And with the wind that has been blowing throughout the empty day – what else can it do but blow? there is nothing to stop it – he knows there will be no traces left by tomorrow. *How* the old man has got away, weak as he was and barely ably to shuffle, no one will ever know.

He is just gone. And now there is no one left in his church.

# 6

## Arrival of the Reverend

IT MUST BE IN THAT TIME, around Brother Cupido's sixty-third year, that the Reverend Moffat of Kuruman decides the time is ripe for his long-promised visit to the mission station at Dithakong. It follows yet another message sent from Dithakong to inform him of the sorry state of affairs at the mission station. It also follows yet another prayer addressed to heaven by the stricken yet unbroken Brother Cupido Cockroach:

'Dear God! Have mercy on this poor sinner. You know I am doing my best, but this is impossible, I have nothing left. No wife, no child, no congregation, nothing. Not even the camel thorn is prepared to listen to me any more. Which is why I am asking you today: Please come down and help us. I know you are a busy man. But this is crushing my balls. And this is a matter for grown-up people, there is no place for children. So I am asking you very seriously, God: Don't send your son. Come yourself.'

Whether it is the message or the prayer that causes the miracle, no one will ever know. All we do know is that the God-fearing missionary Robert Moffat at long last deigns to come from Kuruman and see for himself how things are going at Dithakong.

He arrives alone on an ox-cart, accompanied only by his helpers: a driver, a team leader and two others to take care of tasks like cooking and loading and hunting. He is dressed in shiny black shoes and a dark striped suit with a long tail-coat, three buttons fastened and the bottom one loose, a silk scarf around the high collar, an outlandish crow-like bird in the dun-coloured veld of early winter. Dark hair, prematurely thinning, and high forehead, thick eyebrows. A ruddy, fleshy face, and a deep cleft in his round chin. Bearded jowls, soft and slightly puffy hands, clammy to the touch. Clearly a saved soul.

He comes in style, having received tidings that our brother's situation is desperate. Well, it has been quite a few years since Brother Read had the sheep brought, and there has been a bad drought. Even the thorn trees are becoming scarce, tattered and scorched to a frazzle among the merci-less jonas stones.

From a long way off the Reverend can see that it is indeed going badly, even worse than sporadic reports have led him to believe It makes him feel aggrieved, as it is no pleasant thing for an important and flourishing man like the Reverend Moffat to be faced with deprivation. He has already informed his head office in London that the Society can no longer afford a man like this Cupido Cockroach, such a heathen name. Too old to learn the Kora language and be of any use in the missionary world. Another of the overzealous and intem-perate Brother Read's unconscionable ideas. Too thin and worn out for useful work, and now left destitute without wife or family in this truly godforsaken place. Nothing one could describe as a house or a hut, barely a rickety shelter of desiccated thorn-tree branches dragged up against a tattered camel thorn, and covered with a piece of shrivelled oxhide. To one side, on the grey ashes of a fireplace, a black iron pot (one leg missing, replaced by a few flat pieces of slate). What seems like a few shrivelled tsammas. Some kind of veld food, not something a civilised man would touch. And the brother himself, almost naked, his dusty grey, spare body inadequately adorned with a single flap of skin, looking for all the world like an insect or some veld creature, huddled on his haunches and scribbling with a spiky white thorn on a flattened patch of sand, pretending to write. Waiting until he sees the cart draw up under the camel thorn before he slowly comes to his feet to shuffle closer. Showing nothing of the haste or eagerness or deference a white man, and a missionary to boot — and not just any ordinary missionary but the head of all the LMS stations in this remote and heathen land — may expect after taking the considerable trouble of travelling here to enquire about the situation.

The Reverend Moffat has already made up his mind, even before leaving Kuruman, and his decision has been amply justified by what he has witnessed so far, but he is in no hurry. The mills of God grind slowly and terribly small. He will take coffee first, he proposes; milk, two sugars.

Hopefully the Reverend does not mind white-root coffee? With, possibly, a touch of honey for sweetness? There is no milk.

He has not quite sunk to that yet, declares the Reverend Moffat. Can someone bring some coffee and sugar from the ox-cart? Brother Cupido turns it down: he has already become used to what this lean earth can provide, he explains. Just as well, thinks the missionary; one should not spoil these people. Coffee and sugar today, tomorrow liquor and tobacco.

Behind them the helpers are outspanning the oxen, resting the wagon's draught-pole on a few stones to keep it from the dust.

'How are you coming on here, Brother?' enquires the missionary after he has made himself comfortable on a *riempie* chair provided by one of the helpers, under the spreading branches of the camel-thorn tree which stands listening, all ears for this special occasion. Between his plump white hands a wisp of steam unravels from the coffee mug.

'As you can see, Reverend.'

'I have not received very favourable reports about your work, Brother.'

Brother Cupido shrugs his bony shoulders. The late sun casts his ragged shadow across the white tufts of dry grass, the scorched red earth.

'One cannot expect one's congregation to show respect for the Gospel if you live like a lost soul yourself.' The missionary takes a large white handkerchief from his pocket to dab his moist red lips. One of the servants approaches to take the empty mug from him.

'My congregation doesn't mind, Reverend.'

'Where is your congregation? I haven't seen a soul on the way here.'

'That is so.'

'Brother Cupido, I'm really not getting much cooperation from you.' He leans over to flick a speck of dust from the toe of one shoe. 'You do realise I shall have to lodge a report on you with our head office in London.'

'Do they care then?'

The man in the striped suit and tailcoat rises to his feet, a frown on his ruddy face. 'Do I detect signs of ingratitude, Brother?'

'Ingratitude, never. God is looking after me, as you can see. For God is here, not in London. I speak to Him every day.'

'That sounds blasphemous, Brother, I must say.'

'What has London done for me?' asks Brother Cupido. He isn't looking at Moffat, but right past him, beyond the horizon where the day is beginning to spill over its edges. And as he speaks one can hear that he is – slowly, slowly, without any hurry – beginning to get worked up. 'I got the call when I was still in Bethelsdorp, to trek across the Gariep and go to Klaarwater. Brother Read came with me all the way and gave me a sheep. I was also promised other things. There would be meat for me and my people every month or so. As well as other food. And payment every year, not less than a hundred rix-dollars. And two other missionaries from London to come and work with me. What has become of all that? Or was it promised to me behind God's back, where He couldn't hear? What have I got from you and your Society all these years? In the beginning, at least, I still had my wagon, and my oxen. Those who didn't die were taken away by the Kora. My congregation. Now all gone to hell. But at that time I still had my wife, and our child. Then we had another, but he died. And another, but he was crying all the time. And where is she now, where are the children? Couldn't take it any more, in this poverty. There is no one to look after me, except God. And then you come and speak to me about London?'

'I'll be damned . . .' says Brother Moffat, his face now very rich purple. 'All these years we have tried to make a civilised man out of you. I have read all the reports, don't think I don't know. We trained you to spread the Gospel among the heathen. And this is what we get for it. Base ingratitude. You have sunk lower than you ever were. One might just as well try to tame a wild animal.'

'You can ask Brother Read about me.'

'Don't mention that adulterer's name in front of me.'

'Brother Read walked with God.'

'Today it is *I* who stand before you, in the name of the Lord Our God.'

'*And hath not love*,' Brother Cupido mumbles to himself.

'What was that?'

'Just something a poor apostle once said.'

'I will not argue with a heathen soul,' the Reverend interrupts him.

'All I am is poor, Brother. It is not contagious.'

'Don't you call me "Brother".'

For a moment it seems as if it may get out of hand, but the Reverend Moffat manages to control his just anger. He turns on his heel and makes a wide loop round the ox-cart, stands behind it for a long time staring at the surrounding emptiness, then comes back. 'It is getting dark,' he says with commendable restraint. 'Perhaps you should lead us in prayer first.'

Whereupon Brother Cupido rises to fetch from inside his meagre shelter his curved ram's horn, worn with use. He walks some distance from the camel thorn, presses the horn to his mouth and starts blowing towards the sunset.

At that exact moment the moon rises behind him in the east like a pumpkin that seems to glow very faintly from the inside.

There is a deathly hush on the veld. Not a jackal to be heard, not a cricket, nothing.

Another blast. It resounds, something terrible, in the silence.

Brother Cupido stands waiting. Beside the ox-cart the servants also freeze, as if a sudden cold wind has swept through their bodies.

'You don't seem to have much of a congregation tonight,' Brother Moffat remarks bitingly, the shadow of a grimace around his fleshy gills.

'I haven't had a congregation for a long time now,' says Brother Cupido. 'I wrote to you about it many times. But even if they are gone, one has to keep on shouting in the wilderness.'

'I thought you still had a few Kora left?'

'The last old man is gone now.'

'And do you expect the Society to go on paying until you . . .' He checks himself and tries again: 'Do you think it is acceptable for you to sink into sloth and idleness? If they no longer come to you, then surely you can go to *them*?'

'How?'

'You used to have a wagon.'

'It broke. From travelling after them. The oxen died. We used the wood for fire. Over there you can see the last wheel. As I wrote you ten or twelve times already.'

The missionary begins to look ill at ease, avoiding Brother Cupido's eyes. 'Well, shall we proceed?' he asks gruffly.

From his shelter Brother Cupido brings out a Bible. It is almost too heavy for him to carry, he is staggering on his rickety legs; and the book worn with use, tattered pages spilling from the scuffed binding, past the broken brass clasps.

'Let us read.'

He sits with legs outstretched in the dust, close to the fire, as that is the only available light; the sun has gone down, the pumpkin is not yet giving off enough of a glow. Not that there is much of a sense or pattern to what he reads: he pages forward and back, picking up random bits of text along the way, then forgets about it and gives it up, turns another page, becomes engrossed in a new passage, a list of names perhaps, a text marked in the margin, then rustles among the loose leaves again, here and there, this and that. In the end he just gives up, remaining seated with the bulky book on the sharp knobs of his knees, staring into the fire, as he continues to speak haphazardly about anything that comes to his mind, interspersed with *Praise the Lord*, the same meaningless phrases over and over. The men from the ox-cart sit grinning and mocking behind cupped hands, nudging each other with the elbows.

At last: 'Let us pray.'

It is over before the Reverend Moffat can decide whether he should kneel in the dust or just incline his head (which would expose his balding pate).

'Go and make us something to eat,' he orders his helpers with a wave of his hand. 'We can have our supper behind the ox-cart so as not to disturb our brother.'

Brother Cupido goes to put his book away. The firelight flickers across his furrowed face that looks like the cracked surface of a dried-up lake.

'I think it is time for some straight talking, Brother,' says the visitor, his thumbs hooked into his waistcoat pockets. The silver chain of his watch stretches tautly across his stomach, which is ample for such a young man. 'I have worked through all the reports, as I told you. Thought very deeply about the matter. Asked for guidance from Above. And then decided to come and look for myself.'

'Yes. I been here for eight years now,' says Brother Cupido.

'Now I have seen with my own eyes,' the missionary cuts through his pointed reminder. 'My worst fears have been confirmed.'

'One doesn't need a congregation to preach.'

'Indeed, indeed,' says the Reverend Moffat, unsettled by the gaze in the old man's eyes, the firelight on his face. He is so old, he thinks, perhaps his mind has gone. All the more reason to bring this travesty to an end.

'No one can make a living here any more, Brother Cupido,' he says firmly. He starts walking to and fro, but stepping carefully not to unsettle the dust. 'The Society cannot afford to see you wasting away like this. It seems to me much more useful to move to a more fertile place where you may earn your bread in a less strenuous way.'

'We have enough stones here,' Brother Cupido says quietly.

The Reverend Moffat opens his mouth to ask for an explanation, then decides against it.

'Do we understand each other?' he asks after a pause.

'I don't think so,' says Brother Cupido. 'Are you saying you want to send me away again? Where to this time?'

'That is what I am trying to tell you, Brother Cupido. On behalf of our Society. This time no one is sending you anywhere. You can go wherever you wish. At any rate, it will be better for you to move away from here. It is no longer safe in these parts. Too many outlaws and undesirables coming past into no man's land. Bandits, runaway slaves, escaped convicts, criminals.'

'I have not seen such people around.'

'There is a steady stream of them coming past Kuruman.'

'I shall rather stay here.'

'That is for you to decide. We shall not force you. Whatever we say or do, we say and do out of love. And look, obviously we appreciate what you have done here – or tried to do. Anybody has to be big enough to admit when a mistake has been made. Be assured that we shall continue to remember you in our prayers.'

'Are you cutting me off now, Reverend?'

'If that is how you wish to call it. Provided you do not expect anything more from the Society.'

'I have never got anything from you. How can I expect anything now?'

'Then it is settled. I must go, it is time for supper. We have to be on our way early tomorrow morning. I must go on to Griquatown for an inspection. I shall take my leave now, then I need not disturb you in the morning. I wish you God's blessings.'

The small, old man does not answer. He does not seem

to notice the missionary's outstretched hand aiming irresolutely in his direction, then dropping limply to his side.

The stranger tarries for another moment, then walks away towards the smell of roasting meat from his fire behind the ox-cart. At the last moment he seems to change his mind: this may be his last chance. Without retracing his steps, only half turning, he says in the dark, rather more emphatically than may have been necessary: 'I honestly don't know what has become of the Church in this goddamned country. It seems as if everything is sinking back into heathen misery, barbarism, backwardness, filth, degradation, evil. But I promise you one thing: where the Church has taken root it is not easily dislodged. Whatever it may cost, Cupido, I shall make sure that some space will be opened up for God again.'

'You need not make space for Him. He has been here from long before you came.'

The man has already disappeared into the dark while Cupido is still sitting there as if the words have passed him by like wind. In a way he looks almost content.

Only after the sounds behind the ox-cart have begun to die down for the night does he get up and walk off into the dark. The faint glimmer of the moon is now beginning to rub off on the veld. Wherever it touches the earth among the rocks, it plants its seeds. Long tubers start growing in the dark, black leaves bring the relief of shadows to the night, spreading the smell of fertility in the dust. Brother Cupido finds his way without looking; he does not need light. At the biggest of the thorn trees remaining in the vicinity, far away from his shelter, he stops to pick grapes: the single large bunch that had formed for him during the day, transparent with sweetness. All about him are strewn rocks which in his early zeal he plucked and cast away from a mound of Heitsi-

Eibib when they first arrived here. In the moonlight he selects one of them, a stone which in a time before time was hollowed out like a basin by pristine water; in its rounded cavity he presses his grapes. From his sinewy wrists, down to his pointed elbows, the sticky juice runs down; and when he tastes, his head raised as if in prayer, it is the purest wine. From an anthill he breaks a hard-baked crust which in his hands turns to bread.

In the moonlight that covers him like flour from a sieve, he eats, and drinks. This is my flesh, this is the blood of my son Heitsi-Eibib.

With what is left of his voice he sings to the sky: *Praise ye the Lord*.

Singularly refreshed, he rises, and walks back in the night, his face still turned upward. Which explains why he stubs his foot against something, and stumbles, and falls, badly grazing his knees. The thing he has fallen over seems to be glowing in the dark. Only when he crawls towards it to have a closer look does he discover that it is a fallen star. Well! He cannot quite remember so far back, but somehow it reminds him of the star which as a small child he plucked for his mother: that one had the same slightly jagged edge to one of its lower points. But how did it land here?

Cupido shakes his head. Some things are better not examined too closely. He bends over again and picks it up. It isn't very heavy at all. A child can pick it up. He has always been good at throwing stones, ever since the time he used to tend the goats and sheep. And as far as he can he hurls the shiny object back into the night sky. It leaves a line of shimmering dust past the other stars. Good. So at last this, too, is where it belongs.

He continues on his way. From time to time he stops to look up, noticing with satisfaction that like a thin trickle of milk the dusty path of the star is still streaking through the heavens. With more peace in his mind than he has felt for years he goes back.

The oxen are still quietly chewing their cuds under the camel thorn when he arrives. From the ox-cart comes a sound of snoring. Otherwise everything is quiet. Not even the stars make any sound tonight. A heavy, heavy silence as if a huge black hen sits brooding on her black nest; whatever is to be hatched, is impossible to tell. All one knows is that there is a hatching happening.

On the horny soles of his bare feet Brother Cupido goes round the back of the cart. For a moment the snoring is interrupted, which makes him stop; then the sleeping man under the kaross turns on his other side and the sound starts up again. Like the sawing he used to do when he was still working with wood, at Graaff-Reinet, or with Brother Read at Bethelsdorp, that time of innocence.

To one side, at a little distance from the other sleeping humps — like bundles of baggage dislodged from the cart — he finds the reverend man who has come to see him. In the moonlight his face is glowing as he sleeps. A reddish glow, like an ember lit up from inside.

In the light of the large illuminated pumpkin he can see it very clearly: on either side of the man's forehead, where the sparse dark hair has been stroked back, the two short twisted horns. And at the bottom end of the blanket which he has pulled up against the night cold, the goat's feet. The two brilliant black shoes stand neatly beside the bundle.

'Not that it is much help to me,' Brother Cupido says up to the sky. 'But thank you anyway, God.'

He goes to his dark shelter and sits on the ground before it. Takes up his pipe. There is no tobacco left, but he has learned to use whatever comes to hand: mostly dry grass, mixed with some bitter aloe, a sprinkling of buchu, a precious pinch of dagga.

Until sunrise he remains sitting there. Then he goes over to where the fire was and presses a thin brittle stick in among the smouldering embers, pokes about with it for a while, goes down on all fours to blow it to life, gets his eyes filled with ashes, blows again, until the little blue flames begin to flicker; and then he sets fire to the ox-cart. Returns to his flat stone and watches as the men wake up and start shouting and running about and flapping their arms. And sees how at last they inspan and ride off, the devil Gaunab on the front seat among the flames, the reins in his hands, transparent and burning, the whole lot of them, straight into the sun.

# 7

## Last Letter to God

Dearest Beloved Revrend God

You who made people and stones and caused them to multiply and taught them to talk among themselves

You who live in the Red Sky of dawn and sometimes come to us in the shape of a Lion and sometimes as a Tree and sometimes as a Man

You who can turn water into wine and heal the sick and wake up the dead

You who struck Gaunab on the hip to cripple him and cause him to die and have a good burn in the hell of fire and brimstone:

It is not that I want to complain but God you were Not fare to me and today You must Lissen to me Because this is my last sheet of Paper. I kept it and kept it, all the time I kept it for you, but now it is time for me to take it out of its box and flatten it on this big stone and prepare myself to Write for the Last time. The ink run out Long ago and then I tried to rite with Mud and with the Green of leaves rubd between the Fingers and with Blood snakes blood Tortes blood and today in this place my Own Blood praise the Lord o my Sole. So all I want to ask is if you are Satisfied now? How far can you Hunt a man? Bit by bit you Took away every thing we had. Now my life is what you may call fullempty. It is full as an Egg and empty as a Shell.

All I can still do is pritch. I pritch for Stones and Thorntrees and the Lizzerd on his Rock and the Snake and the Tortes in the dust and I can pritch to the Dust itself and the green Mantiss that is scarce in our Part. But what is the Use? Can a tree or a Stone or a Grasshoper convert Himself?

So now I am come to the End. This is now the End of the Word in the beginning was the word and the word was With god and the Word was god the Same was in the beginning with god. At first I walked in the ways of the Flesh and I hunted and I fighted and I drinked and I went with Woman and then I gave it all up to walk in the Word. But now the Word is no more I got to go past Him I do not know how here I come today to say to you Farewel I am going away. From your Estemed and Honourd and Derely Beloved Brother Cupido Cockrch.

# 8

## The Wings of an Eagle

IT BEGINS AS THE TINIEST SPECK in the most distant distance of the winter veld. Cupido watches it coming. He is sitting among the scattered stones he tore from Heitsi-Eibib's cairn so long ago, his favourite spot to sit and think on his own. This is his writing place, as there are large patches of sand on the plain. Almost without looking he reaches for a twig. But he finds it hard to concentrate. He wants to keep an eye on the speck as it approaches from the horizon. He throws the twig away again. Not today. No longer. The time for writing has passed. He has gone beyond words.

Where beyond? Impossible to tell yet.

He keeps watching the speck. It is like a bird approaching through a bleached sky, gradually growing bigger, but very slowly.

He remembers the story his mother told him so long ago, a story blown by the wind from very far away. Of the *arend* fledgling who thought it was a chicken because it had been brought up in a backyard. Until a man came who took him away to the summit of the highest mountain where he threw him up into the air and said, 'Fly, *arend*, fly!' And the eagle spread his enormous wings and took off and became a mere speck in the expanse of sky, high above the whole world, for ever and ever.

Cupido sits watching. The speck grows bigger, expanding

edited by J. D. Lewis-Williams (2000), *Living Legends of a Dying Culture* by Coral Fourie (1994) and *Return of the Moon* by Stephen Watson (1991). The story of the eagle who was reared by the chickens was allegedly first written down by the Ghanaian James Aggrey, born in 1875.

The episode in which Cupido is apparently betrayed by the letter hidden under a stone comes from John Wilkens in *Mercury, or the Secret and Swift Messenger* (1641) as retold by Umberto Eco in *I limiti dell' interpretazione* (1990).'

The remark of the trader Ziervogel about taking a fork in the road has been borrowed from the American baseball player Yogi Berra.

The biography of Jan Robbertse, the hunter who loved elephants so much that he felt compelled to shoot them, appears in J. von Moltke's *Jagkonings* (*Kings of the Hunt:* 1943, republished 2004).

Cupido's appeal to God at the beginning of Part 3, Chapter 6 is inspired by a prayer which, according to Ryszard Kapuściński, was said by Adam Kok II at Kuruman in 1823 when, together with Robert Moffat, he prepared to do battle against black tribes unsettled by the *difaqane*.

The line from the *Inferno* on page 187 is quoted from the Dorothy Sayers translation which is, of course, anachronistic; but Read wouldn't have known.

Correspondence by Cupido is available in the Cape Archives, but unfortunately translated and transcribed by anonymous and unimaginative officials of the LMS; for the phraseology and orthography in his letters in this text I therefore had to rely on my own intuition and imagination, and I trust that I did not do him an injustice. Cupido may have been spontaneous and unaffected, but he was not a buffoon.

For novelistic reasons a number of adjustments had to be made to the historical material. It is known, for example, that Read paid several visits to Cupido at Dithakong (sadly without making any difference to his situation), and that Moffat, too, went to see him more than once (again, regrettably, without having any influence on his fate), that Cupido was later transferred from Dithakong to Nokaneng (which would have unnecessarily blurred the story), that his second wife did not leave him but, with Cupido, joined forces with the slave Arend in a campaign against the 'Mantatees' (which would have unnecessarily complicated a 'clean' ending).

So many people, over so many years, have been indispensable, in so many ways, to the shaping of the story, that only a few of them can be singled out for special thanks: Tim Huisamen, Dan Sleigh, Annari van der Merwe, Peter Anderson, Jeanette Ferreira, Willemien Brümmer, Susan Mann, Dolf van Niekerk, and Matty Malherbe at Kleinplasie, Worcester.

Cape Town, October 2004

thing of a revision began with Christopher Saunders's 'James Read: Towards a Reassessment' in *Collected Seminar Papers on the Societies of Southern Africa in the 19th and 20th Centuries*, Part VII (Institute of Commonwealth Studies, 1976–7), as well as by Elizabeth Elbourne's *To Colonise the Mind: Evangelical Missionaries in Britain and the Eastern Cape, 1790–1837* (1991), republished as *Blood Ground* in 2002. The shaky documentation on Read's early life was an invitation to imagine what had been omitted or suppressed. The Revd Robert Moffat, long respected as one of the most famous missionaries of the LMS at the Cape, gives an account of himself in *Missionary Labours and Scenes in Southern Africa* (1849). His unsympathetic and even scandalous treatment of Cupido is well documented, even in his own journals.

The story of the runaway slave (Joseph) Arend was told, inter alia, by Edward C. Tabler in 'Addenda and Corrigenda to Pioneers in Rhodesia', *Africana Notes and News* XVII:8 (1967).

For a general contemporary background I could draw on a variety of sources, including notably Martin Hinrich Lichtenstein's *Travels in Southern Africa in the Years 1803, 1804, 1805 and 1806* (Cape Town, 1928–30) and William J. Burchell's *Travels in the Interior of Southern Africa* (2 volumes, 1822; reprinted 1953). Even a seeming triviality like the praying mantis at Klaarwater can be found in Burchell. Further insights into the historical background were provided by *The Shaping of South African Society, 1652–1844*, edited by Richard Elphick and Hermann Giliomee (1989).

For aspects of the way of life, traditions, culture, religion and cosmology of the Khoi and San peoples I made ample use of L. Schapera's *The Khoisan Peoples of Southern Africa* (1930) as well as various texts based on the famous Bleek-Lloyd collection, among them *Stories That Float from Afar*,

# Note

WORK ON THIS NOVEL BEGAN in 1984, but was then abandoned and only resumed in 1992. It was not before 2004 that it found its final form when I decided to write a book for my seventieth birthday.

Although the novel as it stands is fiction, the outline is based on a true history. References to Cupido Cockroach under his Dutch name Kupido Kakkerlak are scattered through numerous documents of and on the London Missionary Society in South Africa, but the most detailed account of his life to date is 'The Life and Times of Cupido Kakkerlak' by V. C. Malherbe in *Journal of South African History* 20:3 (1979). However, it is precisely the reading of such a well-documented account that makes one realise the extent to which the enigma of another's life can only be grasped through the imagination (which is no less reliable than memory).

For the life of the missionary van der Kemp I am indebted, apart from documents of the LMS, to Ido H. Enklaar's *Life and Work of Dr J. Th. van der Kemp 1747–1811* (1988) which provided me with a number of quotations and descriptions. The Revd John Campbell's *Travels in South Africa* (1819; van Riebeeck Society 1974) supplied valuable information on the life of this missionary. The Revd James Read was disgrace-fully neglected by South African historiography until some-

Cupido feels a shiver along his spine, coming from very far away, as if it has been waiting in his body for years.

'I shall come,' he says. 'But I need your help first.' He motions his head towards the scattered stones from Heitsi-Eibib's cairn.

'What must we do?'

'Just help me.'

Together they start working. Stone by stone, until the cairn is repaired and built to its full height again, as it must have been in the time before time.

And something unexpected happens. When at last Cupido straightens his back, Arend points at something in the sky. Cupido looks up. A small feather comes whirling down from very high up, whirling and twirling until it lands at his feet. There is no bird in sight. There are no mountains anywhere near. Nor is there any wind, not a breeze stirring. Just this feather.

He bends over and picks it up.

To Arend he says, 'Come, let us go.'

'Yes, come.'

They get on the cart. The mantis is no longer there. But they do not need him any more.

The day turns old and grey around them, tired at the edges. But they go on, ever further. Yet it does not seem to grow dark. Ahead of them, high above, streaks the star, its dazzling course showing them where to go. That way. That way.

1984. 1992. 2004.

He speaks of Graaff-Reinet. Of Father van der Kemp with the tall bulbous head, of his clothes that became more and more tattered as he suffered hunger and poverty with his flock. And Brother Read, the gentle but determined man who had devoted his life to those who landed between the grindstones of the land but then yielded to the flesh to be cast out into darkness, with weeping and gnashing of teeth.

'What about you?' he asks the stranger.

'I am a slave,' the man announced calmly.

'That is hard to believe.'

'Must I show you?' The man turns his back and pulls his tunic up to his wide shoulders.

Cupido stares at the criss-crossing of old scars on his back.

'How did that happen?' he asks.

'This was done many times,' the stranger says, dropping his tunic again. 'Over years and years. Until I had enough. Then I ran away. First to the Eastern Cape and to the Xhosaland. There I joined a wild white man, his name was Coenraad de Buys. But the farmers were after me, so I went off again, up to the Gariep. And now I am here, still on my way.'

'Where will you hide?'

'No need to hide, the Gariep is behind me now, the laws of the Cape cannot reach here. But there are dangerous people in these parts among the Griqua, the Mantatees, many runaways and criminals. So I am going further. I never want to be a slave again. All of Africa lies up there.' He narrows his eyes against the glare of the sun. 'You want to come with me?'

'How can I?'

'Just get on the cart, then we go.'

'What is your name?'

'My name is Arend,' says the slave who is no longer a slave.

into a small mule cart that drags its shadow after it. A single mule in front, a single man on the cart.

The cart comes closer, draws up to him. The man pulls in the reins. It is a big man, bare head exposed to the sun. A black man, but wearing a white man's clothes. Rather dishevelled, but not in quite such a sorry state as Cupido. Beside him on the seat, upright and haughty, sits a green praying mantis. Is it really sitting there or is it something one can be tricked into seeing by the fierce light?

From the front of his cart the man calls a greeting: 'Good day to you, brother.'

Cupido is staring so hard at the mantis that at first he does not hear. Only when the stranger clears his throat and repeats his greeting does he apologise and say, in his turn: 'Good day, brother.'

The man climbs down. They shake hands. The little mantis does not move.

The stranger asks questions, Cupido answers at length. The man seems interested, and Cupido has an abundance of time, enough to go all the way to the beginning. To his mother. To his birth. How the people thought that he'd died, and began to dig a hole in the hard earth, and how the mantis came to sit on his body and pray. How he returned to life. The years of growing up on the farm, the long walk to the neighbour's place where the letter under the stone betrayed him, which planted in him the resolve to learn to write. How the itinerant trader arrived on their farm with his two loaded wagons. His magic mirrors wrapped in black shrouds. And how he left with the man, on the road of the many names.

Then Anna Vigilant who came to him with fireflies and stars, and who could boil soap like no other living person. Anna who had burned her own foot in the cauldron because she wanted to be white.